Bill froze with his free hand above his head, palm on the trap door. Again, his curiosity and fear were in a wrestling match that his curiosity somehow managed to win. He turned around, his eyes on the floor.

Slowly, his gaze drifted upwards. Bill dropped his candle, barely hearing the smash of the porcelain dish.

He hoped that he was simply tired, and that his exhausted mind was playing tricks on him. He hoped it was his imagination, running wild on fear and paranoia.

He hoped that he was not seeing the four wooden coffin lids slowly opening...

With special thanks to James Noble

To my parents and brothers

ORCHARD BOOKS

338 Euston Road, London NW1 3BH
Orchard Books Australia
Level 17/207 Kent St, Sydney, NSW 2000
A Paperback Original

First published in Great Britain in 2011

Text © Orchard Books 2011
Cover illustration © Simon Mendez/advocate-art 2011

A CIP catalogue record for this book is available from
the British Library.

ISBN 978 1 40831 3 893
1 3 5 7 9 10 8 6 4 2

Printed in Great Britain by CPI Bookmarque, Croydon

The paper and board used in this paperback are natural recyclable
products made from wood grown in sustainable forests. The
manufacturing processes conform to the environmental regulations
of the country of origin.

Orchard Books is a division of Hachette Children's Books,
an Hachette UK company
www.hachette.co.uk

BLACKBEARD'S PIRATES VS THE EVIL MUMMIES

James Black

ORCHARD

Prologue

Somewhere on the Barbary Coast
March 1719

Karim fell to his knees and began to pray. Then he stopped. Why bother? Pirates did not pray. They craved for riches and glory, but a life of sea-robbing and fighting battles on the waves meant that a clever pirate was always aware that, one day, he might end up in Hell.

Karim never expected Hell to come to him.

Tonight, it came in the form of death – wretched, ignoble, agonising death. There was no escape, not from the terrors stalking the *Majestic*. They had killed his shipmates one byone. And now they were coming to kill Karim.

He was in the captain's cabin, at the vessel's stern. Captain Nasir wouldn't need it anymore. He'd been one of the first to die. Above Karim's head, the boards of the quarterdeck creaked – he could hear the thrumming of the abandoned helm rolling over and over at the mercy of the whipping wind; to his left, gentle Mediterranean waves lapped against the hull as the *Majestic* sat almost motionless, wrecked on a lonely, rocky bluff in God knew where. Somewhere on the Barbary coast, Egypt, Karim thought – although, it could just as easily have been Libya, for all he knew. Once the monsters in their midst had begun their murderous mission, the crew of the *Majestic* had been too concerned with staying alive to pay much attention to their heading.

Some had tried to make off in dinghies, only for the little boats to sink under the weight of too many men. Others dove overboard, but with land so far beyond the horizon, Karim knew they had almost certainly drowned.

Drowning was a preferable end to the one that had befallen those who stayed with the ship, out of some kind of pirate loyalty. That seemed utterly ridiculous to Karim now, as he scrambled behind the captain's desk awaiting his own death.

He knew there was nothing for it. He cursed Nasir for accepting the mission from Amir Barbarossa, the self-styled 'Barbary King' who commanded the fleet of which the *Majestic* was a part. Nasir's crew should have mutinied, and told the King to go on his own voyage to take the cursed treasure of the pyramids to the Sultan in Constantinople, rather than pick a crew from his fleet to do it. Barbarossa might have flogged them, but a mutiny would have saved all of their lives.

From beyond the door, he heard them coming – their rotten, swaddled feet dragging along the boards of the gun-deck, their centuries-old, incomplete final breaths escaping their flaking lips in slow, hideous death-rattles.

Several pairs of gnarled, claw-like hands were half-rapping, half-scratching at the cabin door.

They were here. And they meant to break down the cabin door and close in on Karim, just like they had his shipmates. They meant to choke him with lengths of their putrid shrouds, while their hands ripped and tore at his chest and belly, opening them so that they could devour his organs while he still lived, breathed and screamed.

Instinctively, Karim reached for the pistol at his hip, even though he had seen a dozen pirates fire a dozen shots at the monsters, only for them to continue shuffling forward with slow, evil inevitability. He knew the bullet in the barrel would not harm those on the other side of the door. But the bullet was not meant for any of them.

It was meant for Karim.

Part One

Chapter One

Somewhere in the Mediterranean
April 1719

Her name was the *Queen Anne's Revenge*.

She was a floating fortress – two hundred tonnes of timber tearing through the morning mist that danced over the Mediterranean. She was a vessel of vengeance, of mayhem and carnage. Her hull was almost black, like a plague mark sliding across the surface of the sea, and her three masts of square-rigged black-and-red sails promised that Hell would fall upon any who dared share her horizon.

On deck, she bore the scars and stains of countless victories at sea. Some planks seemed almost held together by the indelible blood stains of both brother and enemy, who had fallen during murderous melees. The scrubbed wood of the decks showed the deep wounds made by the tackles that braced the recoiling cannons. There were six of them amidships, three on each side. They stood like silent guards over the pirates as they slept at night, and bellowed the men's rage during the battles they fought.

Beneath the bowsprit that led her relentless charge to the edges of the known world was her ghoulish figurehead: a carved image of a mermaid angel. Her halo dripped stiff seaweed, and her slender hands held a pair of pistols. The sight of the icon breaking the fog over the water could unsettle even the most hardened Naval commander or pirate captain, and prompted the soiled breeches of many a merchant sailor.

Some of her crew reckoned the ghosts of past victims lingered around the ship like the thick mist that greeted her in the earliest hours of morning – defeated enemies who groaned pitifully, their restless souls damned to share every voyage with the pirates who vanquished them.

One thing the crew of the *Queen Anne's Revenge* were not reckoning on was the enemies ahead – the enemies who lurked beyond that mist.

The enemies who were waiting for them.

Chapter Two

Edward Teach, Captain of the *Queen Anne's Revenge*, stood in his cabin at the rear of his ship. At six-foot-six, he needed to bend his knees slightly to avoid knocking himself out cold on the ceiling, which rattled and creaked with each movement issued by the helm, up on the quarterdeck.

He was making himself ready for another day sailing the barren, unfamiliar Mediterranean Sea, on a heading to he didn't know where. He shoved his sixth and final pistol into his leather gun-belt, and then swung the belt like a sash around his broad torso. He inhaled the sweet scent of dirty steel and stale gunpowder as he ran a hand over his face.

I must be the skinniest pirate captain on all the seas now, he thought, feeling his jaw and cheek bones almost poking through his skin and thick beard, which hung to below his heart. He gave the gun-belt a tug, hearing the criss-crossed pistols knock against each other. It was definitely looser than usual. Two months in strange waters with diminishing and carefully rationed food supplies, without ships to plunder, and the weight had dropped off him like dust flicked off his shoulders.

Blackbeard had never needed much food to maintain his tall, broad frame – a bottle or two of rum a day usually kept him going – but even he had lost weight on this voyage. A voyage to nowhere. The rest of the crew was down to a single meal a day, usually stale bread and vegetables swimming in rather putrid, lukewarm water. His crew walked around looking little better than corpses that did not know they were dead.

He stooped to snatch up the leather waist-belt from his hammock, slinging it round his waist. Two clasp-knifes rested at either hip. Even with the belt fastened at the very last notch, he felt the blades drooping lower against his legs than usual. He walked to the cabin door, where his long red doublet hung on a rusty nail. He slipped it on. It was baggier than he had ever known before, but that wasn't such a bad thing – reaching for his pistols would be easier if the doublet was looser.

Instinctively, he reached into a side-pocket and felt around for the stiff length of fuse that he kept there. When taking a ship, he used to fix the fuses to the brim of his hat and set them alight, providing his targets with a vision of Hell, swarming over their gunwales.

But he didn't take them out – it had been a long time since he had had the opportunity to play the Devil at sea.

He stooped to pick up his hat from under his hammock. The leather was cracked and stale – as stiff as a corpse. All the years of placing lengths of lit fuses into the brim to scare merchants and lesser pirates into obedience had given it innumerable black holes, making it look almost diseased. But he would not replace it – not until it had been swiped it from his head by a fierce wind. Or a bullet. The hat was an old friend, that he had had ever since he first went to sea, almost a decade before.

Edward Teach turned to the small, cracked mirror fixed onto the back wall of his cabin, just behind the oak desk at which he rarely sat. Staring back at him was the face of Blackbeard.

A little skinnier, and more tired – but still Blackbeard.

He stepped out of his cabin and moved along the sparred gallery, his broad shoulders brushing the narrow walls. The wood beneath his boots creaked under his heavy steps. The *Queen Anne's Revenge* was beginning to sound as tired as its Captain felt.

Stopping at the rickety ladder that led up onto the quarterdeck, he could see through an open door into the gun-deck. He stopped for a moment, surveying the pathetic sight.

The gun-deck should have been the beating, raging heart of his vessel. The whole structure of the ship should have hummed and swelled with the reverberations of cannon fire it could barely contain; the air should have been thick and heavy with the scent of gunpowder; tendrils of smoke should have lingered like stubborn spirits. But today, the only stench was that of the ship itself – the limp, listless smell of old oak, and the stomach-turning odour of bilge water drifting up from the bowels like an invisible cloud. The deck had been scrubbed clean of the sand that would usually be strewn to help the gunners and powder monkeys keep their balance during a battle, and there was barely a speck of dried blood to be seen.

Blackbeard felt a gentle shudder of disgust in his gut. His gun-deck looked almost...civilised.

The walls of the gun-deck were mottled, each new shade of wood marking the repairs done by the ship's carpenters after the *Queen Anne* had taken a broadside months ago. Each wall had a row of twelve cannons standing at ease, unfired since then. Their muzzles stared at closed gunports, their breeching ropes were unfastened and lying in coils on the deck. The wooden tackles on which they were perched pulled double-duty, not only bracing the cannons, but also providing the dozen idle powder monkeys a place to rest their skinny legs as they dozed, their sleep untroubled by the lurching motion of the ship. The youngest, and generally most useless, members of the crew, Blackbeard kept them sleeping in the gun-deck when most of the mates had opted to sleep up on the waist-deck beneath the balmy Mediterranean night. He wanted them to always treat the gun-deck as their home, because he felt it would keep them ready should a battle ever come upon them unexpectedly.

This morning, he felt they had taken his order too literally.

'On your feet, you imbecilic sea rodents!' Blackbeard yelled. As the youngsters roused and rose, he snapped his fingers. 'All of you, practise before breakfast.'

'Practise what, Captain?' said one of them, a young lad with curly red hair stained with dirt and grease, and pimples bursting from his face.

Blackbeard sighed, stomping into the gun-deck as the scrawny powder monkeys rubbed their eyes clear of sleep, drawing closer together as their Captain loomed. 'Your jobs, lads,' he said. 'Practise your jobs.'

The powder monkeys blinked at him, and then looked at each other, their young faces set with confusion. None of them moved.

'Ready on the guns!' Blackbeard roared, for the first time in months.

The powder monkeys jumped on the spot, befuddled by the command – and afraid of what would happen if they got it wrong. Blackbeard stared them out until one of them – a lithe, lanky lad with dirty blond hair – finally understood, turning to his friends and shouting, 'Form the chain, form the chain!' as he took up his position by the cannon nearest Blackbeard.

The monkeys arranged themselves in their twelve-strong row, stretching all the way to the powder magazine at the far port-corner of the gun-deck, which was towards the bow of the ship. The one at the end, a bow-legged ginger lad – whose name, Blackbeard was pretty sure, was Daniel – disappeared behind the thick, damp curtain that was draped over the door, to prevent sparks from igniting the gunpowder.

The ship may not have seen action for months, but it still held enough gunpowder to blow it to smithereens that would rain on Cyprus.

The bow-legged lad re-emerged from behind the damp curtain, holding a heavy tube of thick leather – the cartridge – in his hand with the same reverence that a civilised man might have held a newborn baby. It was filled with six pounds of gunpowder. He handed it to the next monkey along the line, who passed it to his right, and so on, all the way back to the lanky lad who had got them going. He had a wide-eyed and frantic look on his face – as though the *Queen Anne* really was under attack. He looked from the cartridge to Blackbeard, and back again, then he stepped forward towards the cannon by which he had been sleeping.

'Cartridge, ready, uhm…matey!' he called, miming handing off the powder to an invisible gunner.

As the other powder monkeys looked on, brows creasing in bewilderment, the first one leant forward, a look of complete tension on his face, making a fist with his free hand, pumping it encouragingly. 'You can do it, mateys,' he said to the air. 'Your aim is the best onboard! Sink that ship!'

Blackbeard cuffed him round the back of the head, only gently – but his version of 'gently' was still enough to send the powder monkey sprawling. 'All right, don't take it too far.'

'Yeah, Michael,' said a short, squat one in the middle of the line. He looked to be the oldest of the group. 'You shouldn't talk to imaginary gunners. Surely that's bad luck? What if a ghost were to answer you?'

Michael bounced up to his feet, turning on his heels and looking all about himself, as though he could feel a spirit at his shoulder. Blackbeard shook his head – this young monkey was clearly about as bright as a Jolly Roger at night-time.

The rest of them stared at their captain, unsure what to do.

Blackbeard stared back at them. These were youngsters, who should have buzzed with the vitality of freedom and adventure. But instead, they looked like skeletons with a single layer of skin; skeletons ready to collapse in a heap of useless bones. Their motley jerkins hung loose around their bodies like sails, and their filthy breeches were held up only by rope tightly tied. Their mouths gaped open, sucking in air that whistled as it slipped past broken and missing teeth that were yellow and loosened, ready to fall out any moment.

'Work on your speed,' Blackbeard told them. 'Get a rhythm going. Get faster. Laziness and idleness is a deadlier disease for a pirate than Yellow Jack. Always be ready. Understand?'

The powder monkeys nodded, then continued their pantomime sea battle, passing the cartridge back and forth along the line. Blackbeard turned to walk out of the gun-deck, thinking it was a very good thing his crew had seen no action in so long.

With this rabble on board, he didn't much fancy their chances.

'Oh, and one more thing,' he said, stopping in the doorway. He eyed Michael. 'Stop saying "matey".'

Chapter Three

Blackbeard climbed up the ladder that led from the sparred gallery up out onto the quarterdeck. The salty Mediterranean air was like a warm hand smothering his face. The endless smudge of the horizon, like a glue binding sea to sky, was just becoming visible beyond the morning mist that was clearing at the command of the relentless sun, whose reflection was like an oasis of diamonds in the water.

Above, the square-rigged black-and-red mizzen-sails slapped against the mast and rigging. Ahead, the mainsails, looming dead in the centre of the ship, and the fore-sails by the bow did the same, the canvas rippling and snapping in the growing breeze that was like three godly palms slowly shoving his ship forward.

Down on the waist-deck, clusters of pirates in loose jerkins and filthy bandanas worked the rigging, cupping hands to their mouths to holler directions or insults to the topmen perched high up on the masts. The deck itself almost gleamed in the morning light – hardly surprising, as the crew had had very little to do since they had left the Caribbean the previous

November, and had grown so bored that scrubbing the decks became a pleasant distraction.

Blackbeard turned to face Mister Hands, the helmsman, who gently guided the *Queen Anne*. He was a stocky fellow, whose sausage-like fingers always looked on the verge of snapping the spokes off the helm with too urgent a change of direction. His long brown hair spilled out in tufts from beneath the white bandana he wore, which contrasted sharply with his sunburnt complexion.

'The First Mate gave the order to weigh anchor, sir,' said Hands, his voice trembling a little. 'We didn't know when you'd wake up.'

'I have no trouble getting up these days,' said Blackbeard. 'It's a lot easier when there's no more rum on board to give you a hangover. Maintain this heading, Mister Hands – wherever it is…'

Blackbeard ignored the look on his helmsman's face – a curious look that asked how his Captain could not even enquire as to where they were headed. He moved to the steps that led down onto the waist deck, sitting down and tilting the brim of his hat against the harsh Mediterranean sun.

An older pirate broke from the edge of the ragged group beneath the mainsail. He had not been participating, as a one-fingered man was little good to anyone; instead, he was directing the work – or commenting derisively about its quality. He approached Blackbeard, frustration showing in his one remaining eye, and in the downturn of what was left of his bottom lip.

'What is it, Handsome?' Blackbeard asked.

Handsome Harry, the *Queen Anne's* boatswain – charged with keeping an eye on everything happening up on-deck – half-bowed his head, which had burn scars where other men had hair. 'Permission to be critical, Captain?'

Blackbeard smiled, knowing from the stiffness in his cheeks that it had been a while since his last one. 'When you have ever asked my permission for that?'

Handsome was not in the mood to be jocular. 'The crew are restless,' he said. 'Aimless sailing on a heading to nowhere just will not do, sir.' He pointed the last of his fingers – the little one on his right hand, miraculously not blown off by a bullet fired by a British Royal Navy officer in a battle off the coast of Charleston (who had been promptly captured and keel-hauled) – towards the stern of the ship. 'I would strongly suggest that we turn about, and head back west—'

'Have you forgotten already?' said Blackbeard. 'We

are dead in the west. Literally.'

This was true. Throughout the Caribbean, and all along the east coast of America, word had spread of Blackbeard's death at the hands of the Navy. But, unless he was a ghost sweating at the mercy of the Mediterranean sun right now, he was very much alive. He had struck a deal with Governor Spotswood of Virginia, who had grown tired of trying to arrest or kill the world's most feared freebooter. The deal was, Blackbeard would go on his merry way to new seas, leaving America well alone. The Navy would get the credit for having killed him, and Blackbeard would not be pursued. He would be a free man.

It was the best kind of payment.

'Pirates we may be, and brave ones – but are we stupid, Handsome?' he asked. 'Stupid enough to sail back to the Atlantic and invite the whole Royal Navy to turn the myth of our deaths into reality?'

'Of course not,' said Handsome. 'But—'

'But nothing, you one-eyed sea-mongrel,' said Blackbeard, standing up from the steps, giving himself a height advantage over the older pirate. Not that he needed it. 'There's no point being a dead pirate – an actually dead one. You can bet they don't have any high seas in Hell.'

'Are we any better than dead here? We've not seen a sloop to take in weeks, and the land is barren.'

'I'm starting to wonder about withdrawing your permission to be critical.'

Handsome bowed his head again, his scars gleaming white against his reddish-pink skin. 'I mean no disrespect,' he said. 'It's just starting to look as though they don't even have trade routes in the east.'

'Of course they do,' said Blackbeard. 'We're sailing in the Mediterranean, amidst the vast Ottoman Empire – which means, there's trading going on somewhere. What do you think the Barbary pirates are plundering? Whales?'

'That's another thing we have to think about,' said Handsome. 'The Barbary mob ain't gonna be too happy we're sailing their waters.'

'These are my waters now,' said Blackbeard.

'They don't know that, Captain,' said Handsome.

'They soon will.'

He stomped down the last few steps onto the waist-deck. Handsome stood aside before Blackbeard could barge past him.

He moved down the starboard side, running his palm along the smooth top-edge of the gunwale, and feeling the misty spray of seawater on his skin as the ship rolled with the swells, over and over again like a thrown ball slowly bouncing.

As he passed them, the pirates working the rigging would mutter, 'Mornin', Captain,' and he'd respond with a tip of his hat.

A shadow fell over him, and Blackbeard looked up to see a tall, lithe figure about forty feet above his head, sliding down a loose length of cordage and landing in front of him. The figure was a tall woman, with thick black hair cut in a boyish style, close and uneven; her dark brown eyes and high cheekbones were exactly like the ones Blackbeard saw in the mirror.

She was his half-sister, Mary Bonny.

'Show-off,' Blackbeard muttered, continuing his aimless walk towards the bow of the ship.

Mary followed. 'We're quite close to Cyprus,' she said.

Blackbeard didn't look back. 'So?'

'So, you told us you planned to sail only as far as Spain,' said Mary.

Blackbeard snorted as he stopped just beyond the mainsail, beside a hapless crewmate whose name he thought was Jacob. He was wrestling with a rebellious halyard, the rope constantly fighting free of his grip – a mistake that was drawing the ire from the topman perched high up in the rigging, struggling to keep the sail honest. Blackbeard snatched the rope from Jacob and wrapped it around his forearm twice, then tugged to show that it was now easier to control. 'Like this, got it?'

'Aye, Captain,' said Jacob, taking it from him and doing the same.

Blackbeard raised a hand to pat him on the back, but stopped himself. If he patted one of them on the back, he'd have to pat them all. And who had the time to be that encouraging?

He turned and saw Mary still pouting at him.

'Ah, come on,' he said, continuing to stomp up the deck, tipping his hat to the crew that greeted him. 'If I'd wanted to be nagged left, right and centre, I'd have retired and got myself a family. And anyway – you just want my ship to yourself.'

'Too right I do,' said Mary. 'You promised I'd have the ship if you died.'

'I ain't dead yet.'

'As far as the world's concerned, you are. And anyway, at least, with me as captain, we wouldn't be so hungry – and sober.'

'Oh, you'd do better, would you, sister?'

'If given the chance,' said Mary, as she followed him

up the ladder to the raised end of the bow, above the forecastle, which led back down to the gun-deck. The gun-deck door was ajar, and the cries of the powder monkeys, still engaged in their pantomime battle, drifted up.

'Come on, lads!' he could hear young Michael hollering. 'It'll be a disgrace to be sunk by a French vessel!'

'Take this, Frenchies!' another one shouted, as the whole group simulated the firing of a gun.

'*BOOM!*'

Mary paused at the top of the ladder, staring at the forecastle door. 'Should I even ask?'

Blackbeard just smiled, coming to a stop by the very edge of the ship. He leant over and watched as his hull broke the foamy water, sending spray in every direction. His mermaid angel figurehead had a scrap of real seaweed dangling from one of her wooden pistols – a pistol that was forever brandished, ready to fire, but would never have the opportunity.

Stranded in the Mediterranean, unsure of where they would wash up, or if they'd ever again cross paths with a prize, Blackbeard felt that he could relate to the wooden angel – always ready for a fight that was never going to come.

'At least let's turn about and clear the reach of the Ottoman,' said Mary. 'They won't take too kindly to foreign pirates. We should sail back to Europe – at least we know where we are there, and we'll have more opportunity.'

Blackbeard nodded, his head feeling heavy with reluctance – and a little sadness. Maybe it was time. 'All right, sister. You win. I—' Then he grew quiet. He leant out over the bow, squinting into the distance.

Mary was tapping him furiously on the shoulder. 'You what?' she said. 'Come on!'

'One last score,' he said. 'We give the Old World one more shot and, whatever happens, we turn back for Europe after that.'

Mary followed his gaze, shielded her eyes with her hands. 'What have you seen?'

'Opportunity, sister,' said Blackbeard. 'It is literally on the horizon.'

Chapter Four

A few minutes later, Blackbeard lowered his spyglass and turned round, leaning his body back against the bulwark. His most trusted crewmates – Mary Bonny, Handsome, his First Mate Chris Claw, and quartermaster Brutal Bill Howard – were stood in a semi-circle around him.

'It's a galley,' he told them. 'North African – Barbary – probably. From this distance, I'd say three masts, but no more than twenty guns. Ten less than us.'

'How many on board?' asked Chris Claw, his pale blue eyes alight with the thrill of impending violence. His filthy, jagged nails, that gave him his nickname, scratched at flea bites on his neck.

'I can't tell from here,' said Blackbeard.

Mary took the spyglass from him, peering towards the horizon. 'I still don't know how you spotted it in the first place.'

'That's what makes me captain,' he said, earning a scowl from his sister as she shoved the spyglass back to him, right into his chest. With his skinnier frame and lack of bulk, it hurt more than he was willing to let on.

'This is the opportunity we've been waiting for,' said Chris, flexing his vicious hands. 'Let's meet the locals head on, and rip their throats out. Show 'em who runs these waters now, eh?'

But Brutal Bill was shaking his head, turning his face up into the wind. His complexion was cracked like old leather from a decade of punishment meted out by the Caribbean sun. 'We're downwind of them,' he said. 'That's not good.'

Blackbeard thought aloud. 'They're lighter, faster and upwind of us. Which means they can mix aggression with caution – at the first show of our strength, they'll probably just turn around and sod off.'

'And we won't catch 'em,' said Handsome. 'Not with a ship this size.'

'And not with a crew this size,' said Mary. 'They might sail towards us, but they'll stay well out of our firing range as soon as they see how many men we have. It's a stalemate before we've even had a chance to engage.'

Blackbeard nodded, his thoughts turning this way and that like a ship with an unmanned helm. Idea after idea was considered and rejected in an instant – all because he knew it would take the foolhardiest of pirates to sail right up to a ship the size of the *Queen Anne*, especially when it hosted so large a crew.

There's too many of us, he thought. *Even if we do resemble walking corpses.*

Then an idea struck him. He looked to Handsome and Chris. 'You two,' he said, 'get the all topmen down from the rigging, and tell the men to let the cordage loose. Mary, tell Mister Hands he's relieved of his duties for the time being. Bill, collect the gunners and tell them that they can forget the sails and do their real jobs. There's a dozen powder monkeys down there – tell them to load up and be ready. But do not run out the starboard cannons until I give the signal.'

'What signal?' asked Bill, already turning away. Handsome was gesturing to those working the fore-sail, while Chris Claw was relaying Blackbeard's orders at the main. Mutters of confusion drifted back to Blackbeard, matching the look on Mary's face.

'You won't miss it,' Blackbeard told Bill. 'Now get going.'

As Bill ducked into the forecastle, Blackbeard turned and raised his spyglass at the horizon one more time. If the *Queen Anne* was sailing a straight course east, then by his reckoning, the galley was sailing north, maybe northeast.

Even if they see us, Blackbeard thought, *we might be too far out of their way for them to think about having a go. But if they do see us, and don't at least get a little bit closer to check us out, then they are a disgrace to the very name 'pirate'.*

'Would you mind telling me,' said Mary, 'what on earth you're doing? Taking Mister Hands from the helm, leaving the sails down and unmanned, without dropping anchor? Edward' – she was the only one onboard who used his real name and she did it just to annoy him – 'this is madness.'

'We need them close,' said Blackbeard. 'And they won't get close if they see a big ship with a big crew. And they'll be suspicious if they see a big ship with no crew at all. But if they see a big ship with a *dead* crew...'

Mary looked over the crewmates, seeing what Blackbeard had seen a few moments before. Malnourished men who, from a distance, would make convincing cadavers. 'You're going to bait them into drawing right up alongside us.'

Blackbeard nodded.

'I hate to say it,' said Mary, 'but that's not a bad idea.'

Blackbeard patted her on the head, in a patronising

way that he knew made her blood boil. 'The idea of a captain, you might say.'

Mary just grunted, and moved off towards Mister Hands at the helm, weaving through a mass of mates standing beneath the sails, which fluttered and billowed in the wild wind, the cordage writhing like tentacles. The *Queen Anne* rocked a little, heaving to the left and then the right, but the conditions were mild enough that Blackbeard did not need to worry about capsizing.

He marched amidships to address them. 'A prize is close, lads,' he said, drawing excited murmurs from the men. 'But we need to set a trap for it. And that trap is, that *we* are the prize. We can now consider ourselves fortunate that we've half-starved out here in the Mediterranean – as it means that we can play dead better than most. Now, I'd say we have ten minutes before our deck becomes clearly visible to anyone on board this galley who has a spyglass, so that means you have ten minutes to grab some weapons. Once you've done that, I want you to come back up and then take a nap for an hour or so... Once you lay down, you must not move until I do. Is everyone clear?'

'Aye, Captain,' came the chorused response.

Blackbeard nodded. 'I know it's been rough since we left the New World behind. Starting now, the good days return.'

The crewmates gave a cheer as they dispersed, disappearing below decks. Blackbeard sat down at the starboard side, beneath the ragged shade offered by the mainsail. He angled his hat down over his forehead for further shade. Then he drew one of his pistols and lay down on his back.

The pure blue sky flooded his vision as he settled in to wait.

As the ten minutes drew to a close, Blackbeard saw his crew slithering like snakes along the scrubbed decks. Several dragged canvas bags full of pistols and daggers and cutlasses, handing them out to be passed from mate to mate, everyone staying low against the bulwarks.

Except the ship's resident holy fellow, Chaplain Charlie, who had lost a game of Chuck-farthen against the cook, Mister Peters, and was thus elected to drape himself over the capstan, as though he had breathed his last while desperately weighing the anchor.

'Are you sure this is necessary, Captain?' he had said at the time.

'Aye,' Blackbeard had replied. 'It makes it more convincing.'

'How?'

'Because it will look so uncomfortable, the Barbary pirates will be convinced it has to be for real.'

So the Chaplain had dutifully draped himself over a capstan spoke, and the only part of him that moved was his long, dark hair swaying in the wind.

But he moaned. Good grief, did he moan.

'I think I've squashed my bladder,' he screeched now as, beyond him, at the port bulwark, Mary Bonny laid a musket over her lap and passed a pistol to a young topman, who looked as though he didn't know which end of it to hold.

Blackbeard shot a quick glance at Chaplain Charlie, seeing his lower abdomen yielding to the heavy steel of the capstan spoke. He could believe it had done some damage. It took half-a-dozen men to turn the great wheel in order to lift or drop the anchor. It was not going to lose a battle with a portly pirate Chaplain.

'Any dripping on my deck,' Blackbeard told him, 'and you'll be thrown overboard.'

'This is *extremely* uncomfortable, Captain,' said Charlie.

'Of course it's uncomfortable,' said Blackbeard.

'Did you expect death to be pleasant?'

As the last gun made it around the deck, Blackbeard called to the crew: 'Now, take a rest, mateys. And remember – be as still as you can. If the enemy has spotted us we have between forty-five minutes and an hour before they come up alongside, assuming the conditions remain consistent. Keep your eyes closed and your ears open.'

The crewmates lay down in a ragged formation across the deck, as though they had succumbed to starvation or disease. Their breeches were rolled up above the knees, showing their bony shins, and their jerkins hung open, revealing their ribs.

The Barbary pirates in the galley on the horizon could not fail to fall for it.

He hoped.

He had no way of knowing whether they had taken the bait or not. He and his crew lay still as dead men for an hour, unable to peer up over the gunwale for fear of being seen and giving the game away. Blackbeard did his best to listen for any approach, but his ears were filled with the roar of the wind, and the flapping of his own ship's loose sails. Waves butted the hull on both sides. With his body on the deck, he felt like he could hear and feel every creak and crack of the wood from bow to stern, weather-deck to bilge; like he was hearing the quickening pulse of the *Queen Anne's Revenge* as it anticipated the battle and carnage ahead.

He caught the eye of Mary, who sat slumped against the port bulwark, her musket hidden beneath her right leg. She was motionless, but still able to convey a sense of irritation. She clearly felt their enemies weren't coming.

Blackbeard was about to nod and, reluctantly, command the crew to get to their feet, when his ears pricked at a foreign sound sifting through the cacophony around the *Queen Anne*. More sails, snapping at the command of expert pirates working a rigging with purpose; another hull charging through the sea; coarse commands in a strange tongue; the creaking of an approaching ship as it was pulled hard to port.

The Barbary lot had bitten on the bait! They were drawing up alongside the supposed ghost ship, starboard side to starboard side, bow to stern.

The harsh voice from onboard the enemy galley drew louder. Blackbeard could imagine a Barbary pirate standing at his own starboard side, now able to see more than half the weather-deck, with a clear view of most of the supposedly dead European pirates. Hidden by his own starboard bulwark, Blackbeard drew a second pistol and pulled himself up into a sitting position as quietly he could, the barrels up by his cheeks. The pirates along his starboard side shifted into position, weapons ready.

From behind him came the low whoosh of steel cutting through the air, of rope unfurling and extending before a faint shadow swooped, heralding the arrival of a rusty grapnel that clattered on to the deck, scuttling back towards the bulwark like a crab as it was drawn back to latch onto the gunwale, not four feet to Blackbeard's right. Angling his head, he saw the grapnel twitch as one of the Barbary mob tested its stability.

He grinned to himself, feeling his heart begin to pound with anticipation. Any moment now, more of the grapnels would come, and once the tethers were secure, then would come the boarding planks, on which the Barbary men would run across – right into Blackbeard's trap.

Except, this was not what happened.

Instead, Blackbeard heard the twang of a rope under stress, heard the steel hooks of the grapnel bite a little harder into his gunwale, just before the tall, muscular figure of a Barbary pirate leaped onto his deck, barefoot, with his brown leather waistcoat flapping in the breeze.

And he was carrying a curved sword that looked sharp enough to chop a mast in half with one swing.

Blackbeard was on his feet in an instant, revising his plan as he moved. He tossed both pistols in the air and caught them by the barrels. He swung both handles like clubs at the Barbary man's jaw, knocking out his teeth, which rained down on the deck. He was a tough lad – he managed to keep hold of his sword, and his knees wobbled only slightly at blows that would have left most men asleep for the rest of the week. Blackbeard dropped the pistol in his left hand, before wrapping his arm around the man's neck. He held the barrel of the pistol in his right hand against the knot of the fellow's purple bandana, as he turned to face the rest of the Barbary crew.

There were more than he'd expected.

Chapter Five

When he first saw the Barbary ship up close, Blackbeard was tickled by mild outrage on behalf of whichever European crew they had taken it from. It looked like it had once been a French frigate. It was full-rigged, its black hull smooth and sleek for speed. It had no raised bow, and a quarterdeck that could probably be reached with a small hop. He couldn't tell, because the gunports were closed, but he reckoned his earlier assessment of ten guns was correct.

The corsair's flag flew at the mizzen-mast – a rather splendid design of a two-headed cobra. You didn't get stuff like that in the New World.

The crew were lined up two- to three-deep along their starboard side. Blackbeard's eyes were drawn to a young man roughly in the centre of the first line, who had a blood-stained blue bandana on his head, with tufts of dark, curly hair fighting their way free. He wore a dung-brown waistcoat made of cracked, weather-beaten leather and hoop earrings in both ears. He had a broad dagger at one hip, and a pistol at the other.

Pirate. Or corsair, in this strange part of the globe

in which Blackbeard had found himself – the Old World. And from the way his gaze seemed to draw in everyone on board the *Queen Anne's Revenge*, like they were rickety dinghies drifting into a maelstrom, Blackbeard knew he was the captain.

'Do you know who I am?' asked Blackbeard. It was an odd question to him because it had been many years since he had met someone who *didn't* know who he was.

'Are you Blackbeard?' asked the young pirate, whose English was better than half of Blackbeard's crew. 'The New World villain they call Man from Hell?'

Blackbeard bit his lip to suppress a smile. How long had it been since anyone had used his old nickname? A long time. It had been even longer since he had had a real chance to live up to it. It was a good nickname – who wouldn't be afraid of a six-foot-six pirate called Man from Hell?

Well...this young lad staring him out from the galley didn't seem scared. But then, he didn't look like the easily spooked type, and with good reason – his broad, muscular frame looked like it could do some damage if he got even mildly annoyed, let alone angry.

And he looked very angry now.

'Aye,' said Blackbeard. 'That'd be me.'

The young man did not move. 'Why are you sailing the Mediterranean?' he asked. 'These waters belong to us.'

Blackbeard cast a glance towards Chris Claw, who was flexing his hideous hands, ready to use those filthy nails to rip the cheeks off their new enemy. The line of pistols extended over the gunwale stayed unerringly straight, even though Blackbeard knew his skinny, weary crew must be tiring quickly. He was proud of them – and determined not to sail them straight into a deadly defeat.

But he would have to play this situation very, very carefully.

Blackbeard looked back to the young Barbary captain. 'What's your name, laddie?'

The enemy captain's eyes were as unwavering as his gun-arm. He slapped his free hand to his chest, his dark skin rippling with muscles and filmed with sweat that glistened in the sunlight. This was a successful, well-fed sea bandit. Unlike Blackbeard's crew.

Then the captain said his name as if Blackbeard ought to have heard of him. Not only had Blackbeard never heard of him, he had no idea what language the fellow was even speaking.

'Well, I won't be able to pronounce that,' said Blackbeard, tightening his grip on the toothless corsair when he felt him begin to squirm, blood from his shattered mouth dribbling over Blackbeard's forearm. He dug the gun barrel a little harder into his skull to signal he did not appreciate resistance. 'So, if you don't mind, I think I'm just going to call you…Percy.'

Mary Bonny snorted, despite herself. Elsewhere, some of his crew sniggered. In front of him, the corsair's eyes burned with hot fury, like two white suns.

'What?' said Blackbeard. 'You don't like Percy? I think that's a good name.'

'This is *our* sea,' said Percy. 'We make the rules – and our new rule is: you must go now.'

'I'm afraid I'm going to have to break that rule, my friend,' said Blackbeard.

'You're not my friend,' said Percy. 'You're a trespasser. Go home.'

'Can't,' said Blackbeard. 'My old seas aren't exactly pirate-friendly these days.'

Percy shrugged. 'Not our problem.'

'What's the matter, Percy? You afraid of a little competition?'

Percy smiled, flashing a golden molar or two.

'You're not competition. You try fighting with us, you'll get smashed to pieces. We sail with the fleet of Amir Barbarossa.'

Blackbeard heard a few of his pirates shift uncomfortably, heard someone gasp. They might not have known who Percy was, but Amir Barbarossa's name *had* travelled west.

'The Barbary King, eh?' said Blackbeard. 'I'm impressed. And dubious – not much of a fleet if you boys are allowed to go off wandering on your own.'

'We're on a mission for the King,' said Percy.

'Oh yeah?' said Blackbeard. 'And what mission might that be?'

'None of your business,' said Percy. 'Just leave our waters.'

'No.'

Percy leaned over his gunwale, gritting his teeth as he shouted: 'By sailing these waters, you're insulting me!'

Blackbeard took a handful of his prisoner's leather waistcoat, his eyes never leaving Percy's. 'And you're *boring* me.'

Dragging on the waistcoat, he threw the prisoner to the ground. Then he fired his pistol over the side of his ship.

Chapter Six

The sound of a pistol being fired was ear-shatteringly loud in most situations.

But down in the gun-deck, Brutal Bill Howard barely heard it over the symphony of the sea – the strings of the wind over the percussion of the waves slapping a creaking hull – or the anxious beating of his heart, roaring in his ears as he surveyed the gunners arranged in threes around each of the dozen starboard cannons that were loaded and ready to be run out on his command. Amid such noise, a pistol shot sounded almost incidental, its brief explosion of fire, smoke and charred wadding no more dramatic than a hiccup in a crowded tavern.

Bill hurried along the starboard side, giving a last tug on each of the slightly frayed breeching ropes that were wrapped round the backs of the cannons, fastened to thick metal hooks nailed either side of the gunports. Above his head, he could just about hear the muted pops of pistol- and musket-fire, sounding like a handful of rocks thrown at a wall. The hoarse yelling and coarse threats of the men up on deck fought to be heard through the roar of the sea and wind.

The battle was well and truly on.

Satisfied the breeching ropes were secure, Bill snapped his fingers at the twelve powder monkeys, who stood at the port side.

Dull beams of light crawled in through the opposite gunports as the monkeys threw them open. Even though the weapons on that side would not be fired, the ventilation from the open ports would be crucial once the starboard cannons started spewing their choking smoke.

The powder monkeys then took up their position in the wide aisle between the guns, providing a human chain all the way to the powder magazine. Bill noticed that their formation was perfectly spaced: every single one of them was within arm's reach of those either side, and about three long strides away from the butt of the nearest cannon – close enough to quickly hand off a cartridge when it was needed, but far enough away to not have his legs snapped by the recoiling cannon and tackle. He felt a flush of optimism at their organisation, as well as pride – they must have been practising.

The aisle had been completely covered in sand, to ensure balance amid the carnage – once the *Queen Anne's Revenge* started taking hits, it would rock and lurch and heave, drawing in sprayed seawater to mingle with the blood of the gunners and monkeys that would inevitably drop onto the deck during the conflict. The sand would be crucial to the gun-crew maintaining a decent rate of fire.

Bill turned to the trios of gunners lined up along the starboard side. 'Run 'em out!' he roared.

At each weapon, one gunner moved to throw open their gunport; then he stooped to light the lantern that was left beside the weapon, for visibility once the deck was filled with black fog. His two mates then heaved the weapon forward, the muzzle extending through the open port – twelve of them running out. To the enemy, it would look like the *Queen Anne's Revenge* was baring her teeth.

'Fire!'

The starboard cannon nearest the bow went first, its immediate neighbour firing before it had even fully recoiled. The sequence was continued all the way along to the twelfth cannon, nearest the stern. This was the Captain's preferred tactic, to fire what he called a rolling broadside, that would slowly rip a long gash in the enemy's hull, from stern to bow. It was all very well making twelve holes at once, but reloading all those twelve cannons took time – time during which any opposing gunners that had survived could strike back. But a barrage of shots, one by one, would create a feeling of relentless, unstoppable firepower for the enemy – that he was being swarmed, hit on all sides. As the *Queen Anne's* twelfth shot was fired, the first cannon would be close to ready for its second round. Though single strikes alone were not devastating, the time between shots was minimised – and when they came in from all directions, filling the enemy gun-deck with a storm of splinters and lead, even the most hardened gunner onboard would surely be unsettled.

As each of the starboard cannons unleashed its ire, it recoiled ferociously, the tackle sliding and scraping along the wooden deck. The three gunners manning the weapon would hop aside, as if avoiding a bucking horse, as the breeching ropes stretched taut, threatening to snap or rip their metal rings free.

It was at this point that Brutal Bill ceased to shout any commands – because he knew there was little chance of him being heard. Not in a gun-deck that rattled with the vibrating echo of cannon fire, and not by the gunners and powder monkeys whose ears would be ringing for days from this point on. Now, he just had to leave it in the hands of the gunners, and stay close to provide any assistance or guidance that he could give with physical gestures.

As the gunners hurried to reload their cannons, the smoke from the twelve shots began to fill the gun-deck like fog. The powder monkeys stepping forward to hand off new cartridges were already faint, almost ghostly to Bill's eyes, as were the trios of gunners as they hauled their cannons back and reached for their worms – metal rods with a corkscrew top, shoved down the muzzle to clear any debris left behind by the first round. Once cleared, another gunner cleaned the barrel with a wet sponge attached to a wooden rod. To clear and clean the barrel required two men to crouch right by the open gunport, which – during a battle – was just about the most exposed place onboard. As they worked, the gunners threw anxious glances out of the opening, towards the enemy vessel – surveying the damage, but also checking to see if returning fire was imminent.

As Bill passed the fourth cannon, where gunners Patrick and Francis were finishing cleaning their barrel, he was suddenly bathed in a pool of light that seemed to burn through the smoke; then a shower of splinters which lacerated his face and hands.

As he instinctively closed his eyes against the torrent

of timber flung forward from the hole torn in the *Queen Anne's* starboard side, Bill felt the cannonball slam into his stomach, lifting him off his feet and driving him all the way across the gun-deck.

And he had not heard a thing.

Chapter Seven

While the *Queen Anne's* cannons were being run out, up on deck Blackbeard was leaning over the starboard gunwale and firing the fourth of his six pistols. He ducked as a return shot came close to his head, hearing the breaking of flesh and feeling a splash of blood slap him on the back, just before the dead weight of a pirate fell against him. He shrugged his right shoulder to free it up, and saw the lifeless form of Mister Hands slump to the deck.

The Barbary pirates had killed his helmsman. They would pay for that.

All around him, his pirates were firing shots and then scrambling around on the decks to reload, which was a tricky business amid the flailing arms and kicking legs. Once reloaded, they would spring back up to fire again, then they would duck back down to repeat the sequence. With their pistols only capable of firing one shot at a time, it would be impossible to wipe out an enemy with a wave of lead from up on deck. Especially not with the rocking of the ship throwing off aim.

The gunfire was just the prologue to the main battle,

which would be fought with fists and feet and blades, once the bullets ran out.

As Brutal Bill's gunners unleashed their rolling broadside, the Barbary pirates howled in distress as their deck rattled and wobbled from the impact. They had been caught out completely by Blackbeard's deception – they had been expecting a simple boarding mission, not a barrage of cannon-fire that had great chunks of their hull raining on the surface of the sea.

Half-ducked behind his bulwark, Percy fired a wild shot with his pistol.

'Oh no you don't,' Blackbeard mumbled, aiming his fifth and sixth guns across the sea at the enemy captain. He pulled the triggers just as Percy dropped out of sight behind the bulwark, Blackbeard's shot hitting one Barbary pirate in the gut, and another in the shoulder, sending him spinning.

His last pistols spent, Blackbeard dropped into a sitting position, sliding down to take cover, feeling the bulwark rattle and jolt as the Barbary mob's poorly aimed bullets slammed into it on the other side, the vibrations mingling with those he could feel in his legs and feet as the *Queen Anne's* gunners below began another barrage.

Next to him, Mary Bonny was sat, biting the end

off a small paper tube that contained gunpowder and a musket ball. Holding the ball between her front teeth, she poured the powder into the barrel of her long gun. Then she spat the ball into the air, thrusting up the musket to catch it while, with her free hand, she scrunched up the paper tube into a ball, which was the last thing to be shoved down the barrel to keep the ball in place.

The gun loaded, she held it ready in both hands, diagonally across her chest, while smirking at him across the barrel. 'Bet you can't do that,' she said.

Whoosh!

Blackbeard thrust out a hand to push Mary backwards, just as another grapnel dropped over the gunwale, right where her head had been a second earlier. Had it struck her, it might have knocked her out – or torn three ditches in the top of her skull.

The grapnel was drawn back and hooked onto the gunwale. Blackbeard looked across it at his sister, who shared his incredulous look – were Percy's mob going to try boarding, in the midst of a battle that they were losing?

He was not expecting that.

'Scatter!' Blackbeard cried, as scores of grapnels came soaring over the side of the ship. His crewmates scrambled back, out of the way of the heavy metal claws, which latched onto gunwales. 'Send them to the sea!' he shouted, jumping to his feet and resuming his position. A dozen or more of Percy's pirates were running along the taut ropes that tethered the two ships, as easily as if they were on land. Their curved swords were raised and their eyes burned with fury and hate. Blackbeard was impressed with not only their agility, but their foolhardy bravery, running through the thickening smoke right towards a band of enemy pirates who had the upper hand.

But that did not mean he would spare them.

Taking out the pair of clasp-knifes from his waist-belt, Blackbeard hacked at the two ropes nearest him, watching two of the Barbary pirates plunge towards the littered ocean, right into the path of cannonballs fired from Percy's ship, which tore their bodies in half, right at the tailbone.

But more – many more – of them had already made it across.

Chapter Eight

Brutal Bill himself could not believe it when his eyes opened. The first thought in his foggy, bruised brain was: *Is Hell a gun-deck?*

His second thought was: That actually makes sense.

But then the feeling flooded back into his body and from the dull, repetitive waves of pain in his gut, he knew he was still alive. He was half-slumped against the port side of the ship, his neck bent at an awkward angle, legs splayed in front of him, feet disappearing into the veil of thick smoke exhaled by the raging cannons. It was so heavy, he could no longer see a single one of the gunners, although he knew from the way the ship jolted and hummed beneath his body that those who were not yet dead still worked tirelessly, heroically, to pound the Barbary lot into submission. Faint, pathetic daylight from the holes that had been punched in the *Queen Anne* glowed rebelliously behind the smoke – their enemies were not giving up, and had given almost as good as they had got.

But the *Queen Anne* was still in the fight. More surprisingly, so was Bill.

Just how had he taken a cannonball to the gut and lived to question how he had survived?

As his body grew used to the pain, to the dull ache in his ribs and the lack of air in his lungs, Bill could feel the weight of the cannonball resting on his belly. It should have passed through him – it should have smashed his skeleton into pieces.

He reached down a hand to roll it off him, and felt slick, greasy hair at his fingers. Stunned, he glanced down and locked eyes with gunner Patrick, who looked up at him in the shock of a death he had only just seen coming.

Patrick had been decapitated by a broadside, which had sent his head flying into Bill, moving so fast he had thought it a cannonball. The gunner's neck was now mostly scraps of blood-slick skin, with a shard of skull and jaw protruding from the bottom edge. Somewhere behind the curtain of choking smoke was the rest of him.

Bill sat up straight and laid Patrick's head on the deck, beside an idle port cannon. He got to his feet, his spine screaming in discomfort, his ribs groaning with every breath. At least a few of them had to be cracked, if not broken.

He hacked and coughed, tasting the iron tang of

blood on his tongue and teeth. He spat the red glob out and stumbled deeper into the veil of smoke, feeling the sand slicker beneath his boots, feeling the ship almost reeling back from another hit. His instinct told him to protect his face, and he felt his forearms peppered by shards and splinters as he fought his way to the fifth cannon, which had been torn a new porthole about the size of two stacked rum barrels.

It was unmanned. The light from the ship's wounds shoved some of the smoke back, revealing half a body here, most of a leg there; a head impaled on a sword-shaped shard of timber; scraps of bone in puddles of blood, looking like the most hideous stew had been spilled on the gun-deck – pieces of pirates were all around the fifth cannon, with no way of telling which piece belonged to which pirate.

Bill turned on his heels, wiping his eyes clear of the burning tears that were streaming from them, wanting to shout questions and commands, but knowing he would not be heard. How many gunners did they have left? He could just about see as far as the fourth cannon, where one of the powder monkeys was filling in for a gunner who was either seriously wounded, or dead.

There was no way of knowing.

The powder monkey – the tall, lanky one with blond hair that had been blackened by the smoke – looked around helplessly. Bill saw the problem.

They were out of shot.

Locking eyes with the monkey, Bill gestured that he would search, turning to charge back into the smoke-filled aisle, to the port side, where more cannonballs were stored on racks. But as he moved, he felt the ship heave at the impact of another blow, the force of it making him stumble a few steps. The *Queen Anne's* crew had the superior firepower, but the Barbary pirates were resilient, seemingly content to exchange shots until one of them surrendered, ran out of cannons, or sank into the Mediterranean.

It was going to take more than another simple rolling broadside to turn this battle to their favour. Bill knew they needed to launch a different sort of strike, one that would unsettle the hearts of the Barbary boys in the same way that cannon-fire wobbled their legs.

And Bill had an idea how to do that.

He scrambled through the thick smoke hanging in the aisle between the cannons, back towards port, hoping that – wherever he was – gunner Patrick would forgive him for what he was about to do.

Chapter Nine

The weather-decks of the *Queen Anne* were barely visible for the fighting pirates. They pressed together, swelling and heaving from starboard to port and back again, writhing like a charmed snake. Blackbeard's crew were giving a good account of themselves for a bunch of sunburned, skinny, sober sea-bandits who were rather out of practice. Mary Bonny had climbed onto the back of one Barbary pirate, wrapping her arms around his throat and choking him to his knees. Chris Claw moved through the group like a human axe, his filthy nails swiping at cheeks and necks, sending stubbly skin and scraps of flesh flying in all directions. Handsome Harry defied his age and near-invalidity to duck and dodge slashing knives and driving punches, jabbing his last finger into any open eye within his reach.

Blackbeard himself surged through the tight crowd, forgotten power flowing through his limbs as he uppercut a corsair here, head-butted another one there.

He was beginning to feel like his old self again

Breaking from the mass, Blackbeard held his cutlass

horizontally against the curved sword of a Barbary pirate – who was young, his right eye stitched closed by scar tissue left from what looked like a knife attack. He drove him back to the bulwark and rammed his spine into the gunwale. The Barbary lad gasped in pain, his body going slack, his arms limp. Blackbeard flicked the blade aside and slammed the ridge of his forehead into his enemy's nose, feeling it crumple. He heard the curved sword clatter on the deck as the stunned Barbary pirate leant helplessly back.

Blackbeard gave him a shove and sent him plummeting into the blizzard of smoke and lead that raged in the chasm between the warring vessels. As he watched the Barbary pirate fall, he saw what he was sure was the head of one of his ship's gunners, Patrick, trailing sparks of flame, drops of blood and chunks of brain as it arced over the side of Percy's galley.

It landed among a cluster of Barbary pirates at their bulwark, who cried out in horror and took involuntary backward steps, their eyes leaving the conflict just long enough for an equal number of Blackbeard's crew to get off unopposed shots that cut them down.

I do hope Patrick agreed to that, Blackbeard

thought, as he turned to head off another pair of Barbary pirates who were running along the ropes tethering the ships. They swung their curved swords wildly, eyes ablaze with the adopted fury typical of fighting men who were wrestling with fear.

Blackbeard drove his cutlass into the ribs of the one nearest to him, while thrusting a kick at the second one and sending him stumbling into the path of Mary Bonny, who had turned away from the fighting crowd and now swung her empty musket like an axe, denting the Barbary lad's forehead.

He was dead before he hit the deck.

'Sister!' Blackbeard called, grabbing her by the wrist to pull her clearer of the fight. 'Shoot into their gun-deck,' he said. 'Snipe their gunners – maybe it'll make them think twice about their decision not to surrender already.'

Mary nodded and weaved her way back to the bow, which was about the only stretch of space onboard not covered by the heaving mass of bodies.

Blackbeard turned to throw himself back into it, when a flash of movement in the corner of his eye made him stop. In the time it took him to raise his arm defensively, Percy had covered the last few feet of tethering rope and had launched himself onto the deck of the *Queen Anne*, slamming his soles into Blackbeard's chest and sending him crashing to the deck, so hard he slid back eight feet across the slick timber.

'I kill you!' shouted Percy, charging forward with a two-handed sword raised above his head.

Blackbeard rolled to his right as the blade came down, hearing it punch into the wet deck. Scrambling to his feet, Blackbeard hacked with his cutlass, but Percy was already moving, flicking the strike away and creating some distance between them as they circled each other.

Percy closed down the gap, jabbing his blade at Blackbeard's face. Blackbeard backed up towards the port side; as Percy moved to jab again, he swiped his cutlasses defensively, but deflected only air.

It was a feint.

Percy aborted the strike and stooped, driving forward and slamming his shoulder into Blackbeard's gut, his arms wrapping around his waist. Before Blackbeard could reposition himself, he felt his legs taken away by a quick sweep. He landed on his back on the deck, with the Barbary captain straddling him just below his chest, sword raised to slice Blackbeard's head in two.

But Blackbeard did not bring his own blade up in an effort to protect his face. He swung it in a ferocious arc from left-to-right.

'*Argh!*'

Percy was frozen in agony, unable to move. Unable to do anything except scream and stare at the empty air where his hands used to be. Blood sprayed in thick jets of crimson, hitting Blackbeard's doublet as he shoved the maimed Barbary captain away.

Getting to his feet, Blackbeard picked up Percy's severed hands, which still clutched the hilt of his curved blade. He tossed them overboard, while Percy could do nothing but watch, his breath coming in the heavy, panicked gasps of a dying man.

Blackbeard placed a boot on Percy's chest and raised his cutlass, letting out a roar of victory.

'Look to me!' he shouted. 'See who has fallen under my cutlass!'

His roar carried even over the boom of cannon fire. Slowly, uncertainly, the mass of brawling bandits stopped and untangled themselves, all of them united in their curiosity and exhaustion, as they watched the crimson life of the Barbary captain flow out onto the deck of the *Queen Anne's Revenge*.

Chapter Ten

Two days later
The northwest coast of Cyprus

Blackbeard and his crew sat in a dingy, beachside tavern on the northwest coast of the island of Cyprus. In truth, it was rather a miserable place, that even the pirates – never the fussiest of men – might have sneered at, but it was the first drinking establishment they had come across in months, and they had a victory to celebrate. So it had to do.

The fight had been a fine one, considering his crew had not been at full-strength. Blackbeard would rather his ship had not taken quite so many hits, but he was too euphoric in victory to mind. So euphoric, in fact, that – after plundering Percy's ship – he offered spots on his crew to the brave Barbary lads that had survived.

The gits preferred to take their chances in their vessel's rickety dinghies. As they started rowing away, Blackbeard wished them well. He actually meant it, too.

He raised his cannikin in a silent toast to them,

looking around the tavern again. It was little more than a beechwood shack built on the shore. The timbers seemed so old, so rickety, that they creaked if a patron even hiccupped – and there was a lot of that going on among the pirates who were catching up with their drinking after so many weeks of enforced sobriety. Unlike the taverns Blackbeard frequented in America, or the ones he had grown up with in England, there was no hearth and no roaring fire inside. There was no need. Even with the shade of the beechwood walls, the Mediterranean climate was oppressive, snakes of searing hot sunlight pouring through the gaps between the beams.

There was only one table at the rear of the tavern, at the head of which Blackbeard sat with Chris and Mary to his right, Brutal Bill and Handsome Harry to his left. Elsewhere, the rest of his landing party stood in threes and fours around empty barrels, or sat against the walls with their cannikins in their laps. Or they lay face down on the stony ground, oblivious to the flies circling their heads, or the odd rat scaling their legs.

Yes, it should have been a miserable old place. But it was not miserable today. Because—

'The men are happy,' said Chris Claw as he surveyed

the group over the top of his cannikin, which almost disappeared in the grip of his huge hand.

'Free rum will make anyone happy,' said Blackbeard, turning to take his refill from the landlord, Miko, who had just approached the table. He was a portly man, whose belly rather resembled the barrels in the tavern, and whose jowly cheeks seemed to reach for the dusty floor in reaction to what he had overheard.

'What?' said Blackbeard, with a grin. 'Did you ever seriously expect that hosting *us* would be profitable?'

Among Blackbeard's crew, amused laughter raised into a jeer. Some of the pirates banged their fists on the tables and barrels.

Miko returned to the corner, resuming his position between the barrels. He looked like he was on the verge of crying as Mister Peters carried two armfuls of cannikins for him to refill.

Blackbeard drained his drink in one. 'Mind your head, Mister Peters,' he called, as he threw the cannikin back to Miko. In his haste to catch it, Miko dropped the cannikin he was filling from the barrel. It clattered off the floor, spilling rum all over the stone and leaving an insistent trickle of rum draining from the nozzle.

'Leak!' shouted Mister Peters, his call taken up by

the men. 'Leak! Leak! Leak!'

Blackbeard joined in the sarcastic shouts, laughing along with everyone else. It was not quite like old times. Back then, merry on rum and rich with loot, Blackbeard's crew really knew how to celebrate a haul. They'd have drained this tavern dry and moved onto the next one, while crewmate Mister Jenkins played fine tunes on his fiddle; the local lasses would have danced in the first tavern, and followed them to the next. But crewmate Mister Jenkins had died of dysentery somewhere off the coast of Crete; his fiddle had been thrown overboard with him; and the local lasses here had scarpered as soon as the landing party had arrived. Bedraggled, malnourished and unwashed European pirates were not, it seemed, to the ladies' liking.

But it gladdened his heart to see the men giving it a go. They were trying to make the Old World feel something like home.

From the corner, Miko was fighting his way through pirates dancing jigs and looking bereaved every time one of them spilled even a drop of rum. Blackbeard accepted the refill from him with a grunt that went unheard amid the warbling. He stared into it, inhaling the sweet scent of the drink he had missed so much that it felt like an elixir to him now.

Over the edge of the cannikin, he caught sight of Brutal Bill, who sat directly across from him. The old pirate had hardly touched his rum. Instead, he sat with his eyes down, rubbing a smoke-blackened hand over his jaw as he stared unwaveringly at the length of parchment he had unrolled to cover half the table. The parchment had been among the things they had claimed from Percy's ship – a curious strip of foreign writing on the left side of it, and what looked like a hastily scrawled map on the right.

'Will you stop that?' Blackbeard told Bill, lightly kicking his shin beneath the table. 'You're unsettling me.'

Bill looked up for a moment. 'Sorry,' he mumbled. 'I'm just...concerned. Look at this.'

He turned the parchment around so that Blackbeard could see it, his filthy finger tapping the map. Beside him, Mary leaned around the corner of the table to get a better look.

Towards the top of the parchment – the north – was an unlabelled country, with a smattering of small islands off its western coast, and two larger islands off its southern. An X was marked in black ink in its north. On the other side of the ocean, in the south, was marked the coast of another country, its shoreline broken in the east by a network of rivers that, to Blackbeard's eyes, rather resembled a tree-top.

'I've been trying to figure this out all day,' said Bill. 'Where do you think this is?'

Blackbeard drained the dregs of his own cannikin of rum. Without looking, he tossed the metal container all the way across the tavern. It bounced off the bald head of Miko, who had gone back to cowering in the corner between two rum barrels.

He stared down at the parchment, rolling his shoulders, which were still stiff and sore from the fight with Percy's mob.

'Well, it has to be the Mediterranean,' he said, thinking aloud. 'I doubt Percy would have a map of a sea he wasn't sailing on.'

Mary tapped both of the larger islands in the south. 'Crete and Cyprus?' she suggested.

Blackbeard nodded – Crete had been the last island they had passed before happening upon this wretched rock they now found themselves on.

He tapped his finger on the landmass in the north. 'So that would make this—'

'Turkey,' Bill interrupted. 'Which would make this X-mark—'

'Constantinople,' said Handsome Harry, his voice a weary growl.

Bill nodded. 'Home of Sultan Ahmed III, of the Ottoman Empire.'

Blackbeard reached for the refill that Miko had brought him, with a grunt of thanks. As Miko was pulled away to dance a jig with Chaplain Charlie, Blackbeard turned back to Bill. 'So what?' he asked.

Bill rolled his eyes. 'Has the rum gone to your head already, Captain? Do you not remember what Percy said he was doing at sea?'

Blackbeard took a long gulp, pondering Bill's question. Then it came to him. 'He said he was on a mission for the Barbary King. And when I first spotted him, his galley looked to have been on a northeast heading.'

Bill nodded, pointing at the X-mark. 'Percy was on his way to Constantinople...to the Sultan.'

Blackbeard looked from Bill to the others, all of whose eyes were narrowed in confusion. 'But he didn't have any treasure onboard, so he wasn't paying the Sultan a tribute. So, what was he headed there for?'

'Does it matter?' asked Chris Claw, with a wicked grin as he rapped his fingernails on his cannikin. 'He'll never complete that voyage now, will he?'

Blackbeard smiled, holding the cannikin to his lips. 'No,' he said. 'I suppose he won't.' Then he stood up, drawing to him the glances of everyone present. He raised the cannikin above his head. 'To Percy! A fine foe.'

The gathered pirates paused for just a moment, to be sure their Captain wasn't jesting. Then, as one, they raised their cannikins and echoed his toast, all of them draining their drinks in one, and sending a flurry of metal over to the corner, peppering poor Miko, whose hasty ducking for cover behind one of the full barrels sent it toppling to the ground, where it burst open and sent rum gushing all over.

Blackbeard sat back down as the sound of pirates' laughter filled the tavern. It was feeling more and more like old times.

He looked up when it suddenly faded, like smoke and smog dying away after rainfall. He saw that most of his crew were staring curiously towards the tavern doorway, where a gaunt man in a torn jerkin – that may once have been white – stood, his dark eyes moving over the gathered crew, before they settled on Blackbeard.

Blackbeard appraised the newcomer with the merest

flick of his eyes. He was not a North African pirate – he was Spanish, judging by his black hair and swarthy complexion. He was quite far from home, then.

But not as far as me, Blackbeard reminded himself.

The man took a nervous half-step into the tavern. 'Are you Blackbeard?'

'You obviously didn't see what happened to the last fellow who asked me that question,' Blackbeard told him.

'I did not expect to find you here,' said the Spaniard, walking over dented cannikins. 'Not in Cyprus. I thought—'

'Oi,' said Blackbeard, keeping perfectly still and letting his expression do the intimidation. 'You're awfully talkative for someone I don't know.'

The Spaniard ducked his head. 'Sorry. I come looking for pirates.'

Blackbeard looked to Handsome Harry, whose lone eye squinted back at him, and could see the old man shared his question. *Who goes looking for pirates?*

He glanced back to the newcomer, observing his filthy shirt, and his short trousers that were torn and frayed at the knees. 'You a sailor?' he asked.

The Spaniard nodded. '*Si*. I sail with a crew given license by His Majesty, King Phillip, to—'

'You're a privateer,' said Blackbeard, almost gagging on the word. 'I'd advise you to scurry along, unless you want a bullet in your backside.'

'I'm not a privateer anymore. That's why I come looking for pirates.'

Blackbeard had half an idea where this conversation might be going. And if he was right, he liked the sound of it.

'Mary,' he said.

His half-sister understood, rising from her seat and checking the Spaniard for hidden weapons.

Blackbeard half-turned his head. The first crewmate he laid eyes on was the over-imaginative powder monkey, Michael. Blackbeard nodded at him, and then cocked his head at the tavern door.

Michael nodded, and rose from his stool in the corner, almost bouncing across the tavern with a cat's grace. Then he stopped, and turned around.

'Erm,' he said, 'what do you want me to do, Captain?'

Blackbeard had forgotten that Michael was about as smart as a bag of pebbles. 'Is there anyone lingering on the beach?'

Michael stuck his head out of the doorway, looking left and right. He turned around again. 'Not that I can see.'

'And no ships on the water? Or small boats with any men in them?'

Michael looked again. 'No, sir.'

'That's all right, then,' said Blackbeard, swallowing his exasperation. Michael crossed the tavern back to his table, looking mighty pleased with himself for not messing up a rather simple task.

At Blackbeard's table, Mary was sitting back down. 'He's unarmed,' she said.

Blackbeard looked at the Spaniard. 'All right,' he said. 'So you're not here to cause trouble. What's your name?'

The newcomer cleared his throat. 'Luis,' he said. 'I come from—'

'I didn't ask for your life story,' said Blackbeard. 'Just tell me why you come looking for pirates in a dung-hole like this one.' He drained his cannikin, and tossed it to the landlord. 'No offence, Miko.'

Luis pulled up a stool and made to sit down. 'On the southwest coast, there's—'

Mary's right leg snapped out and kicked the stool aside. Luis hit the stone floor hard, yelping in shock.

'We didn't give you permission to sit,' said Mary.

Luis got to his feet, rubbing his tailbone. Blackbeard saw no anger, or even annoyance, in his eyes. Which meant, he must have been desperate to tell them his tale.

'I know of treasure,' he said, with a grimace. 'On the southwest coast of this island, there's a ship. Lots of treasure, from one of the stranger lands in the south.'

Blackbeard kept his gaze on the Spaniard, noticing that he was not just gaunt and haggard – his eyes were wide, and sunk into his skull. His hands were held in front of him, right gripping left. *He looks haunted*, Blackbeard thought.

'Your ship, is it?' Blackbeard asked. Luis nodded. 'You steal the treasure?'

'We did,' said Luis. 'But it caused us…problems.'

Blackbeard nodded. 'Squabbling, I bet, right? A good haul can do that to a crew if they have no sense of unity. And you privateers never have that, do you?'

Luis took a step closer to the table, casting a quick glance in Mary's direction to make sure she wasn't going to knock him onto the floor again. 'Our captain claimed the treasure for himself. He threatened to shoot anyone who disagreed. My friend and I, we dove overboard to get away from him.'

'And you came here looking for pirates,' said

Blackbeard, 'because you want to teach him a lesson.'
'*Si.*'

Blackbeard held the Spaniard's gaze for a long moment, noticing that the tavern had gone silent. No one was talking, or even drinking, not while their Captain was being informed of potential loot on the other side of this very island.

The silence was broken by Miko, warily creeping to the table with the refill. Blackbeard looked at the cannikin, then at Miko. 'You think I want this now?' he said. 'I've got business to be taking care of. A ship to plunder!'

All over the tavern, his crew were draining their drinks and getting to their feet, whooping and cheering. Far from being intimidated by the boisterousness of the pirates, Miko was withdrawing into his usual corner, his face alight with utter relief. 'Good journey,' he said, toasting Blackbeard.

As his pirates streamed out of the tavern, Blackbeard grinned at him. 'I know you'll miss us,' he said, with a wink. 'I'll be sure to spread the word, make sure all my pirate friends stop in your place if they ever happen to be sailing by.'

Miko's smile faltered. Blackbeard laughed.

'Why wouldn't I, Miko?' he said. 'I bet yours is the

best rum in the Mediterranean.'

Miko smiled again. 'Thank you.'

'So good,' said Blackbeard, 'that I think I'll take a barrel or two with me now.'

From his expression, Blackbeard could tell that Miko's heart had just sunk like a cannonball thrown overboard.

'Look at him. Something's not right – he looks terrified.'

Blackbeard shrugged. 'I have that effect on people.'

Mary Bonny tutted as she guided the *Queen Anne* on a southwest heading along the coast of Cyprus. She was still working the helm after the battle with Percy's crew. 'You haven't been scary since we left Ocracoke,' she said.

Blackbeard pinched her earlobe. 'Watch it, sister.'

Mary swatted his hand away. 'Do that again and it'll cost you a tooth.'

Blackbeard laughed as his gaze settled on the subject of their discussion. Luis was down on the waist-deck, sitting on the capstan and trying to keep out of the way as Blackbeard's pirates crisscrossed the ship in chaotic patterns, Handsome Harry hollering commands. Blackbeard couldn't help the flutter of jealousy in his chest as he looked at the youngsters perched up in the rigging, with the best view of the ship below, and a god's view of the endless sea stretching in every directions.

Blackbeard had loved being a topman when he served under his old mentor, Captain Benjamin Hornigold – where he had first gained some notoriety for his agility, even though he was usually the tallest and heaviest man in the crew. If it had not been so unbecoming of a captain, Blackbeard would have worked the cordage on the *Queen Anne's Revenge* himself – he'd show them all how it was done.

'Would anyone really go this far out of their way just to get back at a cruel captain?' Mary asked him, breaking his reverie. 'It just seems too easy.'

'Of course it does,' said Blackbeard. 'After five hard months, our luck is finally changing – I can feel it. We stumble upon Percy, and take him for everything he had. And now, Luis and his little revenge mission falls into our laps, with treasure as our reward. Fate is just evening itself out, is all, sister – repaying us in kind for months of hardship.'

Mary grunted dismissively. 'I think we should be happy with what we got,' she said. 'We should turn round and go to Spain, like we planned. We should enjoy the new haul, sell some of the goods, relax a bit. And we should set sail when we're strong again.'

'It sounds like you're suggesting we turn down an offer of plunder. As a pirate, I'm insulted.'

'Our luck may be changing, but I don't want to push it. We should be more cautious.'

Blackbeard patted her head, in the way he knew she hated. 'Where's the fun in that?'

Chapter Eleven

'I ain't staying at the helm,' said Mary, as she guided the *Queen Anne* towards the cove that Luis had pointed out on the map. It was a day since they had left the tavern, and their latest prize was close.

Blackbeard was over at the port side, leaning out over the gunwale, the better to stare through his spyglass unimpeded by any of his sails. 'You're the best we got,' he told her. 'Unless Mister Hands recovers from that bullet to the face he took during the fight with Percy's mob the other day.'

Mary scoffed. 'You're just afraid I'll show you up.'

Blackbeard ignored her, focusing his eye on the bluff up ahead – a rocky wall, mostly flat but broken by dents created by the eternal beating by the merciless sea. With the motion of the ship, it seemed to be sliding to the left, like a door being slowly opened to reveal the pirates' prize.

Blackbeard grinned when he saw it: a four-deck galleon, anchored in the cove, sails rolled up, its bulky stern facing the open sea as it bobbed and listed in the gently swelling waves. Blackbeard knew that, a week earlier, this vessel could have smashed the *Queen*

Anne to pieces. But not now – now its bowsprit and beakhead were little more than jagged stumps. Its pine masts leant precariously over its port side.

Immediately, his brain began running tactics – advantages and disadvantages. As far as he could see, there were only advantages: his attack was not one they were expecting; judging by the state of Luis, the crew onboard were probably in an even worse state than his were right up until they encountered Percy; and with the stern facing outwards, they were not going to make any sort of quick escape.

It was almost too good to be true.

He stepped to the edge of the quarterdeck, the thrill of impending plunder filling his chest. If it would not have unsettled his men, Blackbeard fancied he would have allowed himself a stupid grin. He cleared his throat, and prepared to roar a command that he had almost forgotten about. 'Rai—'

'Raise the flag!'

Blackbeard wheeled round on the spot, glaring at his half-sister, who had beaten him to it.

'What?' said Mary. 'I'm just practising…for when I'm in charge.'

Blackbeard shook his head at her. 'You're not in charge yet.' He turned back to face his crew, clustered amidships and looking at him expectantly. He sighed. 'What she said.'

A cheer went up from the pirates, the anticipation of some more action, some more riches, filling their skinny, weary limbs with new strength.

Up went the Jolly Roger, which had been lowered for so long that, now, it spat dust as it fluttered. Seeing it always gave Blackbeard a thrill – the skeleton devil, hourglass in one hand and spear in the other, stabbing a heart that dripped blood. He fancied it was the most ominous, intimidating design on any ship on any sea.

'Keep her steady,' he yelled. He snapped his fingers at Jonesy, a powder monkey sitting disgracefully idle by the bulwark. 'On your feet, you scrawny water rat. Fetch me some fuses. I feel like getting into character again. The rest of you – check your powder. We're going to give these Spaniards a show. Teach them what it means to be *real* sea bandits!'

As his men cheered and stomped their feet on the deck, Blackbeard returned to the helm. 'Once in range,' he said to Mary, 'hard to starboard, sister. We'll fire a broadside, let them know we mean business. Then we shall—'

Mary shook her head, pointing at the prize. 'No need.'

Blackbeard turned, seeing a white flag flapping in the wind above the galleon. He trained his spyglass on the deck, seeing three bedraggled Spanish sailors, waving their arms in gestures of surrender.

He sighed as he lowered his spyglass, his hands gripping it so tight he was surprised it didn't become dust in his palms. 'Well,' he said. '*That* was disappointing.'

Taking the galleon was pathetically easy. The Spaniards did not protest as Mary guided the Queen Anne right up along their port side. Indeed, they were so submissive that the sound of the grapnels latching onto their bulwarks, and the dull clatter of boarding planks dropping down, sounded hideously loud, the show of force and dominance almost crass, even to Blackbeard.

As he watched Brutal Bill lead the boarding party across to the galleon, Blackbeard tried to muster some of the old buccaneering spirit. But it wasn't the same when they didn't try to escape, and never quite as enjoyable when they didn't fight for their lives.

All the same, he grabbed a loose length of cordage to swing across to their waist-deck, making sure to stay in character. 'Surrender, you filthy lubbers!'

Brutal Bill had his pistol drawn, and was backing the three Spaniards towards their capstan, where Chris Claw tied them to the bars. Blackbeard could see that the bars were rusted, presumably from the same water-damage that had left the deck beneath his feet so rotten and creaky. It was like walking on bamboo. *Damned privateers*, he thought. *They don't know how to keep a vessel in good nick.*

He eyed the Spaniards one by one. Like Luis, their faces were gaunt, their eyes wide and sunk into their sockets. Their teeth chattered, and their bodies seemed to quiver, even though it was a warm day beneath the Mediterranean sun. Blackbeard wished Mary was here to see this – and she said he wasn't scary anymore!

Blackbeard looked at Brutal Bill. 'As you please, Mr Howard.'

As Brutal Bill moved past the capstan, towards the bow of the galleon, where he disappeared inside the forecastle, Blackbeard kept a keen eye on the three prisoners. 'Which of you is the captain?' he asked.

The three Spaniards looked at each other, mumbling in their own language.

'There'll be none of that,' said Blackbeard. 'We speak English on my seas, you rotten maggots.

And these are my seas now.'

'No captain,' said the one in the middle, the shortest. He was bald at the scalp, with long black hair streaming from the back of his head. 'He dead.'

'Oh, aye?' said Blackbeard. 'I heard he was a bit of a nasty old git. One of youse kill him, did ya?'

The bald one shook his head. 'He kill himself,' he said.

Blackbeard frowned. 'And why would he do that?'

Baldy and his two cohorts looked down at the deck, each of them shrugging and shaking their heads, to signal that they didn't know. But they had answered too quickly for Blackbeard's liking. They did know. He could tell. There was a story there. Something wasn't feeling right, but—

'Captain!'

Blackbeard's gaze was drawn to the forecastle door, from where Brutal Bill was re-emerging. The smile on his face could light up a night sky. And if that weary, worn-down, miserable old codger was smiling, whatever was down in the hold of this galleon had to be something to smile about.

'You have to see this!' he said.

'Beautiful.'

Blackbeard himself wasn't sure what he was

referring to: the ornate sarcophagus in the galleon's hold, or the face that was carved into it. A young woman's face, her delicate ebony features seeming to rise out of the tomb lid as though she was emerging from bathing in a lake of gold. Her face wore black smudges and splotches, where time had worked away at the carving and paint, but she was still a wondrous sight. Her slender body seemed to flow all the way down to the foot of the sarcophagus, extravagant teal-and-white robes draped around her in lush spirals. She was obviously royalty, maybe even a Queen.

Blackbeard reached out to touch it, to trace the lines and grooves of the carving – but he didn't. He left it hovering, unsure whether he should touch something so... perfect.

'I'd have liked to meet her in a strange tavern somewhere,' said Chris Claw, his eyes alight and his long-nailed fingers steepled like a roof.

'Be quiet!' said Blackbeard, sounding angrier than he expected. He didn't know why, but he didn't like Chris Claw speaking this way, with that leering grin on his face. It made him want to punch his teeth out. 'You get back up on deck and take those Spaniards across to the *Queen Anne*.'

Chris's eyes went from his captain to the

sarcophagus. He took a step forward. 'But I just want to see—'

Blackbeard stood directly in front of him. 'I don't like repeating orders. You don't touch it. You don't even look at it – do you understand?'

As Chris Claw stomped out of the hold, Blackbeard wondered where his anger had come from. He was known for his quick temper, feared for it – but this felt...different. And in a way he couldn't explain.

Which was unsettling.

'It's Egyptian, Captain,' said Brutal Bill, whose eyes had not left the sarcophagus. 'I dunno what era. But it's old, I know that.'

Blackbeard nodded, looking around at the rest of the loot. The sarcophagus was surrounded by four strange wooden structures. They were shaped like coffins, but they stood up like pillars on a wide, heavy base, like a plinth. Blackbeard fancied they were responsible for the slightly putrid smell beneath the familiar bilge-stench wafting up from below. To one side of the sarcophagus, there was an odd little object that looked like a flowerpot with a jackal's head on it. It was ugly and weird, but carved from marble – so it had to be worth something. Laid either side of it were a pair of jewelled swords in what looked like ivory sheaths. Along the walls of the hold were shallow, heart-shaped chests. Bill had left one of them open, revealing amulets and jewels of gold, silver and jade that somehow managed to twinkle even in the dull gloom.

This lady was almost certainly a Queen of some kind.

'It's not actually that big a haul,' said Bill. 'But I reckon that there sarcophagus is the most ancient, most valuable thing we've ever taken. I almost feel bad for stealing it.'

Blackbeard pondered for a moment if he should indeed steal it. But one look at the beautiful face carved into the sarcophagus decided it for him. He *had* to take this on board his ship. It was too valuable, too monumental for him not to. He felt as if his whole life as a pirate had been on a heading towards finding this artefact; that every voyage, scrap and battle had nudged him a little closer to this very moment. He was meant to find it. And he was meant to take it.

He walked backwards, away from the treasure, trying and failing to pull his eyes away from it. 'I'll send the lads down,' he told Brutal Bill. 'You all right to organise the transfer?'

Brutal Bill's eyes never left the sarcophagus, either. He stood rooted to the spot, leaning over it as though he was a nervous man peering over a cliff. 'Aye, Captain,' he said.

With some effort, Blackbeard pulled his gaze away and walked out of the hold. As he climbed the ladder up onto the weather deck, the Mediterranean sunlight hit him like a downpour of rain in a storm. And yet, he felt a chill sail across his chest.

'Stay down, you mangy sea mutts!'

Blackbeard looked across to the weather deck of the *Queen Anne*. Chris Claw was putting the boot into one of the Spaniards, while the two others tried crawling away. As he ran across the boarding plank and back onto his own ship, Blackbeard heard the whimpering cries of the prisoners. He did not need to know the Spanish for 'Let us go!'

He took a hold of Chris Claw's jerkin and dragged him off. 'What are you playing at?'

'They tried to dive overboard, Captain,' said Chris, pointing at the three Spaniards, who were restrained by some of Blackbeard's crew, kneeling on their backs. They beat the decks pitifully.

'So what?' said Blackbeard. 'Where are they going to go? Cliffs on both sides, they're not going to paddle to Crete!' He knelt beside the trio. 'Now, look here, boys... I trust you might have heard of me, and you're right to be scared. That's a very sensible thing to be. But don't believe everything you may have heard. I'm not that bad a bloke, really. Your old friend, Luis, will attest to that – he's been with us a few days, I ain't even locked him up in the hold or anything. He's not a prisoner – and neither are you. And besides, you've brought me my greatest ever haul. That sarcophagus on your ship is the most valuable thing I've ever seen. The most beautiful, too. When we sell it, I'm going to be able to retire on my share. We all could, I'd bet. And you know what else? I promised these lads a few months ago that I'd put me feet up in Spain, and now I'm thinking I might do just that. So how about it, eh? You stick with me, and I'll take youse all home.'

He cast his arm in the direction of their galleon, where a dozen of his crew were straining to move the sarcophagus along the deck. Brutal Bill was at the head of the group, giving gruff commands. 'Consider it a thank you,' said Blackbeard. 'For the treasure.'

The Spaniards said nothing. They just let their faces drop to the deck.

They were weeping.

Two hours later, the *Queen Anne's Revenge* was sailing back west at last.

Blackbeard was at the bow, right by the fore staysail, which flapped ferociously in the gathering winds. The mermaid angel's tail seemed to rip through the water, sending up arcing sprays in all directions as it sailed on a sea that no longer felt quite so strange and foreign; a sea that now seemed to be diving obediently aside as the ship sailed, rather than blithely carrying it towards a new destination. After two successful bouts of plundering – and with a belly full of booze – Blackbeard once again felt like he was the master of his own destiny, that the seas were his kingdom, that the waves were his subjects.

He was feeling like a real captain once more.

The treasure had been transferred, and the petrified Spaniards had been locked up in the hold with it. The crew had also taken boxes of sugar and fruit – not exactly fresh, but it would do – and some caged chickens. Some of the lads were more excited about that than the treasure!

Blackbeard smiled contentedly, and turned to patrol the deck as the crew worked the cordage. As he swept passed the mainsail, he heard Chris Claw – who was running tirelessly from stern to bow – shouting: 'Gybe! Gybe!'

He was sending the call to swing the sails, the better

to catch the wind that had shifted from southwest to northwest. Blackbeard stepped among the crew at the foot of the mainmast, shouldering mates aside as he worked to untie the knot of a lanyard. Once untied, the loosened mainsail seemed to chase the wind, giving a mighty tug on Blackbeard's arms, the ropes cutting into his palms.

He leant back on his heels and, with a snap of his wrists, brought the sail under control as, high above in the topgallant, the young topman, Robbie the Rat – so-called because his two remaining teeth resembled a rodent's – pushed at the yardarm to turn the sail.

Between them, they had shifted the sails only a few degrees, but the entire ship lurched to starboard, picking up speed as she steadied. Blackbeard leant forward to re-fasten the lanyard.

'Thank you, Captain,' muttered the crewmates around him, as he turned and walked towards the quarterdeck. He passed the capstan, on which Handsome Harry sat; one-eyed he may have been, but the old pirate missed nothing.

'That's hardly a Captain's behaviour,' he grumbled, as Blackbeard passed him, climbing up the ladder to the quarterdeck. He was surprised at how fast he was moving. A minute or two of working the rigging, and the energy that had been restored by the plundering had increased even more. This was what it was all about for him – mucking in, and being part of the crew.

It was what it had always been about.

He drew up alongside his half-sister at the helm. Her face was still tight with annoyance.

'I just don't trust anyone else,' he told her, pointing at the wheel she manned.

'It ain't that,' she said. 'Did you mean it this time? What you said, about going to Spain…retiring?'

Blackbeard thought about it for a moment, feeling the charge in his body from his brief work on the sails, wondering if he really did mean it. He was almost surprised to feel himself nodding. 'Aye. There's only so many times you can draw a cutlass on fate and live to brag about it, right?'

Mary eyed him for a long moment, her dark eyes narrowed. 'What will *you* do on land?'

Blackbeard shrugged, turning to look out over the stern. Cyprus was disappearing over the horizon, like a dinghy careering over a waterfall. The rejected Old World was being left far behind. 'I dunno,' he said. 'Might open a tavern somewhere. Make it a haunt for the next generation of pirates – tell them tales to make them jealous.'

Mary smiled. 'I'll have to make sure I take my crew there sometime.'

He grinned back at her. 'You know that you'll be challenged, right? The lads won't take orders from a woman very easily. Especially ol' Chris Claw.'

Mary's jaw jutted out, as it always did when she heard something she didn't like. 'Let any of them challenge me,' she said. 'They'll get their eyes stabbed out.'

Blackbeard clapped her on the shoulder as he moved off the quarterdeck. 'Maintain this heading,' he said. 'I'm going to me cabin to get some shuteye.'

'Edward,' Mary said, 'are you sure this is what you want?' she asked.

Blackbeard smiled, thinking about the quiet life that awaited – and the treasure in the hold that would buy it for him. 'I've just taken my greatest treasure,' he said. 'Things can only get worse from now on, right?'

Part Two

Chapter Twelve

One week later

Blackbeard lay in his hammock, staring at his cabin ceiling, which was coming into focus as the dawn of a new day gushed through his dirty window. His first instinct – as always – was to gain orientation. The sunlight was streaming in at a downward diagonal slant, running through the pane and falling port-to-starboard across the cabin floor. This meant that – with the sun rising in the east – the anchored *Queen Anne* was facing a general southwest direction.

As always, he lay with a pistol in each hand, just in case. That was another reason to seriously consider jacking this all in – when you had to take two loaded guns to bed, it was a rare night that you slept all the way through. Blackbeard was lucky if he got an uninterrupted hour. Even the excitement of being a pirate wasn't always able to balance out the exhaustion that came with rarely sleeping.

His mind drifted to the Egyptian treasure in the

hold, to a vague, hazy future he could purchase with his share of the loot – the tavern he'd idly talked of setting up, in a pirate outpost somewhere.

Yes. He thought he might fancy that – to see out his older days running his own gaff, holding court and telling tall stories to impress the next generation of pirates, and make them a little bit jealous that, no matter what they did, they'd never create legends to rival his.

That's if there even is *a next generation of pirates*, he thought, as he swung his legs out of the hammock and stood up. He slid the guns back into his belt and rubbed the tiredness from his face, wishing he could so easily chase away the sadness from his heart.

The Golden Age of Piracy was coming to an end. He could feel it, even though he was thousands and thousands of miles away from his old stomping ground. His stomping *seas* – the Atlantic and Caribbean. The Royal Navy had got stronger – their ships were newer, and their men younger. The pirates' ships were comparatively ancient, and the men aboard them had become much drunker and lazier.

The end was inevitable.

Blackbeard walked out of his cabin into the sparred gallery, towards the ladder that led up to the

waist-deck. He needed the sea air, the horizon –
the best tonics for the mornings when he woke up
a miserable git. On his left was the door leading to
Mary's cabin – as the only woman on board, she had
her own sleeping quarters. Blackbeard would not
have minded except they had partitioned off about
a third of his own cabin to make it. Each time he
passed it, he considered banging on the door to
interrupt her sleep, but he never did.

Mary was a handful at the best of times.

He reached the ladder, and started to climb up,
stopping when he caught a flicker of movement from
inside the gun-deck. He turned to look, seeing almost
all the crew down there now, sleeping in small rows
of three or four – depending on their girth – between
the idle cannons. The wide aisle between the cannons
was almost completely black, as the deck had not
been properly swept of the gunpowder that had fallen
during the battle with Percy's mob, and its faint scent
seem to cling to walls and ceiling. The portholes had
been left open for ventilation, allowing rods of slanted
sunlight to stab through, their formation reminding
Blackbeard of the oars used on the Barbary pirates'
galleys.

He stepped towards the doorway and squinted into

the gloom. The flicker of movement was a figure, crouched in an awkward crawl, leaning over the sleeping pirates as if looking for something.

'Bill?' Blackbeard whispered. 'What are you doing?

Bill stood up and padded quietly to the doorway. His jaw was tight, his face set with indignant outrage. 'I think we have a thief on board,' he said.

Blackbeard snorted. 'We have a whole crew full of them, Bill – what you on about?'

'One of the crew is stealing from the treasure.'

Chapter Thirteen

'I never like having to do this,' said Blackbeard.

It was just after breakfast – which was a vile-smelling gruel made with oatmeal that had to be staler than the pirates' clothes. It was the type of serving that made Blackbeard thankful he never ate that much. A lifetime at sea, on ships where rations were stretched to their absolute limit, had long conditioned him to go a long time without food. These days, one meal a day would usually do for him, and the sludge that Mister Peters served up that morning was not going to be it.

He had gathered his crew, who now stood in a line along the starboard bulwark. Blackbeard had placed them there intentionally – their backs facing the morning sun, which slowly baked their bare necks. Behind them, the relentless rhythm of the waves rolling at the hull would be a constant threat – a reminder that a wrong answer to one of the Captain's questions might result in them being thrown overboard.

Blackbeard paced the deck, gripping the cutlass at his left hip, as if ready to draw. He had added it to the clasp-knives in his waist belt that morning, for a bit of extra menace. 'Now then,' he said, 'you all know that I do love a nice bit of honest thieving. It's the name of our game, you might say. But there are lines, lads. Clear lines – that you do not cross. You do not steal from your own ship. And that's what seems to have happened at some point yesterday. Thank God for Brutal Bill and his sharp memory, eh? Although, I do have to say, that any pirate who steals treasure off the top of the chest is barely worthy of the name.'

The gathered crewmates looked at each other, muttering – some sounded confused, others outraged. Blackbeard pressed on, hoping to use that to his advantage. 'It seems that at least one of you has forgotten the code that we all live by, the rules that govern us. Let me remind you of one of my favourites – equal shares for all. There's no hierarchy onboard my ship, not when it comes to treasure. Each man gets the same cut as the next. And yet, that does not seem to be good enough for somebody onboard.'

Blackbeard ducked his head a little, so the brim of his hat would veil his eyes in shadow and he could scope out the men with a little bit of subtlety. But the only tell-tale sign of guilt he saw was on the face of Michael, the young powder monkey, who kept his eyes on the deck, and looked like he might chew through his bottom lip.

But could that timid boy really have been the thief? He wasn't bright, but was he *that* stupid? Blackbeard couldn't be sure. He felt a swell of disappointment when he considered that Michael spent most of his time down in the gun-deck, right above the hold. It would have been easy for him to pull off the theft.

'I'm giving you until sundown,' said Blackbeard, raising his head again. The line of men were doing a good job of acting like their necks weren't on fire. 'Leave the treasure on the trapdoor in the gun-deck, and I'll find it in me to forget about all this. I'll put it down to sunstroke. But, if it's not returned...well... Then I'll begin a proper investigation. And I'm sure none of you want me to do that. Right?'

Blackbeard dismissed them, and the crew dispersed. He angled his head down again, not wanting the crew to see where his eyes went. If they got a whiff of him having any suspicion about anybody, there'd be a lynching.

He saw young Michael head not for the gun-deck, but the main-mast, climbing up the cordage. Blackbeard watched him move, supple and agile – fearless. He walked over to Chris Claw, who was stopped beneath the mast, rubbing his sunburnt neck with a grimace.

Blackbeard poked him in the shoulder. 'What's he doing up there?'

Chris looked up to see who he was talking about. Then he shrugged. 'Asked if he could have a go,' he replied. 'We lost a few lads when we took on those Barbary pirates, so I said yeah – thought we could do with training a few of them up, so we could keep the men, er...what'd you call it? Rotating.'

Blackbeard glanced back up at Michael, who was now stood with his feet on the yardarm of the main-topsail, his hands on the yardarm of the topgallant, the two horizontal beams framing him in a glorious portrait against the cloudless Mediterranean. 'He got up there a bit sharpish, didn't he?' said Blackbeard.

'Oh yeah,' said Chris, 'he's a natural. Been working up top for three days, but looks like he's been doing it three years.'

Blackbeard nodded, his mind turning over. Three days, Michael had been working the topsail. This made it less likely he'd been thieving from the hold – of course, he could have done it at night-time, but he would have woken up the whole gun-deck had that been the case.

So he was looking innocent, which pleased Blackbeard. But then, why did the lad look so shifty after the address?

Perhaps he knew something.

Blackbeard adjusted his hat as he made a decision. He knew he could not clamber up there now, for the same reasons he did not want anyone to catch him eyeing Michael right after he addressed the men. He needed to have a word with the lad in a way that would not paint him the thief in the eyes of the crew.

'In about an hour,' he said to Chris, his voice a low mumble that was almost suppressed by the waves and wind, 'have him come down to work the cordage from the deck. An hour after that, make like you need my help with something – tell him to fetch me from my cabin.'

Chris narrowed his eyes at Blackbeard, taking in his instructions. Then his eyes widened and he started to turn to look up towards the topgallant again. Blackbeard reached out a hand to stop him, clasping him round the neck and feeling Chris's skin searing hot and already beginning to flake. 'Don't look,' he said, as Chris gasped in pain. 'Everyone's suspicious enough at the moment, and we don't know anything for sure.'

Grimacing, Chris nodded. Blackbeard let him go, and then turned to walk across the deck towards his cabin, where he would settle in to wait.

'Captain, sir?'

From the other side of the door, Michael's voice was timid, his knock almost silent.

'Yes?' said Blackbeard, crossing his arms over his oak desk. He knew that, with the sunlight streaming in from the window behind him, he would be cast in silhouette, appearing to Michael as little more than a shadow. It gave him the upper hand in any conversation in this room.

The cabin door opened with a creak, and young Michael paused in the doorway, his eyes wide as he took in the sight of the Captain's private sanctuary, and then the ominous, shadowy figure behind the desk.

'Mister Chris says he needs to speak with you urgently, Captain,' said Michael.

'Right you are.' As Michael reached into the cabin to close the door, Blackbeard leant forward, his face breaking the pool of shadow for just a moment as he asked: 'You want to have a drink with your captain, lad?'

Michael froze, staring at Blackbeard as though he had just been asked if he wouldn't mind swimming back to Miko's to pick up another barrel of rum. Then, his face cleared, and he bowed his head respectfully. 'They need me up on deck, Captain.'

Blackbeard bit back a smile as he disappeared back into the shadow. That was the right answer, and Michael seemed quite clearly to be an honest boy, even if he was about as sharp as a wooden spoon. 'They can spare you a few more minutes,' he said. 'Come in.'

Hesitantly, Michael stepped inside, shutting the door behind him. He shuffled across the cabin, coming to stand opposite Blackbeard, the sunlight streaming in through the window making him wince.

'You have something to tell me, son?' said Blackbeard. 'About...the situation we have onboard?'

Michael's gasped. 'What do you mean?'

'I mean,' said Blackbeard, 'that you seemed rather preoccupied after my little talk this morning. Couldn't get up the rigging fast enough.'

'I-I-I was just eager,' said Michael. 'I like being a topman. I hated the gun-deck.'

Blackbeard studied the boy for a long moment. He stood almost to attention, with his arms behind his back, but his face showed desperation and fear. It was obvious he didn't want to upset his Captain, and that he was afraid of being thrown off the crew.

But Blackbeard thought he could have done with a bit more steel about him. He should have rejected the insinuation that he stole from the loot, and swore blind that he didn't know a thing about it. Instead, he had offered an excuse, which just confirmed for Blackbeard that he was right to be suspicious.

'What's going on, boy?' he asked, his rumbling voice like distant thunder in the silent cabin.

Michael looked down at his boots. 'Captain, please… I don't want to be involved.'

'But it seems that you are,' said Blackbeard. 'So you might as well—'

'I saw something,' Michael blurted out. 'But they said—'

'You were threatened,' said Blackbeard, smoothing his beard with one hand.

'Yes,' said Michael. 'And I believed they'd make good on their threat if I told anyone.'

'Who?'

'Two of the gunners,' said Michael. 'Gary Gallows and Bloody Bob.'

Blackbeard leaned forward on the desk again,

letting Michael see his eyes. 'You're a good lad,' he said. 'A well-meaning one. That's rare at sea, let me tell you. But I'm starting to think, maybe you should be reconsidering your choice of career.'

Michael stepped to the edge of the desk. 'I'm sorry, Captain!' he blurted. 'I... I... I didn't know the rules. I didn't know I wasn't supposed to tell. I thought, since you asked me, you wanted to know who the thieves were. Give me another ch—'

'This is no place for a good-hearted kid,' said Blackbeard. 'You need to be ruthless, vicious, to survive on the deck of a pirate ship. You've got courage, Michael, but too much heart. I'm not sure you have the steel to live amongst some of the world's most dangerous and ruthless men. You're not a pirate.'

'But, Captain—'

'No arguments. When we reach Spain, you're going to use your share of the loot to make your way home to England. It will be the best thing for you.'

'Is this because I told you about Gary and Bob?' said Michael. 'But...they stole from you!'

The Captain smiled. 'No, boy,' he said, standing up from his desk. 'It's because I'm looking out for you.'

Blackbeard strode out of the shadows, coming to

stand in front of Michael and tousled his hair. 'I'll see you right,' he said, moving to walk out of the cabin. 'You'll have a good life on land.'

'But I *am* a pirate,' said Michael, following Blackbeard to the cabin door. 'I can prove it. Listen! *Arrr!* Shiver me tim—'

'Don't.' Blackbeard stopped at the closed door, looking at the boy who stood their with tears in his eyes. 'You've seen how tough it can get out here, since we left the New World. The time of the pirate is over. This – this desperate struggle for scraps – is how it's going to be from now on. No time for fun, no time for adventure – just miserable sailing around, waiting for good luck to bless you before bad luck curses you. This is no place for a good-hearted lad. And, deep down, you know that, matey.'

'Why are you doing this?' he asked.

'You know, I'm not sure,' said Blackbeard. 'Maybe, after a lifetime of thieving and fighting and killing, I'm getting the urge to balance the scales a little.' He snorted with laughter. 'Maybe I want to get into Heaven, after all!'

Blackbeard wrenched open the door and marched out into the sparred gallery. *I'm getting soft in my old age*, he thought, as he climbed up the ladder onto the quarterdeck. He looked around and saw what he was looking for – Bloody Bob and Gary Gallows, idle gunners on deck with little to do on a ship settling in for a long, uneventful voyage. They were leaning over the stern and clinking their bottles of rum together in some sort of quiet celebration.

'That's handy,' Blackbeard mumbled, as he walked right up to them. He cracked his knuckles once, the sound silent beneath the strong breeze and the snapping of the mizzen sails.

Bloody Bob was the first to turn, when Blackbeard's shadow slid over him. Blackbeard swung an uppercut that slammed the gunner's teeth together, the loosened yellow gnashers breaking immediately. Then he slammed the elbow of the same arm into Gary Gallows' eye.

Two strikes, one second.

As the gunners toppled backwards over the stern, too stunned to even scream for their lives, Blackbeard caught their bottles of rum.

No way was he going to let them smash and go to waste.

Chapter Fourteen

Brutal Bill placed his last candle on the last corner of the sarcophagus. The beautiful female figure was now illuminated by gentle flame, the rhythm of the flickering shadows passing over her exquisite face matching that of the waves beneath the *Queen Anne*.

He gathered that she must have been an Egyptian Queen. Her coffin looked so ornate, even beneath the cracks in the carving and the black splotches on her cheeks and forehead – the scars of time.

How old *was* this thing?

He was in the hold of the *Queen Anne*, which was directly beneath the gun-deck, accessed by a thick, heavy trapdoor that lay open above Bill's head – not that it provided much ventilation. The air down here was heavy with the smell of damp oak, and with the bilge directly below, the putrid stench was more pronounced; the air was still tainted with blood and cannon-smoke that seemed to coil around Bill's head like a noose.

The light from the candles strained and stretched to reveal more of the hold. A windowless cavern, which played host to the spoils of plunder. It ran the length and breadth of the whole ship, save for a narrow room partitioned off at the stern, which was Mister Peters' domain, and which now hosted the provisions taken from the two ships the *Queen Anne* had conquered – fruit, sugar, fresh water, caged chickens.

And the three Spanish prisoners.

'Please! Let us out! Please!'

Those Spaniards just would not shut up.

Bill crossed to the wall that separated the cook's quarters from the rest of the hold. He banged his fist on the wood, and roared: 'Be quiet, the lot of ya. Or I'll show you how I got the name Brutal Bill!'

The three Spaniards stopped begging to be let out, and got back to what they were doing before – sobbing. Bill shook his head as he walked back towards the sarcophagus – compared to some of the other prisoners they had taken over the years, this trio were being treated like royalty, yet they seemed like they would gladly rather drown in the Mediterranean than be on board the *Queen Anne*.

The Captain's reputation must have been more fearsome than any of them realised.

Bill stopped when he reached the curious, morbid treasure once again. The flickering candlelight stretched and swelled, caressing the four wooden coffin-pillars that he had arranged around the sarcophagus exactly as he had found them on the galleon – one on each side, one at the head and one at the foot. For some strange reason, he felt like this was the right thing to do. The *proper* thing to do. They were obviously servants of the Queen, maybe even bodyguards.

They had to have been special somehow – Bill had never before seen coffins designed to stand up like statues.

From a low table at the starboard side of the hold, he retrieved two lengths of parchment. One length was the notes made by the Spanish quartermaster, an inventory of their haul; the other was blank, for Bill to make his own.

He stepped back to the sarcophagus, holding the Spaniards' parchment beneath the light of one candle. Thankfully, their quartermaster's handwriting was halfway legible; though his Spanish was rusty, Bill fancied he could translate most of the notes and figure out the rest.

But there's a lot of them, he observed. *More than there should be for so few items.*

He should have rummaged around for more candles, to cast more light in the hold so that he could make his translation comfortably.

But he didn't. He simply stood over the sarcophagus, eyes drawn to that beautiful face. Those eyes, seeming to shine like fire even though they were as black as shadows. The long, dark hair flowing like a waterfall all the way down to her heels. Those hands, crossed over her chest in the traditional resting pose of the dead, the fingers long and slender and perfect.

Bill let the two lengths of parchment drop to the floor, stepping closer to the sarcophagus until he was half-leaning over it, staring into the face of the lady as she gazed up at the ceiling of the hold. His own broad body held back the light of the candles at her feet, leaving just her crossed hands and face visible in the muted light. This close, he began to feel a pitiful rage building up in his chest. How unfair it seemed that this spectacular monument to a beautiful creature had to age and wear away like everything else in this world. How cruel it was that this lady's beauty could not be preserved. It was almost as if he could feel her spirit howling in rage at the injustice of it.

He placed a hand on the cold sarcophagus, as though in an effort to soothe her of her eternal anger and sadness.

He could have sworn her saw her eyelids open.

He leaned back, but kept his hand on the lid, feeling tremors tickling his palm. Tremors unlike the usual grunts and groans of a ship beneath his feet. This was something else. Something strange. Something... mystical.

A hand fell onto his shoulder.

Bill gasped and wheeled around, almost knocking over a candle as he raised his arms, ready to fight the newcomer.

When he saw who it was, he let out a long sigh and stooped over, putting his hands on his knees and willing himself not to be sick. 'What are you doing that for, you pesky sea worm?' he growled.

Michael stepped into the candlelight. Tears formed tracks down his dirty face. 'Sorry, Bill,' he said, keeping a respectful distance. 'It's just, I wanted to see the treasure again, while I still could. Thought it might cheer me up.'

'You could have knocked,' said Bill, standing up. 'You could have called down through the trapdoor, "Oi, Bill – it's Michael".'

'I did,' said Michael. 'Twice. You...didn't seem to hear me.'

Bill sighed again, feeling his pulse pound in his neck. Had he been *that* taken with the sarcophagus?

'What do you mean,' he said, '"while you still could"?'

'The Captain says he's booting me off the ship,' said Michael, his voice catching in his throat. 'When we get to Spain.'

'Probably for the best, laddie,' said Bill. 'The captain knows what he—'

Michael wasn't looking at him anymore. All sadness and self-pity had been chased away. Now, his eyes were alight with curious wonder as he stared at the lady's sarcophagus. 'She must have been rich, eh?' he said. 'To get this sort of coffin.'

Bill nodded, stooping to pick up the parchment he had dropped. 'Probably a Pharaoh's wife,' he said. 'If not a Pharaoh herself.'

'What's a Pharaoh?'

'It's a sort of King. But more important and powerful.'

Michael tore his eyes away from the sarcophagus. It seemed to take some effort. 'So, do you know about Egypt then, Bill?'

Bill shrugged. 'I know a little. I sailed along its coast once, with another crew. Learned a bit about their rituals, and that. Long time ago.'

'Is it true that they wrapped people in shrouds before burying them?'

'Rich people, yes.'

'Like her?'

Bill cast a glance back at the sarcophagus, feeling almost outraged by Michael's tone. The lady deserved more respect.

'Yes,' he said. 'It's called mummification.'

Michael frowned, walking closer to the sarcophagus. 'Why'd they do that?'

Bill felt angry – but was it at Michael's questioning, or the fact that he was leering at the lady, breathing on her? Maybe both.

'Superstition,' he told him. 'The ancient Egyptians believed that, after death, there was another life – a better life. They wanted to make sure that they were ready for it. So they would be buried in a tomb with their riches and things. They were wrapped up in a shroud so that their bodies could be preserved. Can't enjoy the afterlife if you're a skeleton, can you?'

Michael nodded. 'All your food would fall right out of your belly, wouldn't it? It'd be like being hungry – forever.'

Bill looked at him for a long moment. Nope – there was no sarcasm on the boy's face, or in his voice. His head was as empty as the hold of the Spanish galleon after the pirates had been at it.

Michael stepped away from the sarcophagus, crouching beside the odd little jackal-statue. 'What's this thing, then?' he asked. 'A monument to her favourite pet?'

With a bored sigh, Bill went to crouch beside him. He looked over the curious object. It was about two feet tall, as round and wide as a cannon. At the back of it was a series of crude, carved lines running alongside a painted blue streak that moved in an almost perfectly horizontal line, north to south. He had wondered if it might have been some sort of code.

He ran his fingertips over the carved jackal's head, finding it cold and smooth. 'It's definitely marble,' he said. 'Maybe, in the next world, this thing was supposed to come to life and protect her.'

'From what?'

'How should I know? I haven't been to the next world, have I? And I hope not to, for many years.'

Bill examined the statue some more. At the point where the jackal's neck merged with the base, he felt a groove running all the way around. 'It's not a statue…' he said. 'It's a jar. The head is the lid.'

Michael slapped a hand on the top. 'What's inside it?'

'Don't!' Bill swung his arm, the back of his hand

catching Michael flush on one cheek and sending him sprawling.

'What's the matter with you?' Michael cried, rubbing his cheek.

Bill stood up. 'Sorry,' he said, feeling a shudder shift through his shoulders. He often gave Michael a hard time – he often gave *many* of the crew a hard time – but he didn't know where that flash of anger came from. 'It's just…we don't know exactly how valuable this stuff is, nor do we know how fragile it might be. If you broke something, you'd be in serious trouble.'

Michael nodded. 'So… You slapped me for my own good?'

Bill bit his tongue. 'Erm… Yeah.'

Michael actually smiled. 'Thanks, Bill.'

Bill shook his head as he watched Michael climb out of the hold with his typical monkey-like grace. It was a good thing that boy's missing half a brain bolstered his heart.

Bill cast one more look at the sarcophagus. Then he rolled up the parchments, and walked backwards away from it. It really was beautiful.

He turned to follow Michael out of the hold.

He saw a shadow slide across the wall, the room growing darker just before he heard something behind him smash. He wheeled around, arms raised against he knew not what. Had one of the desperate Spaniards woken up and somehow got free? Nothing else could be in here with him. Right? Of course nothing could.

So why did he think there might be?

Looking back to the sarcophagus, he saw that one of the candles he had placed by the lady's face had fallen off. The candle had broken into two, and its porcelain dish into many more pieces than that.

How did that happen? The *Queen Anne* was sailing smoothly, and the candle was placed a good six inches away from the edge. He stepped back towards the sarcophagus, as though he might find an answer upclose. In the dim light of the three remaining candles, Bill found his eyes dragged back to the carved face of the Egyptian lady.

She was so very beautiful, even in this darkness. He placed a hand on the lid, looking closer, feeling those tremors again. He was less concerned about where they came from now.

Such a beauty. And now, she lay dead – long dead – in this ornate sarcophagus. Mummified, no doubt. As he had explained to Michael, that was the Egyptian custom for the rich and powerful. A complicated procedure, involving evisceration and embalming, before the corpse was wrapped in a shroud, awaiting the next life, whatever lay there for them.

How did she look now, this beautiful lady? Was she perfectly preserved, or had the centuries taken their toll, even with the Egyptian protection? Was she shrivelled, withered, a twisted lump of black and grey flesh? Had time made a mockery of her beauty in life?

Somehow, Bill knew that this was true. And the thought of it made him strangely angry.

I have to get out of here, he told himself, his mind's voice tiny amid the images rampaging through his mind. *I have to get out right now.*

But he could not pull his hand away from the golden sarcophagus. The tremors he felt were getting stronger, like some kind of claw gripping his arm and keeping it still.

Get out, you fool! he told himself. But still he could not move.

His eyes were locked on the lady's as though linked by a belayed length of rope, her gaze fixed on the ceiling, unmoving.

They were black, and yet they seemed to glow. She looked less like a carving, and more...*real*. Her painted skin seemed to have more texture, her eyes seemed to be open wider, with more depth to them.

With a grunt of effort, Bill wrenched his hand away and dragged himself towards the trapdoor, telling himself that it was just his own talk of Egyptian superstition and mummification that had got inside his head, tricking him into thinking that something strange was going on when it wasn't. It couldn't be.

Could it?

William.

He froze again. It couldn't be, he told himself – it could not be a voice in the hold, whispering to him. He was the only person – the only *living* person – in there, except for the Spaniards in the cook's quarters.

Bill clambered up through the trapdoor, walking briskly to the forecastle and out onto the weather deck.

He was too scared to look back.

Chapter Fifteen

For the next three nights, Brutal Bill's head was invaded by visions of places and things he had never seen before, not even in drawings. But his mind conjured them as if from memory. Dreams of Ancient Egypt so vivid he could taste the dry desert air, and feel the relentless heat of the sun on his slick, sweaty skin. He would wake up, sweating and gasping, in the gun-deck, the rest of the crew curled up between cannons, feet resting on tackles, snores louder than the waves outside.

Then he would lay back down, listening to the creaking and cracking of the ship, the rattling of the timber sounding like the groan of the dead. He would feel the pull of the dreams as sleep washed over him again. His dream-self would wander through the streets of a small desert city spilling away from the bank of the River Nile, somehow knowing that the sharp, unnatural mountains of sand and stone in the distance were the near-mythical pyramids he had heard of on his travels along the Barbary Coast as a younger man. He knew that most of the toiling slaves he saw, hammering at the structures and lugging heavy stones, would die before the job was complete.

And he knew that the shadowy silhouette walking beside him, holding his hand and guiding him through the visions, was the lady from the golden sarcophagus. On the second night, the shadow had begun to peel off the lady's form like smoke, revealing the face of the carving. That beautiful face, as it was meant to look – no cracks of time, no worn paint. Her delicate, ebony skin seemed to shine, sucking in the sunlight and then throwing it back over the desert, as if brightening it further.

The feel of her hand in Bill's was stronger. He could feel her skin and flesh; it was cold, like the sarcophagus lid, and with the same tremors that tickled him all the way up to his elbow. When she looked ahead to the desert horizon, Bill followed her gaze. In the distance, was a cluster of four pyramids, arranged in a diamond formation. The sight of them stole the breath from Bill's lungs, even though he should not have felt such a sensation.

Is this really a dream? he wondered.

'It is, William.'

It was the same voice that he had heard in the hold. A hissing, snake-like whisper, at once seductive and terrifying. And now, it came from beside him.

It was the lady's.

Bill almost dared not look at her, but the pull of her eyes was irresistible. She smiled at him, her teeth a perfect white.

'You'll help me, won't you?'

Bill simply looked at her, confused. Help her with *what*?

The lady seemed to understand his doubts, and answered them by gazing back to the horizon again. Bill's eyes followed, just as a rumble rippled through the desert earth beneath his boots. One of the four pyramids seemed to shake like a tree in a storm. Clouds of dust rose off its sides as it began to sink into the ground.

Bill knew without knowing that he had just seen the lady's tomb disappear.

The ground where it once stood seemed to cave in on itself, before spewing up a torrent of sand and debris that swirled and writhed in a sandstorm that fell upon the desert city. As the residents of the city burst from their houses, running for the Nile, the writhing, swirling sand began to come together in the solid shape of a strange-looking creature, with the powerful body of a lion and the terrifying head of a crocodile.

Before Bill could say anything, or ask any questions,

the sky grew dark as the sandstorm raged. He looked up to see the form of a giant, four-legged creature eclipsing the sun. The lady gripped his hand tighter as the creature's thin legs paddled on the air as it got closer and closer to them. But she was not gripping Bill in fear – she was stopping *him* from running away.

The light from the sun seemed to flow around the flying creature now, bathing it in a harsh golden glow, allowing Bill to see exactly what it was.

The jackal. The creature from the marble jar. Was Michael right? Was this thing a pet of the lady's?

The jackal opened its mouth, hideous black drool flying from its cruel teeth. The lady's grip on Bill became even tighter, somehow seeming to hold down not just his hand, but the rest of his body, too. With a hungry growl, the jackal chomped at the air, its teeth seeming to snag on the very surroundings. Bill gasped as he saw a pool of darkness flood out across the sky.

The jackal had torn a hole in the air.

It tugged once and dragged the whole desert away as if it was simply removing a tablecloth, leaving Bill standing among very different surroundings. Now, Bill stood beside the lady in a vast, cavernous stone chamber with a ceiling so high he could not see it for the shadows.

The lady's tomb.

Dead in the centre was the golden sarcophagus, which was open – its lid was propped against the wall to Bill's right. It looked exactly as it did now, except that the beautiful, carved face of the lady wore no splotches or scratches – because the carving, the whole sarcophagus, was brand new.

And it was waiting for her.

Next to the sarcophagus was a bare table, around which stood three topless, shaven-headed Egyptian men holding square wooden buckets, their lips pursed and eyes wide in fear. And around both, positioned exactly as they had been aboard the Spanish galleon, and exactly as they were now down in the hold of the *Queen Anne's Revenge*, were the four standing wooden coffins on their plinths.

The walls of the chamber seemed to be cut into a perfect triangle, and Bill was positioned at a corner, directly opposite a wall broken by an archway. The walls to his left and right were lined with a different class of man. To his left was a platoon of soldiers, in long linen kilts, armed with swords or bronze spears, and shields of wood and ox-hide. They were stood to attention with their expressions as fixed and blank as statues, as though they were in a trance.

All around the floor of the tomb were curious, eerie little figurines – miniature soldiers holding spears and swords and shields. Their armour was painted onto their wooden bodies, and their faces were carved into fixed scowls of rage and violent intent.

Somehow, Bill knew that these were the *Shabti*, who would come to life in the next world, to protect their mistress.

But *how* did he know this?

Through the archway in the rear wall, came a group of six soldiers. Like the ones lining the wall, these men were bare chested, with linen kilts wrapped around their waists. But Bill guessed they were some kind of senior, elite soldier, from the gold bracelets around their muscular arms, which were raised high above their heads as they carried the lady into the chamber, towards the table. Her teal-and-white robes spilled down over the two soldiers at the rear, while her long, beautiful black hair hung between the front pair, so long it almost brushed the dusty ground.

They were followed by an imperious-looking fellow, walking in their wake. His upper body was adorned with curious sashes of gold and silver chain-links, as well as a long oval jade pendant with the head of a lion emerging as if from a lake. His linen kilt was not white, but black, and longer than the soldiers'. His head was adorned with a head-cloth of gold and silver stripes, that stretched all the way down to the middle of his back. In his large hands he clutched a thick papyrus scroll as if it was the handle of a sword. His black eyes did not blink as he watched the soldier's progress. Bill felt a storm of rage in his heart as he stared at the Pharaoh – was *he* responsible for the lady's physical death?

'No,' came the hissing voice. 'My husband served my greatest wish.'

The soldiers brought the lady to the table, and laid her upon it, crossing her arms over her body in the exact way depicted on the golden lid of the sarcophagus. The three men with the square buckets stood, seemingly transfixed by the beauty who lay before them.

Even dead, she was magnificent.

Three of the six soldiers stepped back from the sarcophagus, marching to join their comrades at the wall to Bill's left. The remaining soldiers were joined by the Pharaoh, whose eyes bored into the three men at the table.

'Begin,' he barked.

Bill's whole spirit was shuddering with the urge to

leave this dream, this vision – whatever it was. He wanted to break free of the lady's grip. He wanted to run, even though he didn't know the way out of this tomb. He knew what was coming next. Getting lost out in the cave tunnels beneath the Egyptian desert had to be preferable to seeing what was about to happen.

But the lady would not let him go.

'Stay,' she commanded. 'Observe what I endured for life eternal.'

Bill wanted to scream, but he couldn't. He wanted to close his eyes, but it was impossible. He had no choice but to watch 70 days of Egyptian funeral rites and preparation flow past him in a bewilderingly rapid sequence, the vision of the tomb repeatedly shimmering and dissolving over itself to show the same place and the same people – just minutes or hours or days later.

First, the lady's robes were removed and the three shirtless men set about upending their wooden buckets over her body, washing her in palm wine.

Next, the three men went at her left ribs with large, thin knives, with which they made a long, deep cut. Unlike the wounds Bill had seen on pirates – the wounds he had made – the lady's blood did not gush forth, for she had long been dead. Instead, it merely trickled lazily over the side of the table and onto the chamber floor.

While two of the men held the gaping wound open, the third dug his hand in, halfway up to his forearm. He rummaged inside the lady's torso as if he was looking for doubloon in a sack of grain. One of the priests stepped forward, the falcon-headed marble jar nestled in the crook of one arm. He knelt beside the table, lifting the lid off and extending the jar.

With a grunt of effort, the embalmer drew his hand free from the lady's torso, bringing with it a length of large intestine. He pulled at it, hand over hand, like he was working a halyard. The sound of squelching organ as it slipped past skin and snagged on bones, the hollow, wet slap and plop as it was dropped into the marble jar, was unnaturally deafening.

It was repeated three times, the embalmer plundering the lady's body for her stomach, liver and lungs and dropping them into separate jars adorned with the heads of a jackal, a baboon and a human soldier. Bill felt like he heard the hideous sounds of the evisceration not just in his ears, but in his mind and bones, too.

The four priests took a jar each to the standing,

wooden coffins and stood it before the plinth, to be guarded for eternity.

'Four of them.'

The lady's voice was soft, but insistent. Bill knew without knowing that she wanted the remaining three jars.

She *needed* them.

I understand, he told her, wanting her to release him from this terrible dream, to spare his eyes and soul the horror of what he had just witnessed.

But the plundering of her body was nothing compared to what came next.

A long, steel rod was brought to the lady's face. It glowed red from where it had been held in a fire. The hooked end threaded up the lady's nose. Bill heard the bone break before two of the embalmers twisted and pulled at it, like they were taking a crowbar to a particularly sticky barrel-lid. He saw the lady's face heave and swell before the red-hot hook came free – taking her brain with it.

Brutal Bill felt his soul shudder. He was grateful that, within this nightmare, he was unable to vomit...

He woke up in the gun-deck, gasping as he had done the previous two nights. The rest of the crew were asleep, and did not stir as he got to his feet and tip-toed along the sparred gallery to the ladder leading up to the weather-decks. He walked to the starboard bulwark and leaned on it.

The sky was dark, the moon full and as white as the lady's teeth. There was a lot of night left. Bill knew it was going to be a long one for him.

He did not know – *could* not know – that the following night would be the longest night of the pirates' lives.

Chapter Sixteen

'I just don't understand,' said Blackbeard.

The *Queen Anne's Revenge* was becalmed in the open sea of the Mediterranean. By Blackbeard, Mary and Handsome Harry's reckoning, the coasts of Crete and Libya hid behind the horizons on either side.

And they had been on either side for some time now.

The ship wasn't going anywhere. The winds had vanished, as though the cloudless blue sky above them had breathed in and stolen all the air from the world. The sails on all three masts were still, with not even the merest flutter or ripple to be heard. Blackbeard's ship was as stationary as if she had dropped anchor.

He stood next to Mary at the helm. She had the same quizzical frown that he could feel on his own face. She shrugged at him. 'The sea is an unpredictable friend,' she said.

'Don't talk such nonsense,' he told her. 'When have you ever known the air just become still so suddenly? I don't like this.'

'Calm down,' she said. 'The winds will return soon, and we can be on our way.'

Blackbeard shook his head again, eyes roving over his idle crew. At the bow, Brutal Bill sat leaning against a bulwark in the shade of a flat sail, his head drooping. 'Look at him,' he said, with a tut.

'He's up most of the night,' said Mary. 'Says he's working on translating the Spanish notes, but he must have done it twice over by now. And he's in the hold most days, with them Egyptian coffins.'

'I never took Bill for a ghoulish one.'

Blackbeard strode down the steps of the quarterdeck to the waist-deck, his heavy boots battering the boards with loud bumps. Bill did not stir at his Captain's approach. He did not even look up. Standing over him for a second, Blackbeard jabbed a toe into his shin.

'Guuh, wha—' Bill rubbed his face, shielding his eyes to look up at Blackbeard. 'Did I nod off, Captain?'

'Yes,' said Blackbeard. 'What's going on, Bill?'

Brutal Bill looked back down at the deck. He mumbled, 'Nothing.'

'Come on, Bill,' said Blackbeard. 'Don't tell me that. Word is, you've woke up grunting and gasping from night terrors three nights in a row. I heard you myself last night, all the way down in me cabin – I thought it was those blasted Spaniards at first.'

133

Bill sighed, but did not look up. Blackbeard sat down beside him, planting a soft fist in his shoulder. 'What's the matter with you, you craggy-faced numpty? You're Brutal Bill Howard – your nightmares are supposed to be scared of *you*, not the other way around.'

'The long journey must have got to me,' said Bill. 'Or maybe I'm just getting old?'

Blackbeard shook his head. 'That's a scary thought.'

Bill glanced to his right, briefly meeting Blackbeard's eye and then looking back down at the deck.

Blackbeard gazed at him. 'Come on. Let's go have some dinner, eh?'

He lifted Brutal Bill up by the arm, as Mister Peters came up on deck with a big pot of chicken stew – a luxury they had not been able to imagine for almost half a year. As the pirates sat down in clusters on the waist-deck, Blackbeard decided that he would not push Bill to talk just now. The quartermaster was one concern – one mild concern – among a crew that was seeing their luck changing. Except for the sudden lack of winds. He told himself that was also nothing more than a mild concern.

But he would keep an eye on Bill. That was for sure.

'They don't shut up, do they?' said Chris Claw,

dipping his nasty fingernails into the stew to shovel scraps of chicken into his mouth.

Blackbeard grunted as he tried to ignore the hoarse cries of the Spaniards down in the hold. Thanks to the unnervingly still conditions, he could hear them all too clearly. Their cries to be released – in a mixture of Spanish, English and plain old gibberish – drifted up from the hold to the waist-deck like a bad smell. 'I've got used to them by now,' he said.

He was sat in a wide circle on the rear of the waist-deck, against the wall that raised to the stern. A bloated shadow of the unmanned helm was slung across the deck, looking like a black sun. To Blackbeard's left was Chris Claw, then Handsome Harry, who balanced his bowl of stew in the crook of his left arm while miraculously using his dextrous last finger to spoon it into his mouth. With barely any lips left, he was unable to stop most of it tumbling down his chin and onto his jerkin.

To Blackbeard's immediate right sat Mister Peters, who regarded his fellow diners with an anxious glare as they wolfed down the meal he had so lovingly prepared. Beside him was Chaplain Charlie, whose bald head was dappled with yellow blisters that looked ready to erupt like volcanoes. And between Charlie and Handsome, sitting directly opposite Blackbeard, was Brutal Bill, who looked more likely to fall asleep in his dinner than polish it off.

'Just give the word,' said Mister Peters. 'I'll finish them off myself. Do you know how hard it is to slaughter chickens when you've got three prisoners babbling at you? Why can't we just tie them up and leave them in the hold?'

'Not near the treasure,' said Brutal Bill, without looking up.

Luis, the Spaniard from the tavern, turned around from his position, sitting on the capstan. 'They're not used to hardships,' he said. 'And, with respect, Captain – I don't think they trust you not to kill them.'

Handsome Harry drank from his bowl. 'Fools,' he said. 'How long they been down there already? Don't they think we would have thrown them overboard by now, if we were going to?'

'I know,' said Blackbeard, gulping some rum from his cannikin. The chicken stew – which smelled better than what Mister Peters usually put together – was not going to be his one meal for the day. 'And I ain't even tried frightening them in any of me usual ways. My reputation must be—'

Mary Bonny appeared among them as quickly as

a cat pouncing on a mouse. She swung a boot at Chris Claw's face, sending him flying across the deck. His bowl of stew flew overboard as the gathered pirates scrambled to their feet, cheering and jeering.

Except Mister Peters, who was scrambling for the bulwark, shouting: 'No! No! Don't waste it!'

Chris was trying to wrestle himself free as Mary fought to wrap a choking arm around his neck.

'I got a doubloon on the Captain's sister!' shouted one of the crew.

'I'll match that,' called Michael, who had fought his way to the edge of the group. 'Chris will turn this one around.'

No he won't, thought Blackbeard, as he shoved Luis off the capstan and took his position on it.

Chris had managed to turn over, but Mary's fists were too fast. Blood was already streaming from Chris's face in both directions. Blackbeard kept an eye on the bone-handled knife in his sister's belt – when the frenzy took her, she was liable to draw it. He did not want that.

Michael was shaking his head in disappointment. Most of the other pirates were cheering on Mary, except Brutal Bill, who had not bothered to stand up, and Handsome Harry, who crouched beside the brawlers.

'Come on, Chris,' he said. 'Don't be having this! Not from a lassie!'

Mary took two handfuls of Chris's hair, while glaring at Handsome. 'Shut that mangled mouth of yours,' she snarled, 'or you'll be next.'

'Yes, Mary,' said Handsome, backing away as Mary's head plunged downward.

Chris screamed as she bit into his nose, his legs juddering as though he was having a fit, palms slapping the deck in a gesture of desperate submission.

Blackbeard counted to five, then he looked to Michael. 'That's enough,' he said. 'Drag her off before Chris's hooter goes overboard.'

Michael took a cautious step forward and tapped Mary on the shoulder. Mary rose up from Chris and swung a massive roundhouse, that Michael avoided by cart-wheeling to his left, much to the delight of the crew.

Breathing heavily, with Chris's blood on her knuckles and chin, Mary glared at the rest of the pirates. 'Who's next?' she shrieked. 'Who else thinks they'd be a better Captain than me? Eh? Try it, you scurvy wretches. I dare you!'

The pirates looked at the floor, shaking their heads and mumbling 'Not me, not me.'

Blackbeard smiled, and raised his cannikin. His half-sister had taken his warning about the men challenging her authority and made sure it would never again be a problem. 'To your next Captain, lads!'

A cheer went up from the men, although Blackbeard could see and hear that not all of them put their whole lungs into it. Clearly, some were thinking she was crazier than her brother.

She just might have been.

The cheer died away to silence.

Complete silence.

Blackbeard looked to his half-sister. 'Do you hear that?' he asked.

Mary wiped her chin clear of Chris's blood. Then she shrugged. 'Hear what?'

'Exactly.'

'Careful of the sarcophagus!' shouted Brutal Bill, as Blackbeard dropped through the trapdoor into the hold. It was dark apart from the weak, floating puddle of light limply drifting out from the four candles placed on the golden sarcophagus.

He heard some of his crew following him.

'Careful!' said Bill again.

Weaving in and out of the standing wooden coffins, Blackbeard led the crew through the hold to the cook's quarters, where he had kept the unruly, very loud Spanish privateers.

Who had not made a sound for several minutes.

With practised ease, Blackbeard lifted the wooden beam from out of the brackets nailed into the door, then wrenched the whole thing open.

The body of the short, bald Spaniard slumped at his feet. Blackbeard recoiled, barely registering that he had backed into one of his crew. In the cell, the other two Spaniards limply fell on top of their compatriot.

Blackbeard crouched down beside them.

'Be careful, Captain!'

Blackbeard half-turned to glare through the gloom at Michael. 'What do you think they're going to do?' he said. 'They're clearly dead, boy.'

'But there's not a mark on them,' said Mary, crouching next to him.

Blackbeard looked them over. The prisoners didn't seem to be bleeding, nor did they have bruises. He reached out to take Baldy by the shoulders, dragging him clear of the other two, and turning him over.

The man's eyes were almost as wide as his mouth, which hung open in a grisly 'O'. Blackbeard had seen dead men's eyes before – more of them than he could count from memory – and these were like none he had ever seen. They held not the blank, vacant stare of the 'long sleep' – the bald privateer's eyes looked like he was staring at something.

He's staring at whatever it was that frightened him to death.

Blackbeard shook his head clear of the ridiculous thought. And it was ridiculous – the only person on board who might have been able to frighten three privateers to death was him, and he hadn't been down there to do it.

But if it was not him, then who?

Blackbeard closed Baldy's eyes and stood up. Even in the gloom, he could see the faces of his crew. They were pale with shock. Blackbeard cleared his throat, and said: 'Michael, find Chaplain Charlie. Tell him he's got a service to conduct. The rest of you – get these men up on deck, quick as you can.'

He followed Michael to the trap door, muttering: 'It's bad luck to sail with corpses on board.'

Chapter Seventeen

'One... Two... Three!'

Chris Claw heaved the third Spanish corpse over the port gunwale. As Chaplain Charlie aimed an air-crucifix at the sea, Blackbeard locked eyes with the dead man, who stared up with the same fixed expression of desperate fear, before the sea claimed him as it had his two friends.

Beside him, Luis muttered something in Spanish, and then crossed himself.

As one, the pirates that had gathered at the bulwark for the impromptu funeral turned away walked aimlessly about the decks. The conditions remained as lifeless as the sinking Spaniards, so there was nothing for anyone to do except exchange sheepish, confused glances and shrugs.

Except, Blackbeard noticed, Brutal Bill, who sat on the steps leading to the quarterdeck, staring vacantly out at the expanse of ocean, as if trying to pick out something in the emptiness. What was going on with that old geezer?

'Get off me!'

Blackbeard looked towards the forecastle door,

where he saw Vicious Vern, an ageing gunner who had been with Blackbeard's crew since he had overthrown his old Captain, Benjamin Hornigold, carrying one of the powder monkeys up onto the waist-deck. The young lad – the ginger-haired one with the angry red pimples all over his mug – beat his little fists uselessly against Vern's back, before Vern tossed him onto the deck as though he was a sack of potatoes.

'What are you doing?' Blackbeard asked, walking over to them and hearing the chorus of footsteps as others walked in his wake. All around the deck, idle pirates closed in on the scene.

Vern's face was red, and not from sunburn. He was in his fifties, and lugging the boy up the ladder from the gun-deck looked like it had almost killed him. 'Gonna question 'im,' he wheezed, his chest heaving rapidly. 'The monkeys must know something.'

'Why?' asked Blackbeard.

Vern swiped a hand at Michael, who had bent to help up the powder monkey. Michael ducked his head and hopped away, shooting Vern an accusing look.

'Because they spend most of their time in the gun-deck,' said Vern. 'So they be the closest to the hold, and the closest to the dead men.'

An angry mutter moved through the gathered mob.

Blackbeard shook his head as he called to the men: 'Don't let your heads run away with you. You know most of you lot get headaches by the time you've had a second thought.' He stepped between Vern and the ginger monkey. 'And you, you should know better – you know you need my permission for something like this.'

'But Captain,' said Vern, 'we have a killer onboard.'

Another mutter from the pirates, this one louder and more panicked. Blackbeard held up a hand for calm: 'The Spaniards had no marks on them,' he said. 'They were not murdered.'

'No,' said Chris, his voice sounding strangled because of his battered nose. 'They were frightened to death.'

Blackbeard stared down at the cowering boy with the spots. 'So it's hardly likely to be... What's your name?'

'Owen,' said the lad.

'It's hardly likely to be Owen, is it?' Blackbeard sighed, lifting his hat and smoothing his hair back from his eyes. 'This is why I tell you lot to let *me* do the thinking. When you think, this is the sort of thing that happens.' He extended a hand to Owen. 'Come on, up you get.'

Owen hesitated for a minute, but then he accepted

Blackbeard's hand and stood up.

'No more of this,' said Blackbeard, eyeing each of his crew in turn. They had regained their weight and their strength since their hard times a couple of weeks before, but the anxious glint in their eyes gave them a look that was equally pathetic.

'But how could they have died that way, sir?' asked Vern. 'The chickens hardly could have done it.'

'Maybe they tried to eat one,' said Mister Peters, smiling. 'They're a bit feisty, them chickens – they peck, like. It's almost as if they don't want to have their heads cut off.'

Mister Peters stopped smiling when he caught Blackbeard's eye. He ducked his head and mumbled, 'Sorry.'

'Your jokes go down about as well as your stews,' said Blackbeard, drawing a guffaw from some of the men. But most were too anxious to engage in humour. 'So, what is it?' he said to them. 'Come on, speak up.'

'Why has the weather died, sir?' asked Chaplain Charlie. 'We've never seen anything like this.'

'And we have sarco… Sarc…' said Michael, shaking his head as he struggled with the word. '…big coffins onboard!'

'That can't be good luck,' said a voice among the

crowd, that Blackbeard couldn't pick out, because another one was crying: 'Have we stolen a curse?'

'What does it mean?' shouted a crewmate behind Blackbeard.

'Enough!' he roared. 'I won't hear anymore talk of curses. We are not cursed. It's just treasure, that's all. The Spaniards...probably just starved. Maybe we should have fed them a bit more regularly.'

But the crew were not sated by his words. They stared at him, their chests heaving with panicked breathing.

Blackbeard sighed. 'Fine,' he growled. 'I shall tell you what. I will go down to the hold, and I will sit among the coffin treasures for one hour. And, when I emerge from the hold in one piece, anyone who hasn't stopped this talk of curses will be left behind at the next port.'

Ten minutes later, Blackbeard sat down in the hold as Brutal Bill placed the last candle at the fourth corner of the golden sarcophagus, then walked back to the open trapdoor, where he paused.

'Are you sure about this, Captain?' he asked.

Blackbeard grunted. 'It's the hold of my ship,' he replied. 'Nothing's going to happen to me down here.'

Bill accepted the hand of Chris Claw, reaching down to pull him up into the gun-deck. Mary closed the trapdoor with a loud clatter that startled the surviving chickens in the cook's quarters.

Now, the only light was from the four candles as they illuminated the beautiful face of the painted lady. Blackbeard sat down at the foot of the artefact, beside one of the standing wooden coffins. Just in front of it was the curious marble jar with the jackal's head, and the maze of grooves etched into one side.

Blackbeard reached for it, suddenly curious as to what it might have contained.

But he did not pick it up. He paused, with his hand hovering over the jackal's pricked ears, its painted black eyes glowing with the gleam of the candlelight. Blackbeard drew his hand back, chiding himself for even considering opening the jar.

It was precious. Essential.

But to what?

Blackbeard shook himself, forcing out a laugh at the ridiculous thoughts drifting through his mind. Of course it was precious – it was treasure, and it was worth a lot of money. So, of course, it was essential – because that money would fund his well-earned retirement.

He told himself, that was all he meant when he had the thought. It was just his tired brain, playing tricks on him, latching on to the vague idea that there might be a curse on board – something powerful and deadly.

The only powerful and deadly thing on board this ship is me, he thought.

Then he took a deep breath and settled in to see out an uneventful hour, letting his senses focus on nothing but the sounds of the sea.

Except, that there was barely any of that. The only sound to be heard was the listless waves of the almost still Mediterranean, sounding no more magnificent than water in a bathtub.

That was something to worry about. The unnatural way the conditions had suddenly just…died. He had never seen anything like it. He sat forward, resting his elbows on his knees as he pondered. How to sail anywhere if the sea and wind was uncooperative? At this rate, they'd have to fashion oars out of something – and make their own holes in the hull through which to use them.

Old-school pirating, he thought, with a smile, wondering how many crewmates it would take to actually move a two hundred-tonne, thirty-gun ship.

His smile fell off his face when he heard a low

scraping sound behind him. Like something moved along the deck, just an inch or two. He twisted in his sitting position, staring at the ghoulish arrangement of coffins. Perhaps one of those weird, standing structures had shifted...

...in the near-motionless hold.

Blackbeard stood up, feeling a knot of unease build in his gut. He stepped back from the coffins, staring at each of them in turn. He told himself, he was getting old, that was all. He was hearing things. Silly superstitions. He turned his back on the treasure, and bent to sit back down.

Creak...

He stood up and spun on his heels, staring again at the treasure. Had any of it moved? It was impossible to tell – the floor of the hold was hidden beneath the lake of shadow cast by the candles; and he was on a vessel made entirely of oak, which meant it could have been any one of hundreds – thousands – of timber beams and planks that might have creaked just then.

It didn't necessarily mean that it was one of the four wooden coffins.

Did it?

Creak.

Thump!

'Edward!'

Blackbeard started, instinctively taking a deep breath through his nose to calm himself when he heard Mary's voice from above. He turned, and saw her leaning down into the hold.

'The wind is picking up,' she said. 'The *Queen Anne* needs her captain.'

Blackbeard paused a moment, waiting for his heart to stop pounding. He could feel the ship lurching as the seas heaved and swelled as they were supposed to, could hear the howl of an insistent wind.

'Take over for now,' he said. 'I'm staying here until the hour is up.'

'It *is* up, Edward,' Mary replied.

'Nonsense. I've been here no longer than ten minutes.'

'No, you've been down here an hour. Now, come on.'

Blackbeard walked to the trapdoor, reaching up to get a handhold and haul himself into the gun-deck.

Mary was standing up, grinning at him. 'So,' she said, 'no curse, then?'

Blackbeard closed the trap door, stamping on it once to make sure it was secure – something he had never done in all his time captaining this ship. 'That's right,' he told her. 'Now, everyone can get back to normal.'

He followed her towards the sparred gallery and, as his sister climbed the ladder up onto the quarter-deck, Blackbeard told himself: *No one else is going to die.*

Chapter Eighteen

Did she *do it?*

For the fourth night in a row, Brutal Bill Howard had trouble sleeping – but this time, it was not night terrors waking him up. The terrors on board the *Queen Anne's Revenge* were more than enough to keep his eyes open in the dark. He felt like no amount of rum could ever hope to chase away the fear that filled his skull.

He sat up, reaching out for the cannon to his right to pull himself to his feet. Duelling snores sounded from the crew as he stepped over curled-up bodies and made his way to the trap door in the centre. He pulled it open as quietly as he could and slipped down into the hold, letting it gently close over his head.

The candles at the corner of the sarcophagus had almost burnt to their bases, the dishes in which they stood now small puddles of wax.

Did you *do it?*

He stepped closer to the sarcophagus, the light from the candle at the bottom left corner spilling over one of the standing wooden coffins. As he passed it, Bill froze, desperately wanting what he thought he had just seen to not be true. It *couldn't* be true.

But as he slowly looked to his left he realised, with a hot and bilious feeling in his throat, that it was true. He *had* seen it.

The lid of the coffin to the lady's left – it was slightly ajar.

His breath coming in shallow pants, Bill reached to pick up the small candle at the lady's foot. He held it over the standing coffin. *How is this possible?* he thought, staring at the lady's face as if expecting her to respond.

Breathing quicker, and heavier, Bill side-stepped along the coffin, letting the candlelight sail from bottom to top, then all the way around. As he moved along the left edge of the coffin, doubt and urgent suspicion tickled his mind. Something wasn't right about these coffins, and hadn't been since he had first seen them on the Spaniards' galleon.

He took a step back, the light from the candle in his hand swinging over the hold in a chaotic pattern. His lips smacked together as he gasped for air – he had realised what was wrong with them.

The coffin lids were not nailed in. There was nothing keeping them on. But how could that be possible? They should have slid right off when Bill and the boarding party transferred them onto the *Queen Anne*.

He stared at the wooden coffin in front of him for a long moment, his free hand inching forward, driven by a foolish curiosity that thumbed its nose at the fear tingling and prickling in Bill's belly and chest. Something told him, he *had* to see.

Holding the candle closer, he ran his fingers over the sides of the coffin, searching for hidden nails. But there was nothing. The wood was smooth, except where it was dented or rotten. Bill slipped his fingers into the sliver of a gap and tried opening the lid.

It did not give. Not even an inch.

It's like it's being held tight from the inside.

The second he had the thought, Bill somehow knew it to be true.

He stepped around the coffin, back to the lady, as though her golden sarcophagus might give him an answer – but what kind of answer could it possibly give? The light from his candle merged with those either side of her face – it wore fewer black splotches than before. The lines of time were fainter, shallower. It was like the carving of her face had got younger.

Bill half-gasped, half-shrieked as he pulled his body

away, using every ounce of strength he could muster to head back to the trap door.

He didn't know what was going on down here in the hold – he didn't even know what was going on inside his own head – but he knew it was something wrong, something unholy.

Some kind of...*curse*.

With his free hand, he reached to push the trap door open, moving fast and not caring if he woke up the rest of the sleeping crew. He had to tell the Captain that his precious treasure was cursed; he had to tell the captain to consider throwing the whole blasted lot overboard.

'William.'

Bill froze with his free hand above his head, palm on the trap door. Again, his curiosity and fear were in a wrestling match that his curiosity somehow managed t???o win. He turned around, his eyes on the floor.

I've failed her, he thought, without knowing why he did.

Slowly, his gaze drifted upwards, as though puppet strings were connected to his skull.

Bill dropped his candle, barely hearing the smash of the porcelain dish.

He hoped that he was simply tired, and that his

exhausted eyes and mind were playing tricks on him. He hoped it was his imagination, running wild on fear and paranoia.

He hoped that he was not seeing the four wooden coffin lids slowly opening.

Chapter Nineteen

Blackbeard held one of his pistols close to his chest as he gazed out into the wall of darkness in his cabin. He was laying in his hammock, which gently rocked side to side; he was trying to shake the images of the dead Spaniards from his mind. But they wouldn't budge. They seemed planted there like weeds.

He had seen many things during his time as a pirate, but he had never seen men frightened to death before. He knew he was scary, but he was not that scary.

But if it wasn't him, and it wasn't the fear of what the pirate Blackbeard might do to them, then what had put fatal terror into those privateers?

Could the ship really be haunted by spirits? After all, they had brought five coffins on board with them a few days before. Maybe—

He shook his head. What a ridiculous thought! It was just treasure, that's all. Fancy, valuable treasure. And Blackbeard had sat down in the hold for an hour, and nothing strange at all had happened.

Not really.

He shifted in the hammock, aiming the barrel of his pistol in the general direction of the cabin door. If anyone so much as knocked, he fancied he'd fire. He closed his eyes and tried to drift off, hoping the dull noises of the ship would shepherd him to sleep.

It was beginning to work. Blackbeard felt his eyes grow heavy as he felt the ever-so-gentle rocking of the hull as the anchor and seawater made it dance. He listened to the familiar creaking and cracking of his vessel…

…and the frightened scream of a pirate in the hold.

Blackbeard bounced up to his feet, pistol ready – although, if the *Queen Anne* actually *did* harbour ghosts and spirits, he didn't know what use it would be.

He pulled open his cabin door and ran down the sparred gallery into the gun-deck, where most of his crew were already disappearing *down* through the trapdoor. Blackbeard did not break stride as he hopped down into the hold, which was dimly lit from short candles placed on the golden sarcophagus.

'Outta the way,' said Blackbeard, as he pushed past the pirates who had not made a lane for him. They shrank back, mumbling and muttering in high-pitched, frightened voices. He took a candle from the sarcophagus, and angled the small flame at the floor beside it – at the spot where all the pirates were looking.

Brutal Bill lay on the floor between the sarcophagus and the wooden coffin to its right. He was dead, his mouth open in scream of unimaginable terror – that he did not live long enough to finish.

Just like the Spaniards.

In one hand, he clutched the marble pot with the jackal head on top; in the other, he held his length of parchment, the one on which he had been making his notes about the special treasure.

Mary appeared by Blackbeard's side. 'Bill, too?' she said. 'What is going on?'

Blackbeard said nothing. He handed her the candle and pushed back through the pirates, reaching up to drag himself out of the hold and into the gun-deck. He walked to the capstan and leant on it, gripping a bar in each of his meaty hands, feeling such angry strength in his arms, he felt like he could weigh anchor all by himself.

He was trying to catch his breath. He was trying not to be sick. He looked to the heavens, seeing the first sliver of the Mediterranean sun – like a bump in the horizon – dribbling light over the dark sky. Another day was coming.

The longest night of the pirates' lives was over.

But worse – much worse – was still to come.

159

Chapter Twenty

'You know...I used to think that no one on God's earth could ever be as free as us. That sailing was the most liberating life there was. But now... I feel more trapped than I have ever felt before.'

Perched at the stern of his ship, Blackbeard couldn't decide if he actually preferred it when his half-sister was griping all day about when he was going to retire so she could inherit the captaincy. The whole morning since they had discovered Brutal Bill's body, all she talked about was the horror of finding him, and how it had changed her view of life as a pirate.

'It's just some form of sea madness,' Blackbeard said, not for the first time that morning. 'One we ain't seen before.'

'Maybe,' said Mary, who stood at the helm, casting a quick glance back at him over her shoulder. 'It seems like our lives and crimes are finding new ways to catch up with us.'

'Balderdash,' said Blackbeard. 'It's just this place, these unfamiliar seas. The Old World is a deadly mystery to us.'

On the waist-deck and up among the rigging, the

crew went about their jobs in almost total silence. Blackbeard reckoned that, if they didn't want to simply get out of the Mediterranean so badly, most of them might not have had the stomach to sail. He wasn't sure he did either.

It was one thing for the Spanish privateers to suddenly turn up dead – they were strangers, prisoners, who none of them really cared about – but one of the crew? And Brutal Bill, to boot!

Blackbeard hopped down onto the quarterdeck and cast his eye over his topmen, turning his attention to captaining his ship so that he could keep his mind occupied, hoping the horrors of the night before might slip from his mind. Up among the mizzen-sail, he saw the unexpected figure of the Spaniard, Luis.

He strode down to the waist-deck to find Handsome Harry. He tapped him on the shoulder. 'What's he doing up there?' he asked.

Handsome shrugged. 'Said he wanted to contribute. He's not actually that bad.'

'Where's the lad, Michael?' Blackbeard asked.

'Down in the hold,' said Handsome, shaking his head. 'Poor little twerp won't come out. Devastated, he is.'

Blackbeard ran a hand over his face, feeling his jaw

and cheekbones no longer threatening to stab through his beard. He wasn't a gaunt, exhausted captain anymore, but his mind was still clouded with the anticipation of hard times ahead. For the first time he could remember, he was looking forward to reaching land. 'I need this like I need gangrene,' he said. 'I'll go talk to him.'

He walked along the deck to the forecastle, feeling the eyes of his crew on him. His hour in the hold counted for nothing now that Brutal Bill had turned up dead in the same way as the Spaniards. He kept his shoulders square, his head high and his stride brisk. If he looked confident, unbothered, then maybe the men would start to feel it, too. Maybe they would get through this.

He moved through the gun-deck. The gunports were open, and when he crouched to pull up the trap door, long spokes of light stabbed through the gap, illuminating the hold – the treasure, the barrels of food...and the body of Michael on the floor.

'No!' Blackbeard breathed as he jumped down. It took him two strides to reach Michael's body. The boy lay flat on his back, one arm thrust out to the side, the other clutching Brutal Bill's parchment to his chest. Just like the others, there was not a mark on him. His face was pale, his closed eyes ringed with deep purple, and his cheeks caked with dirt and grime from the tears he had shed for Brutal Bill.

Blackbeard fell to his knees and shook the young topman. 'Michael? Michael?'

'Hnnnuuuhhh...what?'

Michael's free hand moved to rub his face, opening bleary, reddened eyes which narrowed. 'Captain?' he asked.

Blackbeard let out a long sigh, feeling his chest shudder as he started laughing in relief. 'You gave me a scare, boy,' he said. 'I thought you'd gone the way of Bill and the Spaniards.'

Michael sat up, still clutching the parchment to his chest. 'I just fell asleep.'

'What are you doing down here by yourself?' asked Blackbeard, looking around the hold at their treasure. The golden sarcophagus sat beneath the gentle blanket of light from the four candles, the flames waving and pulsing with the motion of the ship. Even amid his tiredness, his memory of his own eerie experience down here the day before, and his grief for Bill, Blackbeard was struck once again by how beautiful it was. As Michael spoke again, he had to pull his eyes away from it.

'I wanted to read Bill's work,' said the boy. 'I was interested in the treasure, and Bill said he knew about Egypt. I thought...' Michael's voice caught in his throat. He looked away for a moment and took a deep breath to compose himself.

Blackbeard felt a swell of pity for him, but also pride – Michael was still young, but he was learning to control himself, his emotions. Essential skills for any self-respecting pirate. Maybe he was cut out for it, after all.

'...I thought that, if Bill never finished his work, maybe I could finish it for him.'

Blackbeard smiled and ruffled Michael's sandy blond hair. 'You're a good lad,' he said. Then he asked: 'So...did Bill finish?'

Michael said nothing. He simply held out the parchment. From the look on the boy's face, Blackbeard knew that there was something on there that he had to read:

Six dead. I darent tell anyone what I think might be happening. If Im wrong, they will ridicule me for the rest of the voyage. But Im more frightened of being correct.

She is controlling us... Must stay away... Captain

wont throw treasure overboard... He is a fool
  She is in my dreams
  They came, as I dreamed they would.
  Three more jars will give the answer. To the greatest
treasure of them all.

Blackbeard put the parchment down on the desk in his cabin, even more confused and worried than before. It was not just an inventory – it was the rantings of a mad man. But who was the mad man – the Spanish quartermaster, or Bill himself?

Where was Bill getting all this information from – about the 'three more jars', that gave the 'answer to the greatest treasure of them all'? Blackbeard had very little Spanish, but it did not take more than a quick glance at both pieces of parchment for him to see that Bill's translation stopped at the Spaniard's proclamation that someone had come to him in his dreams.

Therefore, Bill could not have simply been copying the notes of his Spanish counterpart. Also, there were several references to Blackbeard himself in the second half of Bill's notes, rendered in handwriting that got progressively less legible as it went on. Several times, his quill appeared to have torn thin holes in the parchment. Something was compelling Bill to write down his rambling, fevered thoughts. It was very unlike him – and that was the most worrying thing of all.

'What could this "greatest treasure" be?' Blackbeard wondered aloud, knowing that he needed to keep this information in his cabin for now. It would surely not do for the crew to know that Bill had seemingly gone mad over the course of several days. They were spooked enough as it was.

Blackbeard sighed and picked up the parchment again, quickly casting his eye over Bill's translation, at what had been the first warning sign during his initial reading of them:

Six dead. I darent tell anyone what I think might be happening. If Im wrong, they will ridicule me for the rest of the voyage. But Im more frightened of being correct

He could not ask Bill what that might have meant. He could not ask the Spanish quartermaster, either.

But there was someone on board the *Queen Anne* who might have an answer.

Chapter Twenty-one

'No! No! Not down there... Not with them!'

Blackbeard looked up to the trap door as Handsome Harry and Chris Claw dragged Luis towards the edge. The two pirates shoved him and the Spaniard fell into the hold, hitting the floor and giving a loud gasp as the air was driven from his body. He spluttered and spat as he tried to get up. Blackbeard marched over to him and gave him a fierce kick in the ribs, sending him rolling, as Harry and Chris hopped down to join them, dragging the door closed and leaving just the light of the candles.

This was how Blackbeard wanted it. An eerie, spooky setting would loosen that tongue of Luis's. So he hoped.

'You say "them",' said Blackbeard. 'Who do you mean?'

Luis coughed as he pushed himself up to his knees. He looked up at Blackbeard, trying to suck in air and looking like he was contemplating whether he could charge right through the hull and swim clear of the *Queen Anne's Revenge*.

'I don't like asking twice,' said Blackbeard.

Luis's head dropped. After a moment of silence,

Chris Claw stepped forward. 'You better answer the Captain,' he said, grabbing Luis's hair and pulling him to his feet.

'Easy, Chris,' said Blackbeard. Chris Claw took a step back, his chest heaving with angry breaths that he took through his mouth, because he could not breathe through his nose. Not after the beating Mary gave him yesterday. His eyes were also ringed with deep black.

'Let's try this another way, Luis,' he said. 'Before he died, your quartermaster wrote that six of your crew had snuffed it. In his notes, he said that he had an idea about what might have been going on, but was very afraid of being right. Do you happen to know what he meant?'

Luis tried to shake his head, but he could not stop his eyes going to the Egyptian treasure in the hold. Blackbeard stepped aside to give him a better view of the golden sarcophagus.

'Something to do with the treasure?' he asked. 'I remember your other three boys weren't all that happy to be locked down here with it.'

Luis looked at the floor again. Blackbeard had had enough of this already, and drew his pistol. 'Fine,' he said.

'Cursed!' cried Luis, raising his arms in a gesture

of surrender. 'The quartermaster believed we had angered the Gods of Heaven.' His voice fell to a strangled croak. 'The treasure... is cursed.'

Blackbeard shoved the pistol back into his sling. 'Certainly explains why boarding and plundering your ship was as easy as it was.'

'We were desperate,' said Luis. 'Within days of us taking the treasure, strange noises plagued the ship at night. The men had bad dreams first – then they began dying. We had no other choice!'

'You tricked me. When you turned up in that tavern, you said you were looking for a pirate. You weren't lying, were you? You were looking for a pirate to pass your curse onto!'

'It was supposed to be the North Africans,' said Luis. 'I did not expect to find Blackbeard in Cyprus, of all places!'

Blackbeard snorted. 'No, I suppose you wouldn't have. Serves me right for sailing into the Old World.'

Handsome Harry took a step closer to Luis, his mangled face set in a grimace of rage. 'You set us up, did ya?'

'Our crew were dying!' said Luis. 'One by one. We had no other choice.'

'I'll kill you!' Harry snarled.

Blackbeard stepped in front of the older pirate and shoved him back. 'No, you won't,' he said with a wink, letting Harry know he had something else planned for the treacherous Spaniard. 'Any man has a right to try and lift a curse off himself, wouldn't you agree?' He turned back to Luis. 'But, if you thought the treasure was cursed, how come you didn't try diving overboard like the rest of them?'

'You said you'd take me back to Spain,' said Luis. 'I thought that, if I stayed away from the hold, I might be able to avoid the curse long enough to see out the voyage. It felt like a risk worth taking.'

Blackbeard stared at Luis for a long moment. There was something not right about this privateer. Just moments before, he was gasping and whimpering and begging to be taken out of the hold. Now, he seemed calm as he explained his story, even after admitting betraying the most notorious pirate on the seas.

'Well,' said Harry, 'when we get to Spain, you best hope I never run into you in a dark alley. If I do, I'll have your intestines for a necklace, so help me.'

'We're not going to Spain,' said Blackbeard.

The other three men looked at him sharply.

'What are you talking about?' said Chris Claw. 'Spain was the plan.'

'But the plan did not include us getting saddled with an Egyptian curse,' said Blackbeard. 'So we need a new plan now.'

'What is it, Captain?' asked Harry.

Blackbeard sighed, shaking his head as he examined his choices. He could sit tight, barricade the hold, and ride this out – make it to land, abandon his ship and hope that distance put between his crew and the curse would save their lives.

Or, he could find a way to look this curse in the eye, and put a bullet or a blade in its heart.

'Not here,' he said to Harry. 'Up on the waist-deck, five minutes – make sure everyone is there.'

Blackbeard and his two mates climbed up onto the gun-deck. As Chris Claw and Handsome Harry made their way to the forecastle, Blackbeard turned on his heels, seeing Luis's hands thrust through the hole in the floor. With a grunt, the Spaniard starting climbing out.

Blackbeard brought his boot down on his fingers. Luis howled. 'If this curse is real,' he said, 'I'll make sure you fall to it. Nobody double-crosses Blackbeard.'

He reached down to grab a handful of Luis's hair, which he used to pull him up out of the hold, setting him down with another thump.

'It's just my bad fortune that I need your help.'

Chapter Twenty-two

'I'm about to give a command that none of you are going to like.'

Blackbeard stood on the quarterdeck, looking down at the gathered pirates on the waist-deck. All thirty-odd of them crowded together, their pale, haunted faces looking to him, so attentive they dared not even whisper among themselves. Their motley jerkins flapped in the northwesterly breeze, which swept their hair across their faces.

It was good sailing conditions, but the *Queen Anne* wasn't going anywhere. The anchor had been dropped, the sails rolled up to reveal the network of black cordage looking like a bare tree in autumn – the skeleton of the sails.

The ship's heading was in the balance, awaiting the outcome of the impromptu meeting that had been called.

At the fore of the group, Handsome Harry and Chris Claw stood together, faces still wearing the confusion they had shown down in the hold. Next to them, Mary stood with an almost motherly arm round Michael, who looked ready to fall asleep again.

'I'm going to recommend that Mary turn the ship about,' Blackbeard continued, 'and sail back the way we came.'

Thirty pairs of eyes flitted left and right as the crewmates tried to figure out if their captain was playing some kind of joke. One by one, they looked back at him quizzically.

'I know it doesn't make much sense right now,' he said. 'And I know that we will put this to a vote that I might lose. If that happens, I will accept it. But, I ask you all to hear me out before we vote.'

There was silence among the men. Blackbeard took this as a good sign. Twisting his beard with his fingers – as he always did when he was thinking hard – he began pacing the quarterdeck.

'As you all know, some strange things have been happening down in the hold. Things we can't explain. First, them three Spaniards die, and then our own beloved Brutal Bill. Four men, not a mark on them. And what's more, they looked like they had been frightened to death. None of us have ever seen anything like this. Now, our adopted friend, Luis, here—'

Blackbeard pointed up to Luis, who was tied to the main mast about thirty feet off the deck. He gently swayed back and forth in the light wind, grimacing at the tightness of the rope wrapped around his wrists.

'—told me why he thought his compatriots were so eager to simply let us take their treasure. Why they tried to dive overboard when we brought them onto the *Queen Anne's Revenge*. And why they did not shut up the whole time they were down in the hold.'

Blackbeard stopped pacing, and stopped fiddling with his beard. He could not undersell this moment. 'The Spaniards believed that the treasure was cursed.'

Now there was mumbling from the men. 'We plundered a cursed ship?' shouted Mister Peters. Chaplain Charlie crossed himself and clasped his hands together, throwing his eyes to heaven.

'I knew it!' shouted Vicious Vern. 'I should have been listened to!'

'They shared your opinion, Vern,' said Blackbeard, raising his voice and speaking quicker to make sure their attention came back to him. 'But that does not mean that I do.'

'You still think it's not a curse?' asked Vern, shouldering people aside to reach the front of the group. Chris Claw shot him a look of angry contempt.

'No,' said Blackbeard. 'I agree...we *are* cursed.'

A stunned silence fell over the group. It was one

thing for them to be paranoid, but it was another for their captain to so calmly tell them they were damned.

'But unlike you, Vern,' Blackbeard continued, 'I shan't run around shouting about how we're doomed. I'll do what I do every time I face danger, be it physical or otherwise. I'll cut it down.' He addressed the group as a whole: 'Now...I brought you all here, to the Mediterranean – to the Old World. It was my choice, and that means that, if we are indeed cursed, then it is my fault. And I want to do everything in my power to lift this curse from the two things I love most in this world – my ship, and my crew.'

The mates had fallen silent again, looking at him in rapt attention.

'And that means that we must turn about. We must follow the guidance of brave Bill Howard, and find the answers he was looking for. To do that, we must head deep into the Old World, and follow this curse back to its source, wherever that is. For I believe that is where we will find the means to lift it. I know it must sound reckless, even foolish. I don't disagree with you. It is both of those things. But, I'm sure you lads know me well enough – I am not one to simply stand by and accept fate without a fight. That attitude is for land-lubbers. And none of us is that! Now, there is a long way between here and Spain – and no guarantee that we will survive that journey, curse or no curse. So I say, why not turn about and sail straight into the wrath of fate, and we'll see who emerges victorious!'

The mates' gazes were still fixed, their expressions still confused and concerned – but Blackbeard detected a ripple of nods amid the wide-eyed, incredulous glares.

He was winning them round.

'We shall vote it now,' he said. 'All in favour?'

As one, the men yelled: 'Aye!'

Blackbeard grinned. 'Mary – turn this ship about, if you please.'

As his sister jumped up onto the quarterdeck towards the helm, Blackbeard drew his cutlass and raised it high. 'You are the bravest of men,' he said. 'Your courage will not be squandered by your Captain. And if we are cursed…if we are under attack from those who Luis here calls the Gods of Heaven, then I say this: let's see how they deal with the Men From Hell!'

Part Three

Chapter Twenty-three

One week later

On the seventh morning after the vote, Blackbeard gave the order to drop anchor, just off the northwest coast of Egypt, close to the Port of Alexandria, judging by the markings on his map. Although, having never had need of studying maps of the Old World before, he could just as easily have been staring at the coast of Australia, for all he knew.

Not that he was going to tell anybody that. The crew did not need another thing to worry them. Almost nobody dared venture into the hold now, especially not alone. The men spent their nights sleeping on the weather-decks, rather than below in the gun-deck. Two mates would stay up, in watch-pairs that changed every two hours.

Just in case.

They had seen nothing, but more than a handful of the men complained of hearing strange noises from down below. A grating, scraping sound that definitely was not the groaning or cracking of timber with which they were all familiar. Changes in the wind direction that almost turned the Queen Anne in a somersault.

A hissing voice that sounded more like a snake's than a person's, uttering a language that none of them recognised.

Seven mornings had seen a mate come to him with these questions, and each morning, Blackbeard had given the same response: 'You're imagining it, matey. We're all a little spooked, that's all.'

But, if they experienced one more troubling night, Blackbeard suspected even he wouldn't believe his reassurance.

Standing at the bow, flanked by Handsome Harry and Chris Claw, he raised his spyglass. 'Definitely a Barbary ship,' he said, 'one they captured. But I recognise that cobra flag. I tell you what, I rather fancy stealing that design for myself!' He narrated for his mates: this new ship was stranded on a rocky bluff, only this one was wrecked and barely afloat. Foamy waves slapped against the hull in a listless rhythm. Its torn sails fluttered uselessly in the wind. The sense of emptiness and desolation seemed to waft off it like a bad smell, even from a distance.

'Get Luis,' he said.

Chris Claw disappeared below decks, returning a few minutes later with their Spanish prisoner, dumping him before Blackbeard.

Luis was groggy, half awake with his head lolling as though it was about to fall off. Blackbeard extended his foot, lightly shoving Luis at the shoulder to turn him on his back. He was the palest, gauntest man on board, which was hardly surprising – he was the only one who was made to sleep down below.

With the treasure.

'When was the last time we fed him?' Blackbeard asked.

'Dunno,' said Harry, with a shrug.

'Oi,' said Blackbeard, crouching beside the prisoner. He slapped his face, hard. Luis's skin was slick and almost papery – Blackbeard was surprised it didn't slide off at his slap. 'Don't fall asleep on us. You're actually useful today.'

Luis groaned and stirred, shielding his eyes against the rod of sunlight that pulsed almost unbearable waves of heat down on them. 'Am I to be released?' he muttered.

Blackbeard smiled grimly. 'A week alone in the hold must have made you delirious,' he said. 'We seem to be at the location you marked off on the map.' He showed him the spyglass. 'I need you to have a look and confirm.'

Putting a hand under Luis's shoulder, Blackbeard pulled him to his feet. Luis took the spyglass and peered through for less than five seconds before he spoke.

'That's it,' he said. 'That's the Barbary ship where we found the treasure.'

'And are you sure they're all dead?' said Blackbeard. 'If you're leading us into another trap—'

'I promise you I'm not,' said Luis. 'The only thing you'll find there is a bunch of dead Barbary pirates, and the treasure our ship could not bear.'

'Is that all?' said Blackbeard, making sure to give the man his best death-stare. He found it got the truth out of most people.

Luis shrugged. 'There's also the cargo of cotton that was ours – we decided to transfer that to make room for more of the Egyptian treasure.'

'Don't get smart with me, you treacherous little worm,' said Blackbeard, tapping the butt of one of his pistols. 'Your usefulness to us is running out fast, and I will not think twice about putting a hole in your skull if it happens to be the most convenient option.'

He nodded at Chris to signal that Luis should be

taken back below deck. Chris wrapped one hand around Luis's neck as he led him away.

Handsome Harry marched down onto the waist-deck. 'Weigh anchor!' the old pirate cried, before he began directing the crew.

Blackbeard walked with him, continuing on towards the helm. 'Straight ahead, sister,' he said, as he walked up the steps. 'If you please.'

'In the future,' said Mary, 'I'd appreciate it if the important conversations took place up on the quarterdeck.'

Blackbeard playfully ruffled her black mop of hair, which had grown longer, almost falling over her dark eyes. 'You'll not be at the helm much longer,' he told her. 'This is almost over. I can feel it.'

Chapter Twenty-four

After Mary drew the *Queen Anne* along the wrecked vessel's starboard side, Blackbeard led the boarding party in place of the late Brutal Bill. He hopped across from one gunwale to the other, his heavy feet coming down on the weather-deck of the corsair ship, where he felt the battered planks of wood dip and rattle beneath him.

'Halt!' he commanded, raising his voice to be heard over the relentless, rhythmic roar of the waves that attacked the bluff like a battering ram. He turned to his men, just as Chris Claw was preparing to launch himself. Others were clambering up to do the same. 'This ship is ailing. It might not bear the weight of all of us. Better to be cautious. Chris, Handsome – with me. The rest of you—'

'Ahem!'

Blackbeard did not need to look to spot his sister among the line of pirates at the bulwark. He could feel her glare. 'Chris, Handsome and Mary,' he corrected himself, 'with me. The rest of you, watch our backs. Check your powder, and keep your eyes peeled. I don't believe Luis is foolish enough to have told us more lies, but it's better to be safe.'

As his three most trusted pirates cautiously made their way from one ship to the other, Blackbeard drew one of his pistols and turned around, closely examining the deck of the Barbary ship for the first time. Walking across from starboard to port was like stepping up a gentle incline, the vessel listing and leaning, the deck soaked and slippery from seawater that had arced over the hull at high tide. Looking along the port bulwarks, Blackbeard saw that its gunwale was smashed and broken in several places, where the ship had come upon the bluff. Somehow, a cannon had been ripped from its tackle and had rolled halfway across the deck, knocking against the thick base of the capstan with each dip and rise of the ship, its metallic *thunk* providing an eerie, almost maddening rhythm to accompany the scene. Towards the stern, it seemed to have snagged on a minor outcrop. It may well have been what was keeping the damned ship afloat.

'My God...'

Blackbeard spun round at Handsome Harry's gravely voice, looking towards the port bow. Not much could turn the stomach of the most feared pirate in the world, but what he saw then seemed to melt his insides into a hot, prickling mess. He swallowed hard to stop the insurgent vomit from flying out of his mouth. Behind him, he heard Mary gasp.

The contorted figure of a Barbary pirate was lying on the deck at the port bow. His brain was over at the starboard. He was face down, with his muscled arms splayed to the side, but his toes pointing to the sky. It was almost like his body had been unscrewed at the hip, his flesh seeming to have burst open. A length of jagged spine protruded at a hideous angle, scraps of skin stuck to it.

'Had to have been a fall,' said Blackbeard, casting his eye up to the sheer bluff. 'This lad must have been near enough at the top when he slipped.'

'There's no way anyone could climb that,' said Chris, appearing at Blackbeard's side.

'If you're desperate,' said Blackbeard, 'you can find a way.'

'Question is,' said Mary, the first to dare step a little closer to the dead man, 'what made him so desperate? What was he trying to get away from?'

Blackbeard said nothing, because the only possible answers were ones that might undermine the confidence of the crew, compel them to vote again. He needed them strong, he needed them determined.

'Let's go below deck,' he said. He drew a brace of pistols. 'Weapons.'

Mary drew her pistol, while Chris Claw held a dagger in one hand. Handsome Harry had not the hands and fingers to hold a weapon – but he rarely needed one, anyway.

Blackbeard led them to the forecastle door, which opened with an eerie creak that seemed to be warning the pirates against their exploration. Walking slowly, with his pistols held out in front of him and his fingers on the triggers, he moved below decks into the sparred gallery of the Barbary ship.

As a sleeker, lighter ship, the gallery walls were narrower than the *Queen Anne's*. Blackbeard had to walk almost side-on to move with any speed. The walls were lined with more windows than the *Queen Anne's*, and strong shafts of sunshine stabbed through them like spears, making pools of light at the bottom.

And in each pool was another dead body.

Seven corsairs lay face down, one arm extended and the other limp, down by their sides. They had been crawling away from something.

The same thing that had frightened the Spanish prisoners and Brutal Bill to death?

What could it be? Blackbeard asked himself, unsure

if he actually wanted to find out.

'Let's move them over,' he said, crouching and taking the first one by the waistcoat to drag him to one wall, rolling him over onto his side, 'so that we can— Stone me!'

Blackbeard recoiled, standing to his feet and driving his makeshift boarding party back several steps, all of them muttering in horror. The dead corsair's belly was as wide open as his brown leather waistcoat. Scraps of broken ribs dribbled out of him and onto the floor, becoming lodged in the dried puddle of blood and flesh.

He had been hollowed out.

'We should get back to the *Queen Anne*,' said Mary. 'Only bad luck can find us here.'

'It's already found us,' said Blackbeard. 'We should meet it head on.'

'Brother—'

'Captain!' Blackbeard corrected, turning on his heels to glare at her. 'If your stomach and heart fails you, Miss Bonny, you have my permission to return to our ship. But I have a unanimous crew behind me, who voted that we do whatever we can to lift the curse that is upon us. If this damned corsair ship contains answers that will help me do that, I will find them –

no matter how many corpses I have to step on.'

Mary bit her bottom lip for a moment, thinking. Then she nodded. 'Aye, Captain,' she said. 'Forgive my doubt.'

Blackbeard nodded at her to show that he was not angry. He knew he was asking a lot of his crew, especially when he could not give them a clear, logical reason for why he was so determined to sail deep into the Old World, in search of misfortune and hexes. He didn't really know himself. He was compelled, fascinated, working on instinct.

But more than that, he was Blackbeard – and no one, not even Egyptian gods, were going to rule his life.

The pirates moved on, placing their foot in the gaps between the dead Barbary pirates' elbows, ribs and knees. At the end of the sparred gallery was an oak door that had been forced open, standing half-mangled on its one remaining hinge. It was dented, as though on the receiving end of fierce blows, and scored with what looked like the claw marks of some kind of wild predator.

Blackbeard turned his body side on, nudging the door open with the barrel of a pistol. He slowly walked inside, finding himself in the captain's cabin.

It was ringed with large windows, duelling beams of sunshine crisscrossing over the floor, the chairs and the ornate carved desk at the far wall to his left – where a puddle of caked blood had formed, gluing the remains of another dead corsair's skull to the deck. In his lifeless hand, the dead man held a pistol.

He had put a bullet in himself rather than face whatever it was that had eviscerated his compatriots.

'So much death on this ship,' said Handsome Harry. Blackbeard heard the others slowly following. 'Looks like we got off lightly.'

Our journey isn't over yet, Blackbeard thought, but did not say. Pointing that out could do no good.

'Edward.'

Blackbeard turned at Mary's voice, seeing her crouching and pulling on a steel door-handle. A small square of the floor came up. 'I think we're above the hold.'

The hold was empty apart from the boxes of cotton that Luis had mentioned. Trickles of water drained from holes in the ceiling – not surprising when the ship had stood still and took a pounding from the sea for so many weeks.

Blackbeard and his pirates moved through the hold,

the timber beneath their boots wobbling and groaning. Down at this level, the battering waves were almost unbearably loud on the starboard side, while the port side groaned and rattled as it was forced against the bluff over and over again.

The sea will claim her soon, Blackbeard realised, moving quicker through the maze of boxes. He wasn't sure what he was looking for, he just thought he might find something here – after all, if he could stumble upon such bad luck, who was to say he couldn't stumble upon some good?

'There's nothing here,' said Mary. 'We should—'

'*Gnuugghh...*'

All four of them stopped dead at the hideous groan sounding from somewhere in the hold. Blackbeard held his pistol out straighter, moving the barrel in wide arcs as he scanned left to right.

A cotton box fell to the ground, making them jump. Looking in its direction, Blackbeard saw the body of a Barbary pirate.

And – somehow – he was still breathing.

Chapter Twenty-five

Blackbeard shoved his gun back into his belt as he went to the fellow.

He lay face down in a corner of the hold, his waistcoat covered in dust and blood, tracks of grazes and scabs at his throat and jugular. Something had been wrapped around his neck, trying to choke him.

Blackbeard could tell from the sag of his skin, the way his tattoos drooped, that he had lost weight. How long had he been lying here, just waiting for a death that cruelly never came?

It had to have been weeks.

'Do you speak English?' Blackbeard asked, getting on all fours and dropping his face low, so as to be at eye-level with the dying pirate. 'English?'

The man did not open his eyes. His lips barely parted as he spoke: 'You...must...go...'

'We can't,' said Blackbeard. 'We've inherited your curse.'

Now, the man's eyes opened, but his gaze seemed to go through Blackbeard. 'Then you are dead... You and everyone with you... Dead...'

Blackbeard heard his companions shifting

uncomfortably behind him. 'What's your name, friend?'

'Nasir,' said the man. 'Captain…Nasir.'

'Right, Captain,' said Blackbeard. 'What is this curse?'

'Ancient curse,' said Nasir, closing his eyes again as his words fell away to an agonised groan. 'As old as time…'

'What can we do about it? There must be something.'

'The King… Amir… Tell him it is no good… She won't ever let us…reach the Sultan…'

Blackbeard reached out to place a hand on Nasir's back, half to comfort him, and half to shake him alive the same way he might shake a lazy pirate out of sleep. 'What do you—?'

His voice fell away to a gasp as the whole galley was heaved to port by a powerful wave. A low groan sounded from the timber as clouds of splinters were spat from the hull. A wound opened up, revealing the jagged rocky bluff, punching its way through.

'Edward,' said Mary, her voice carrying the warning. They could not guarantee that this ship would stay afloat much longer.

'Start gathering things up,' he told her. 'Anything that you think might help. Take it back to the *Queen Anne*. I'll follow you.' He turned his head and saw that the others hadn't moved. 'Now!' he barked.

As the others got to work, Blackbeard turned back to Nasir. 'Captain,' he said. 'Stay with me for a moment. Please... Tell me your story.'

'King Amir...' he croaked, his voice slick with blood that had filled his mouth. His lips smacked together as he tried to spit – but he barely had the energy. 'He charged us with a mission, by the Sultan. Plunder the tomb of Sakhmet. Bring the most valuable of all Egyptian treasure to Constantinople, or...'

'Or what?' said Blackbeard, laying his cheek on the deck, trying to find Nasir's eyes. '*Or what?*'

But Nasir's eyes were closed. He had grown still. Blackbeard swallowed the urge to shake him again. He could see there was no use.

He was dead.

And Blackbeard was no closer to figuring out what could be done to lift the curse from his crew, except to 'Follow the map'.

But what map?

'Edward!'

Blackbeard snapped out of his reverie and looked across the hold, over the cotton boxes. Mary was crouched in the opposite corner, a look of fearful wonder on her face.

He got to his feet and marched across, coming to a stop and feeling some of the tension drain away when he saw them – two of the jars, like the one they had on board the *Queen Anne*. They were made of marble, about the size of a cannon, only they had different heads on them – one was a falcon, the other what looked like a baboon.

Reaching down to pick up the falcon-headed jar, Blackbeard turned it over and almost cried out in joy. Like their jackal-headed jar, this one had a web of grooves in intricate patterns, with a curved blue streak running diagonally from top-to-bottom down one side.

And just like that, Blackbeard understood the fevered ramblings of two dead men – Brutal Bill, and Captain Nasir.

'It's the Nile!' he said. 'The River Nile.' He crouched back down to place the jar next to the baboon-headed one. Side by side, their blue streaks merged into each other perfectly.

'How can you be sure?' asked Mary. 'We've never seen the Nile for ourselves.'

'These lines are a map,' said Blackbeard, pointing. 'This is what Nasir was talking about. "Follow the map". And it has to be the Nile – look how it runs downward across the jars. With the street- and road-markings branching off alongside it. Bill made a note that these jars would provide the answer to…'

He felt all the excitement bleed out of him in an instant. His head dropped.

'What's wrong, Captain?' asked Harry.

'We're missing one,' said Blackbeard. 'Bill's notes said there were three more. We've only found two. Damn it!' He stood up and gave one of the cotton boxes a kick, the wood caving in beneath his boot. He took a deep breath to compose himself. 'Search every inch of this ship – I want that other jar. And if you don't find it, then look for logs, maps – anyth—'

His voice collapsed into a grunt of surprise as the ship heaved again. He staggered, instinctively reaching out for a handhold and finding nothing but a pile of boxes that toppled like a felled tree.

'No,' said Mary. 'We need to get off this ship, before we go down with it.'

Chapter Twenty-six

'Steady!' Blackbeard yelled to his crew as he gazed over the stern of the departing *Queen Anne*, watching as the mighty sea claimed Nasir's vessel. First, its bow leant forward, disappearing into the surface as the water invaded it through the gashes in its hull. The bulky stern slowly came up, up, up as the loose and torn cordage flicked and snapped in the breeze, as though desperately trying to escape the doomed vessel. Slowly, the whole ship slid into the Mediterranean, like a blade put back into its sheath, leaving nothing behind but flotsam in the ripples.

Man and sea would wrestle for all of time. But there would only ever be one winner.

Blackbeard said not a word to Mary as he passed her, nor did he return the sad faces of the crew whose eyes looked to him for help as he disappeared below decks, marching back to his cabin and slamming the door shut behind him.

On and around his desk was everything they recovered from Nasir's vessel. They may not have found the fourth jar, but Mary and Chris did take from it piles of parchment – maps, the captain's logs, the quartermaster's logs. Blackbeard took his seat and rifled through them, observing in only a few seconds that they were more or less useless to him. Every bit of scribbling on every bit of parchment was in Arabic.

No help whatsoever.

Blackbeard tossed a roll of parchment onto the table in his cabin, picking up a map from the pile.

'I don't believe it,' he muttered, as he leaned forward to look closer. It was the same map as the one they had taken from Percy's ship – the route to Constantinople.

It was starting to make sense, without making much sense at all.

When Blackbeard had first seen Percy, he'd estimated the vessel was on a northeast heading – the general direction of Turkey and Constantinople. Percy's group was well-fed and healthy; they did not look haunted, or in fear of a curse – which meant that they had probably never had this treasure onboard their ship.

But Nasir did – at least, until the opportunistic Spaniards had come across him, when he and his crew had already been torn to pieces by...

By what? What evil, hideous menace stalked the poor Barbary captain's galley?

Blackbeard rubbed his forehead, which was beginning to ache. This was not the time to focus on what he didn't know. He had to concentrate on what he *did* know.

Nasir had said the Barbary King, Amir Barbarossa, was trying to get the Egyptian treasure to the Ottoman Sultan, all the way in the capital – Constantinople. Percy had bragged that he was on a mission for the King – which, Brutal Bill had figured out, was getting his ship to Constantinople.

But if Percy did not have the treasure that Amir was delivering to the Sultan, then...

He was looking for Nasir.

That was it. Percy was sailing the Mediterranean, searching for Nasir – because the King had grown concerned that Nasir may not have completed his original mission. Anticipating that he might have come upon a shipwreck, Percy was armed with a map to the capital – it would have been his duty to complete the mission.

But why? Why did the Sultan want this treasure? Did he not know of the mystical risks it held?

And why was the great, feared Barbary King going to such lengths to make the ruler of the Ottoman Empire happy?

Blackbeard did not like so many unanswered questions.

He was startled by a gentle knock at his door. He set the map down on the table and crossed his cabin, opening it and revealing Chris Claw, who looked annoyed.

'It's that Luis,' said Chris. 'He's really insistent, Captain.'

Blackbeard half-sighed, half-growled. 'All right, bring him in.'

Chris turned and walked down the sparred gallery, as Blackbeard sat down. Within two minutes, Chris had returned, dragging Luis by the scruff of his neck.

That week or so in the hold had really had an effect on the Spaniard. He looked like he hadn't slept in that whole time. He had probably been too scared to. His face bore almost no expression – his sunken eyes were vacant, their stare distant.

Blackbeard didn't mind. At least he wasn't wailing to be let out of the hold – not that he had done much of that while he'd been down there.

'I overheard the men talking,' said Luis. He must have been really tired – his words blended into each other in a strange hiss. Like a snake. Blackbeard almost had to lean forward to hear him. 'They say that you recovered two more jars, but not the last one. And that you have maps and logs from the North African pirates.'

'What of it?' said Blackbeard.

'I imagine you'll be having trouble reading them. I offer my help to you.'

Blackbeard shared a look with Chris Claw, both of them trying to figure out what Luis's angle might be.

'That's very good of you,' said Blackbeard. 'But why do you offer to help the man who is keeping you prisoner?'

Luis's pale, cracked lips parted in a smile that was almost...smug. 'So that he won't keep me prisoner anymore.'

'Don't get smart,' said Blackbeard. 'And anyway, they're all in Arabic, not Spanish. What good are you?'

Luis took a step forward. He no longer had the hunched posture and shuffling gait of a starved prisoner. He moved with confidence. 'I'm familiar with the Barbary coast,' he said. 'I've sailed up and down it many times. I have picked up some of the language.'

Blackbeard regarded him for a long moment, still trying to figure out what the angle could be. Perhaps he was planning to get close to Blackbeard so that he could kill him?

But that was a stupid move – Blackbeard had about thirty men onboard. Luis would never make it off the ship alive – and even if he did, where could he swim to?

All the same, Blackbeard drew a pistol as he stood up from his desk. 'By all means,' he said, gesturing at the stool he had vacated. 'Have a go.'

Blackbeard and Chris Claw stood guard over Luis as he sat in Blackbeard's chair, rifling through the parchment, eyes sailing over the scribblings, lips moving as he translated Arabic into Spanish – which did not help Blackbeard at all, because he barely spoke Spanish.

'Well?' he said, after an hour. His pistol was still aimed at Luis's head.

Luis let the parchment he was holding drop back onto the table. He turned his face to Blackbeard, his eyes unreadable. 'Big trouble,' he said. 'Big, big trouble. The Barbary Pirates believed that the worst of luck had befallen them – that they had angered an Ancient Egyptian goddess.'

Blackbeard nodded. 'Sakhmet?'

Luis's eyes widened as he took a sharp intake of breath. 'You know the name?' he asked, his strange, hissing voice setting Blackbeard's teeth on edge.

Blackbeard nodded. 'Nasir said it – before he died. Who was she?'

Luis's eyes narrowed for a moment. 'Hmmm,' he breathed, nodding to himself. 'It doesn't say here, not exactly. But I believe she had to have been the most wondrously beautiful of all Egyptian goddesses, who seeks a righteous resurrection from the horrible purgatory of—'

'Get on with it,' Blackbeard growled.

Luis nodded. 'The Barbary pirates sailed from the Port of Rosetta, down the Nile. They found Sakhmet's tomb and stole away her burial treasure. They made for Constantinople. But they had not been at sea more than five days when the curse began taking hold. They tried to run, but it caught them. They tried to fight – and they lost. It was too strong for them to outrun.'

Blackbeard stared at him for a long moment. Luis stared right back, letting his last sentence speak for itself.

'So now that curse is on us?' said Chris Claw. 'How do we lift it?'

Blackbeard let his pistol-arm drop. 'We shall pay

a visit to the man Nasir answered to. Amir Barbarossa.'

Chris Claw scratched at his temple, leaving behind an angry red mark. 'What for?'

'Because he charged first Nasir and then Percy with the mission to take this treasure to the Sultan,' said Blackbeard. 'Which means, it was his crew that plundered the tomb of Sakhmet in the first place. So he can show us the way there.'

Blackbeard spun round at the sound of footsteps from the sparred gallery. As the cabin door opened, he drew a pistol and thrust it towards the newcomer.

'Whoa!' yelled Mary, dropping to the floor. 'Careful, you lumbering numbskull!'

Blackbeard lowered his gun again. 'Sorry,' he said, reaching down to help her up. 'You startled me.'

'I just come to ask if you were coming up on deck any time soon,' she said. 'If you're going to leave me stuck on the helm, you can at least tell me where we're going.'

Blackbeard nodded. 'The Port of Rosetta.'

Mary frowned, her hands going to her hips. 'Eh?'

'Luis will show ya,' said Blackbeard, stepping towards his hammock. 'I need to lay down for a bit.'

Luis gave an oddly formal half-bow. 'Yes, Captain,' he said, as he stepped around the desk and crossed the cabin towards Mary. As the Spaniard followed her out into the sparred gallery, he gave her an appraising look.

Blackbeard felt a scowl on his lips as Chris Claw closed the door behind them all. It didn't matter if Luis led them to the Barbary King's lair – if he laid a hand on his sister, Blackbeard would send his whole arm to the bottom of the Mediterranean.

Chapter Twenty-seven

Three days later
The Port of Rosetta, Egypt

Amir Barbarossa weighted the ivory-handled dagger in his hand, and tried not to think of what it symbolised. But that was impossible. How could a father not think about his ten-year-old son, locked up in a cell all the way in Constantinople, under the threat of death? That was the fate looming over Amir's son Beni, unless his father, the Barbary King, completed a mission on behalf of the Ottoman Sultan, Ahmed III.

Amir set the dagger down on the arm of the throne in which he sat. It was carved from the same oak as his ship, the *Gallant*, and was big enough to seat two large men. Usually Amir would sprawl in the seat, one leg over the side, as he lorded it over his unruly pirate crew as they indulged all their favoured vices of food, music and fighting in the place he called his 'Palace' – a cavernous hall in the caves just west of the Port of Rosetta.

But not now.

The year he had been given was over in two months'

time, and he had not heard word of either Captain Nasir or Captain Djeema.

Amir's restless hands fiddled with the necklace he wore, from which the teeth of his most prized victims and enemies dangled. He was thinking the same thought that had dominated his mind for the last year.

Some 'King' I am. I charge those loyal to me with the task of saving my son. Even if I did not trust the Sultan's word that he would spare our lives, I should have accepted the responsibility myself. And now, I'm paying for it.

His First Mate, Omar, stood at the bottom of the carved stone steps that led to his throne. Behind him, the rows of wooden tables stood empty, chairs idle or capsized, with the bear- or tiger-skin coverings left carelessly on the stony ground. When full of celebrating pirates singing songs, playfully wrestling, fighting, and chasing women, it felt no bigger than the hold of the *Gallant*. Now, it felt as lonely as a deserted city.

'Permission to approach,' Omar said, with a bow.

Amir gestured for him to do so, and the gangly young man climbed the eight steps two at a time, coming to a stop at Amir's side.

'There is still no word from Nasir,' said Omar. 'Nor

Djeema. Who shall we dispatch next? And where should we even send them?'

Amir could not stop his eyes going to the dagger briefly before he responded: 'I don't know. Nasir should have returned from Constantinople by now. He should have my...' He bit back an anguished sigh, running a hand over his shaved scalp, all the way down to the plaited ponytail that stretched from the back of his head.

'There's something that's been worrying me,' said Omar. 'What if... What if what the Sultan believes about the treasure is not true?'

'It doesn't matter,' said Amir, shoving the ivory-handled knife into his belt and leaning forward, elbows on his knees. 'All he asked for was the treasure, we've found that... Doesn't matter if it tells him the secrets of immortality or not. It probably won't. But we've done our part of their deal. As long as it gets to him...'

His voice trailed off. Was the treasure going to get to the Sultan? What price would Amir pay for putting his son's life in the hands of his pirate crew?

'But how can we even keep up our end of the deal?' asked Omar, his long, spindly arms spreading in a gesture that begged for a good answer to his question. 'We don't even know where the treasure is right now.'

'I wouldn't be so sure of that!'

Amir and Omar turned towards the chamber archway that led off into a maze of tunnels, veiled by the thick cave shadows. One of his boy minions – Jamal, he thought his name might have been – had burst from the shadows, running up the aisle towards Amir's throne with a look of glee on his face.

'What is it?' asked Amir.

'A visitor,' said Jamal, standing breathless at the bottom of the steps. He put his hands on his hips, his skinny chest glistening with sweat. 'From the New World. He seeks a parley with you. He says he has the treasure of Sakhmet.'

Amir stood up, feeling his muscular chest swell with the purest rage. His hands balled into fists so tight, he thought he might shatter his own bones. 'A foreigner dares rob a ship of my fleet!? He puts the life of my son in danger!' He fingered the necklace of teeth. 'What is the name of this sea-bandit who seems to have grown tired of being able to chew his food?'

Jamal's voice shook with awe as he answered: 'He calls himself Blackbeard.'

Chapter Twenty-eight

Now this *is how a proper pirate lives.*

Blackbeard hoped that his face did not show how impressed he was with what he was seeing. A cavernous stone chamber strewn with chairs draped in animal skin covers, open chests along the walls, bursting with treasure. A steep stone staircase leading up to a throne, beside which was a low table piled high with plates of bread and cuts of meat, and a goblet of what Blackbeard was sure was the finest wine or ale or rum in Egypt.

This was *style.*

Like the other Barbary pirates Blackbeard had encountered since he had set that trap for Percy, the one who sat on the throne wore a brown leather waistcoat. The difference was, he was so muscular it barely covered his ribs. His torso was adorned with a deep, black tattoo of a cobra with two heads stretching out in opposite directions from his sternum, the familiar Barbary symbol seeming to come to life every time his muscles rippled – which was often.

He was the Barbary King – Amir Barbarossa.

Blackbeard drew to a stop at the bottom of the

stone steps, Mary at his side. She had threatened Chris Claw with the loss of an ear if he didn't agree to her accompanying Blackbeard for this impromptu meeting.

'The famous Blackbeard,' said Amir, standing to his feet. He held no weapon except an ivory-handled dagger in his belt. Nevertheless, Blackbeard felt a jolt of apprehension – it was one weapon more than either he or Mary had on him. As a show of peace, they had left their weapons in the dinghy they had rowed to reach the shore. The rest of the crew remained onboard the *Queen Anne's Revenge*, which was anchored out of sight in the Mediterranean.

If this parley went bad, Blackbeard knew he could be in serious trouble.

For one thing, it had taken them fifteen minutes to be shown into the chamber, what with all those caves leading to it. Blackbeard did not reckon he'd find his way back out in a hurry.

The chamber was empty of all the Barbary pirates except the King, and who Blackbeard assumed was his First Mate – a tall, shaven-headed lad with limbs like bamboo, standing next to the King's throne.

'Good day to you, Mr Barbarossa,' said Blackbeard.

Amir smiled grimly. 'In these parts, I'm usually

referred to as King Amir.'

Blackbeard took a moment to choose his words carefully. He was here for the man's help, and he was willing to play nice – within reason. But he would not call another man 'King' anything. 'I'm not disrespecting you,' he said. 'Kings are kings of their territory, and the people in them – I'm not from this territory.'

'How did you find me?' Amir asked.

'I came across one of your boys,' said Blackbeard. 'He pointed me in your direction. Name of Nasir.'

The First Mate walked down two steps. 'You saw Nasir?'

'Omar,' the King growled. Omar grew still, but stayed at the lower step, his eyes alight with concern.

'Where is Nasir now?' asked Amir.

'About twenty miles west of Alexandria,' said Blackbeard. 'To be more specific, he's at the bottom of the Mediterranean.'

Amir's thick, powerful arms fell to his sides, hanging loosely. 'He's dead?' Blackbeard nodded. 'How?'

'Murdered,' said Blackbeard.

'By who?'

'I was hoping you could tell me.'

Omar came down the stone steps with the chaotic

grace of a scrabbling spider. 'Don't play with us,' he snarled. 'Tell us what you know.'

Blackbeard did not take a chance. As soon as Omar was within reach, he slapped a hand to the side of his scrawny neck – a strong blow, but not a deadly one. It stunned the First Mate, whose bandy legs wobbled. Blackbeard wrapped him up in a choke hold, forcing the lad's left arm behind his back. An inch further to the right, and it would snap in two.

He looked over Omar's shoulder, into the inscrutable eyes of the Barbary King. 'I come here unarmed,' he said. 'But I don't need a weapon to snuff out this little runt. Now, Mr Barbary King, are we going to parley or not?'

'You have my treasure,' said Amir. 'Where is it?'

'It's safe,' said Blackbeard. 'On board my ship. Close, but not so close that you can steal it. And I warn you, send any ships out to sea to look for it, the *Queen Anne's Revenge* will turn about and disappear, and you'll never find it. And you'll never get that treasure to Constantinople.'

'I want it back!' Amir roared.

Blackbeard could tell that Amir's own mission was not only an important one, but highly personal judging by the incensed look in his eyes. He tightened his grip on Omar's neck, hearing him gag and splutter as he tried to wrench Blackbeard's forearm off. 'I'm willing to trade.'

Amir regarded him for a long moment, before finally he nodded and made his way, slowly and deliberately, down the stone steps. 'Omar will give you no more trouble.'

Blackbeard nodded, shoving Omar forward. He stumbled as he went to Amir's side, turning and baring his teeth at Blackbeard in an angry glare. 'You'll pay for that,' he said. 'I promise—'

Amir moved so fast, Blackbeard barely saw his right arm thrust out, his massive fist catching Omar on the temple and knocking him unconscious.

And the Barbary King had not taken his eyes off Blackbeard. 'Now we can talk,' he said, shaking his hand loose and rubbing his knuckles. 'How did you come to be in possession of my treasure? Did you capture Nasir's ship?'

'No,' said Blackbeard. 'The treasure had already been stolen from him by some Spaniards. I took it from them.'

Amir shook his head. 'Not possible. Nasir was the most capable Captain in my fleet – mere Europeans could not have overpowered him.'

'It wasn't the Spaniards,' said Mary. 'It was... something else.'

'What?'

Blackbeard puffed out his cheeks, taking off his hat and tucking it under his arm. 'I don't know, exactly,' he said. 'But I came upon Nasir's ship weeks after it had been plundered by the Spanish, and most of the crew had been dead for a long time. Torn to pieces, most of them. Hollowed out. If I didn't know better, I'd say a wild animal had ripped through them.'

'What do you mean,' said Amir, '"know better"? What else could it be?'

'Again, I don't know,' said Blackbeard. 'But I reckon it might have something to do with that canopic jar you have in your possession. The one with the map on the back.'

Amir could not keep the flicker out of his eyes. He clearly knew what was being discussed.

'Cursed treasure,' said Blackbeard. 'Apparently.'

Amir smiled grimly as, at his feet, Omar sat up, rubbing his temple. 'You're trying to frighten me out of reclaiming it, aren't you?'

Blackbeard was having trouble keeping still. He felt like he had lost fifty pounds of body weight when he left his weapons back in the dinghy. Amicable, cagey discussion was not how he was used to operating.

'On the contrary,' he said. 'I know you want the treasure back, because I found the map you gave your boys, directing them to Constantinople.'

'Boys?' Amir echoed, his eyes narrowing. 'You encountered Djeema, too?'

Blackbeard shared a confused glance with Mary. Then it hit him. 'Oh, Percy!' he said. When Amir and Omar, who was getting to his feet, looked at him blankly, he flapped a dismissive hand: 'Never mind. Yeah, I ran into what's-his-name off the coast of Cyprus. Nice fellow – bit temperamental, though.'

'Where is he now?' asked Amir.

'Dead.'

Omar's face fell. Amir winced, his eyes going to the ground and his mighty fists balling up for just a second. 'Do you know what happened to him?'

'Oh yeah,' said Mary. 'We—'

Blackbeard shot her a sharp look, but it was too late. The Barbary pair took a step forward.

'You what?' asked Amir.

Blackbeard grimaced, as he put his hat back on, angling the brim down over his eyes. He needed to reclaim some status in this parley. 'I'm afraid that was my doing.'

Omar sprang forward, shoving Mary aside to get a clear run at Blackbeard. He drove his shoulder into his ribs, trying to upend him in the same way that Percy had on the deck of the Queen Anne.

Blackbeard took a long step back and put all his weight on his front leg, stopping Omar's momentum stone dead. He boshed him in the back of the head. For the second time in several minutes, Omar hit the ground, out cold.

Mary was up on her feet. 'Let me at 'im,' she growled.

Blackbeard stepped away from Omar's prone body and took her by the shoulders, lifting her off the ground and placing her on a stool draped in a bear skin covering. 'Sit down!' he said. 'You're going to get me killed.'

He turned back to Amir, gesturing towards Omar. 'He took that a bit personally, didn't he?'

'Djeema was his brother,' said Amir.

'Oh dear,' said Blackbeard. 'Listen – I had no choice. Your boy was hot-headed, and tried to take my ship. He started a fight with me, knowing the consequences.'

'What do you want?' Amir asked.

'I believe you have in your possession the fourth

marble jar,' he said. 'Am I right? The jars with what looks like sections of a map marked on the back?'

'You obviously know why the jars are important,' said Amir.

'Actually, I don't,' said Blackbeard. 'Not entirely. I know the map leads somewhere. I can't figure out where, though.'

Amir sighed, staring at the ground, his eyes flickering as he considered his options. Then he looked up at Blackbeard. 'Sit with me, Mr Teach.'

As Blackbeard followed him to a table in the chamber, chairs covered with the dried-out pelt of a tiger, he asked: 'You know my birth name?'

'Nothing sails the seas faster than legend,' said Amir, as he sat down.

Blackbeard took the chair opposite, both of them resting their forearms on the table.

'The jars,' said Amir, 'do not provide a guide to any city or village on land.'

Blackbeard grinned. 'Don't try to con me, Mr Barbarossa,' he said. 'I may not be a native, but I know the River Nile when I see it marked.'

Amir nodded. 'The three jars you have mark the route down the Nile, this is true. The fourth jar – in my possession – shows the destination. A place below ground. Far below ground. The fourth jar will guide you through the tunnels and caves beneath the pyramids of an empty city of the Nile...to the lost pyramid of Sakhmet.'

'You know this for sure,' said Blackbeard, 'because you've been there already.'

'We plundered the pyramid, yes,' Amir replied. 'So I can vouch for the jar's authenticity.'

'I need that jar.'

'You need to leave the Mediterranean – after you return the stolen treasure to me.'

'Can't do that. According to Nasir, I've inherited a curse – and the only way to lift it off my head is to either let it kill me, or find the source of it and destroy it there.'

'You don't even know what you're looking for.'

'I'm a pirate. I'm used to that.'

Amir sat back in his chair. Blackbeard saw that, behind him, Mary leaned forward in hers, alert and ready to pounce if Blackbeard gave the nod. He got the feeling that Amir sensed this, too.

'You don't even know what you're looking for, Mr Teach,' he said. 'For you, it would be a suicide mission. And anyway, surely – if you give the treasure back, the curse will be returned to me.'

'Funny thing about this curse,' said Blackbeard. 'It don't seem to know when it's been "transferred". Besides, I have my own reasons for wanting to find this pyramid. If this Sakhmet lass has been doing her evil work, then she's responsible for the death of a very close friend of mine. That won't go unpunished.'

'I could say the same thing about you.'

'Yes, you could.'

Amir sat forward again. 'What do you propose?'

Now it was Blackbeard's turn to sit back in his chair. He had the bargaining power now, and he was going to let this 'King' know about it. 'This is your territory,' he said. 'You know the Nile, you know the desert. You found this sunken pyramid, plundered it, and got out alive. You take me and my crew there, help us do what we need to do to snuff out this curse, and you can have your treasure back. And if the curse is lifted, you should be able to get it to Constantinople without losing any more ships.'

Amir stared at the table, his muscular arms flexing and relaxing as he pondered Blackbeard's offer. He looked up. 'How do I know you didn't kill Nasir?'

Blackbeard shrugged. 'How do I know you won't just kill me and take the treasure the first chance you get?'

The two pirate leaders regarded each other, neither of them moving, neither of them blinking. Finally, Amir nodded. 'Very well. It seems that we are, ourselves, cursed to depend on each other. But we must make haste. We don't have much time. The voyage down the Nile will take a week.'

Blackbeard extended a hand, which Amir took in a strong grip. 'We have a deal?'

'Yes we do,' said Amir.

Blackbeard nodded, and told him. 'Follow me.' He stood up from the table, and gestured to his sister, who stepped over Omar as they set off down the aisle, back the way they had come. When they reached the archway, Amir's voice stopped them:

'Mr Teach.'

Blackbeard turned around and stared at the man who, even all the way down at the other side of the chamber, cut an intimidating figure. And he had not even stood up.

'I will join forces with you to solve both our problems,' said Amir. 'But I promise you this: if we make it out of Sakhmet's pyramid alive...I'm going to kill you.'

Blackbeard just smiled. 'Have you not heard? I'm already dead, Mr Barbarossa.'

Chapter Twenty-nine

Blackbeard stood at the bow of his ship, staring ahead over the stern of the *Gallant*. When he had seen it for the first time, he had asked Amir, 'Do you not have any ships of your own in this part of the world?', for it was yet another stolen European frigate.

Amir just smiled, and asked Blackbeard in turn if he had ever asked a crew of pirates in the 18th century whether they'd like to be oarsmen?

Blackbeard couldn't argue with the logic.

To be fair, the Barbary leader had made the ship his own. His figurehead was his familiar design of the two-headed cobra, which was wrapped around the bowsprit. A larger version of the Barbary flags was painted onto the stern, which Blackbeard stared at now as they sailed west along the Egyptian coast, towards the Nile Delta. Progress was slow, because conditions were maddeningly mild, so Blackbeard killed time watching the Barbary pirates at work. They were an efficient lot, but they didn't talk much as they went about their business. They just did their jobs.

They were following the *Gallant* because Amir knew

where they were. And they, in turn, were followed by another, smaller Barbary ship, called the *Brave*. Amir had insisted on bringing another of his fleet along – and Blackbeard could understand why he might want the numbers – just to be safe.

But that did not mean he was especially fond of being surrounded bow and stern by Barbary pirates.

He raised his spyglass and spied beyond them, seeing the dappling of lush, wide banks of brilliant green seeming to rise up out of the water, which flowed almost obediently around it.

The Nile Delta was getting closer. Beyond it, the river itself, almost sucking the pirates in.

When he lowered his spyglass, he saw that Amir had come to the stern of the *Gallant*, making a pushing gesture with his hand. He was signalling that, with the sky growing dark, they should drop anchor.

Blackbeard nodded, turning to relay the command to his own crew, and telling Chris Claw to let the boys on the *Brave* know.

Blackbeard stepped down onto the waist-deck as Vicious Vern and Chaplain Charlie worked their capstan, veins pulsing in their temples as their faces went a comical shade of purple.

'She is the most evil woman in history.'

Blackbeard turned at the sound of Omar's voice. The Barbary pirate was standing beneath the mainsail, arms crossed while young Michael worked the rigging, the sails being rolled up for the night. All around Omar, crewmates dodged him, walked around him, scowling the whole time in annoyance. Blackbeard shook his head. Omar was one of three Barbary lads that Amir had insisted be onboard the *Queen Anne*, in exchange for three of Blackbeard's own crew – apparently this would encourage trustworthiness, so said Amir. But, unlike his two compatriots, who could not do enough up on deck, Omar had done sod all except talk of how unimpressed he was by the vessel.

And now he was telling tall tales.

In one day's sailing, he had annoyed every member of Blackbeard's crew.

Except Michael, whose eyes alternated between his task at hand and the Barbary lad beside him, a mixture of fearful fascination on his face.

'She wished to die young,' said Omar, 'so that she would not enter paradise as an old woman. She wanted to be the most beautiful woman in the next world. And so, she took her own life.'

Michael turned away from the cordage, much to the chagrin of the topman, who Blackbeard saw slap a crosstree in frustration. 'How did she do it?'

'She drank a poison,' said Omar. 'As soon as her husband, the Pharaoh Ankhotep and his priests had compiled her own special Book of the Dead, she took her own life at the height of her beauty.'

'She doesn't sound that scary,' said Michael.

'She was not when she was alive,' said Omar. 'But now, three thousand years later, she controls an army of the dead. At her command, all the servants who built her tomb, all the soldiers who stood guard over her body, all the priests who made her preparations for the afterlife – they will all rise and destroy any who seek to steal her treasure.'

'Mummies?' asked Michael.

'Yes. We— How do you know about mummies?'

Michael's open expression tightened, his voice catching: 'Old Bill told me about them – before he...'

Omar grinned. 'Before the mummies killed him?'

As Michael's gaze fell down to the deck, Blackbeard decided he'd had enough. He marched over to Omar and wrapped a huge hand around the scruff of his neck.

'I warned you before,' he said, 'if you're not going to help, keep out of the way.'

'I was just giving Michael a history lesson,' said

Omar, legs kicking as Blackbeard lifted him off the ground.

'Lesson's over. If I see you trying to unsettle any of my boys again, you can join your brother.' With a flick of his arm, Blackbeard sent him stumbling over to the port bulwark. 'We're dropping anchor for the night. Get back to the *Gallant*.'

Omar barked something in his own language. The two other Barbary pirates – teenagers with excited smiles on their faces – broke from the gathered crew, waving to some pirates they had made friends with, as they followed Omar to the bow.

'Supper!'

The call was familiar, but the voice was not. Blackbeard turned and saw Luis, the Spaniard, emerging from the forecastle with Mister Peters, both of them carrying a big pot of steaming stew.

Blackbeard walked over to them as they set down on the waist-deck, pirates crowding round for their serving. 'What's all this?' he asked.

'I wanted to show my gratitude,' said Luis, his hissing voice almost swallowed whole by the night air. 'To you all, for letting me out of my...prison. You are most kind.'

Blackbeard peered into the pot. It was an odd, black

and grey concoction, with chicken and vegetables floating like flotsam. 'Spanish, is it?'

Luis smiled. 'No. But you'll like it.'

He dunked a bowl into the pot and held it out. Blackbeard took it and nodded in thanks. 'I'm going to take this to me cabin,' he said. 'I have some thinking to do.'

'If there's any left over,' Luis was saying to Mister Peters, as Blackbeard walked away, 'we should give it as a gift to the crew of the *Brave*. It would be a nice gesture, no? Help us all get along.'

As he went below decks, walking along the sparred gallery to his cabin, Blackbeard felt troubled thoughts battering his mind.

Something about this just wasn't right. What was Amir up to, exactly? If he knew the treasure had the legend of a curse attached to it, and that the way into the sunken pyramid itself was fraught with unimaginable dangers – as Omar had just suggested to Michael – why would he agree to make the journey a second time?

And what could the Sultan possibly want with the loot?

And why would a proud, strong pirate such as Amir reduce himself to the level of little better than a privateer, sailing in the name of a Sultan who was based on the other side of the Mediterranean?

There's more to this than Amir's letting on, Blackbeard told himself, as he entered his cabin and set down the bowl of Luis's stew on his desk. He had only taken it to be polite. As usual, he wasn't that hungry. Right now, the only thing he felt like was a nice drink.

Blackbeard found a bottle of rum beneath his hammock. He used his teeth to pull out the cork. He took a long swig, and instantly felt the tension of the day began to recede.

Just a little bit.

He slept an oddly sound sleep, by his own standards. A dreamless sleep, which was the best – and most helpful.

In dreams, your mind could explain away strange noises happening around your sleeping body. In a dreamless sleep, every noise heard was not supposed to be there. Every sensation was a reason to wake up.

Like the feeling of the ship weighing anchor, and sailing away.

Blackbeard sat right up in his hammock, the momentum almost sending him tumbling out. The empty rum bottle on his chest rolled away and smashed on the cabin floor. He drew two guns as he got to his feet and moved to the door. Anxiety filled his gut – they had dropped anchor for the night not long after Luis had served up his dinner. They weren't due to resume sailing until morning.

It was *not* morning.

'What are you doing?' he hollered, at no one in particular. He tucked one of his pistols under his arm, so he could wrench open the door, then he moved to climb up the ladder to the deck.

He stopped when he saw a pair of boots in the doorway of the gun-deck.

Creeping along the sparred gallery, Blackbeard held his pistols out ready. Was this Amir's game? To kill Blackbeard's crew in his sleep?

No, it couldn't have been that. He would have gone for Blackbeard first.

He stopped in the doorway, lowering his pistols when he saw no foreign danger – just two rows of his crewmates, sleeping as soundly as he would have expected between the cannons. Nearest him was Chaplain Charlie. Blackbeard crouched beside him, placing two fingers to his jugular, and feeling a good, strong pulse.

'Charlie!' he yelled, giving him a shake.

Charlie did not move. Did not even stir. He just snored.

Blackbeard moved to the next pirate along, Mister Peters. He got the same result, even after slapping his face a couple of times.

'Wake up, you maggoty sea dogs!' he bellowed, firing one of his guns in the air and feeling a faint shower of splinters rain on his shoulders.

None of the pirates moved. They were in the deepest of sleeps. But how was this possible? It wasn't like they'd been drinking rum all day, and were now all in some kind of stupor.

They haven't drunk too much... But what about what they ate?

Luis's supper!

Blackbeard rose to his feet, dropping his empty pistol and sweeping the other one over the sleeping bodies, looking for Luis. But of course he wasn't there. He was hardly likely to have eaten food he had tainted. He had to have been up on deck, helming the ship.

Blackbeard turned around and hustled back down the sparred gallery, climbing the ladder and bursting onto the waist-deck, pistol raised and ready to fire.

But from waist to bow, he saw no one to aim at. There was no one up on deck.

'What?' Blackbeard breathed, his eyes going to the sails. They were rolled up, as they had been when he had left the pirates to their poisoned supper.

'Am I going mad?' he asked himself, as he moved to the port side. He was thinking that maybe he wasn't sleeping so soundly in a dreamless sleep after all – maybe he was having a night terror. How else to explain the state of his crew?

He looked over the port gunwale, squinting through the night and seeing that, yes, the sails were up and the ship was moving through the Mediterranean.

It had to be a nightmare, then. Blackbeard straightened up and turned away, almost laughing to himself at the absurdity of the Man From Hell having a nightmare.

He stopped dead when he looked up towards the quarterdeck.

A figure was at the helm.

A tall, broad figure, with arms like modest tree trunks. Its huge, stiff fingers were wrapped around the handles of the helm. Its black, vacant eyes stared out over the deck; its half-rotted teeth chomped together as animalistic snarls escaped its mouth. Broken strips of its white linen shroud fluttered in the night breeze, which ferried to Blackbeard the hideous stench of death and decay.

An Egyptian mummy was steering the *Queen Anne's Revenge.*

Chapter Thirty

Blackbeard took aim with his pistol. But before he could fire, another shrivelled, blackened hand came down on his gun-arm, gripping it tightly. His head whipped to his right, where he looked into the face of another standing corpse. Its grey-black features poked through rips and tears in the long strips of its rotten shroud, which danced and fluttered at the command of the breeze on the Nile. Its eyes were the deepest, darkest black imaginable. Its nose was little more than a hole in its skull, lined with what looked like scraps of dried brain. Its neck wore a deep slash at the left jugular. The wound that had ended its life, Blackbeard could tell.

Its body was smaller than the mummy at the helm – narrow shoulders and skinny limbs. Dangling low on its chest was an oval jade amulet, with the golden carving of what looked like a lion's head emerging from it.

And then there was the noise it made. A pained groan. A rattling breath, like the final one exhaled by a dying man – except it did not end. It did not even pause or break. It just kept on going.

Blackbeard gritted his teeth and tried to pull his hand away, but found he couldn't. The mummy's grip was too tight. He transferred his pistol to his other hand and fired right at the mummy's forearm, seeing lumps of dead flesh and greyed bone spray in all directions. With a growl of exertion, he was able to pull his hand free, reeling away from the mummy's stumbling lunge.

Blackbeard staggered back, his foot slipping on the wet deck. As he toppled, he felt the dull, powerful prod of a capstan bar in his spine, knocking the wind out of him and sending him spinning. He landed with a thud, right on top of one of the pistols in his gun-belt, almost breaking his ribs; the side of his head slammed against the wood. He was left prostrate and winded, his vision blurred.

And the mummy was advancing. Its feet dragged along the deck, knees always straight in a shuffling stride. Its arms lowered as its waist slowly bent – its gnarled hands were reaching for Blackbeard's throat.

'Let's finish that death of yours,' said Blackbeard, as he reached for another one of his pistols.

It was stuck.

Blackbeard yanked at the gun handle, but it was snagged. Panic rising in his chest, he reached for another one, just as the mummy leant down to take hold of his neck. A dusting of decomposed skin pattered onto Blackbeard's face, that pained, endless death-groan filling his ears.

He was going to die. He knew it. He was going to die on the deck of his beloved ship, at the clawed, rotten hands of an Egyptian mummy.

As Blackbeard froze, unable to decide whether to reach for another gun, his cutlass, or simply try to punch and kick his way free, a hole exploded in the mummy's chest – a broad blade stabbed through it from the back, plunging and stopping with the tip just inches away from his face.

'Roll clear, Captain!'

Blackbeard half-rolled, half-crawled to safety, feeling like he could have cheered. Young Michael – a shred of luck! He must not have eaten any of Luis's tainted meal, either. Blackbeard bounced up to his feet, coming by Michael's side as he yanked at the cutlass. It would not come free.

The mummy stood up straight, turning slowly. Blackbeard grabbed Michael by the jerkin and pulled him clear.

'What do we do, Captain?' Michael asked.

Blackbeard said nothing. He hadn't a clue in his

head. A gunshot did not stop the mummy, and nor did a blade through the chest. What else could they try? A cannon, maybe. But they were all down in the gun-deck, along with Blackbeard's comatose crew. Even if they did lure their corpse attacker down there, there would be no way to get off a decent shot – not without risking killing or maiming one, or several, of their pirate brothers.

The only option was the one he had long said he would never, ever take. 'We have to abandon ship.'

Michael clutched at his arm. 'What about the others?'

Blackbeard felt hot anger in his chest and throat. His crew were still alive, last he checked, but there seemed to be no way of waking them up. And even if there was, there were far too many of them to rouse – no matter how much they stumbled and shuffled, these mummies would eventually get their hands on them.

And Blackbeard remembered all too vividly the state of the men they had found onboard Nasir's ship.

'Too late,' he said. 'There is nothing to be done.'

'But, Captain, we can't—'

Michael's words died away when the forecastle door opened with a loud whine. Another mummy was shuffling forward, a third death-groan harmonising with the others'. This one was as tall and muscular as the mummy at the helm. It also wore no amulet.

'No time,' said Blackbeard, taking Michael by the scruff of the neck. 'Dive overboard.'

'No!' Michael tried to dig his heels in, but he was powerless against Blackbeard's strength.

Blackbeard hurled the lad over the side, hearing him hit the sea with a splash. Then he climbed up onto the gunwale, preparing to jump in himself. Preparing to abandon the ship he loved – the crew that had relied and looked up to him; the sister who had taken his word that she would one day be Captain Mary Bonny. How could he leave her here, at the mercy of these monsters?

Because, if I don't, he told himself, there will be no one left to avenge her.

And avenge her, he would.

Blackbeard bent his knees to jump. Then he froze, his jaw tight with futile anger. This was not any kind of glorious end for the greatest pirate of them all. It was a pathetic, desperate retreat. A humiliation.

Blackbeard drew the two pistols at the bottom of his gun-belt, turning around on the gunwales and taking aim. The two advancing mummies were within ten feet of him now, shuffling forward side-by-side.

Blackbeard fired two shots simultaneously, the bullets passing right through the chests of his targets. It stopped them for the briefest of moments before they continued their slow, inevitable charge.

Blackbeard dropped the pistols on the deck. Then he turned and dived into the Mediterranean.

Chapter Thirty-one

Blackbeard kicked out his legs and thrashed his arms underwater to turn his body upright. When he broke the surface, he shook his eyes clear and gasped – and not just because he needed to take in a deep breath.

A frigate was sailing right towards his head, its black hull given a ghostly glint by the light of the moon and stars in the cloudless sky.

Blackbeard threw his body to his left, kicking for all he was worth and wishing he had thought to remove his boots and doublet before he abandoned the *Queen Anne*. The ship glided past him like rolling thunder. Blackbeard was yanked back by the slipstream. He heaved his body against it, not wanting to be dragged beneath the hull.

'Wait!' he cried. 'Throw down a rope!'

But the ship did not stop. It just continued to sail, in the path of the *Queen Anne's Revenge*, which was just about disappearing in the darkness.

It was following her. But it wasn't *chasing* her.

As Blackbeard trod water, the grip of the slipstream loosening around his legs, he heard a desperate splashing punctuated by panicked pants.

'Captain!' It was Michael, fighting his way over.

'Are you a strong swimmer, boy?' Blackbeard asked.

'Aye, sir,' said the boy, stopping alongside Blackbeard, and treading water with him. 'But I don't know if we can make it to that delta.'

Blackbeard had to agree with him. He looked back into the night, at the stern of the treacherous Barbary galley. Now that he had some distance, he could see quite clearly that it was the smaller of the two vessels, the *Brave*.

'We should turn back,' said Blackbeard, 'and see if we can find the *Gallant*.'

Michael was looking back towards the disappearing ships. 'The *Queen Anne* is moving faster than I have ever seen her.' he said.

Blackbeard said nothing as he turned away and began paddling back the way they had come. He was trying to understand what had happened. Not just the speed of his stolen vessel, but everything leading up to it. Answers that should not have made sense suddenly seemed plausible – simply because they were the only answers there were.

'It can't be natural,' he said. 'Someone – some*thing* – must be controlling it.'

'But how is that possible?' asked Michael, raising his voice over the splashes of strokes and kicks. 'How is *any* of this possible?'

'If I knew that,' said Blackbeard, 'I'd put a ruddy stop to it. I'd...'

Blackbeard's voice fell into the sea when he picked out the glow of small torch-flames, floating high in the air through the thick night. Their glow illuminated the faces of the two-headed cobra beneath a bowsprit.

'We heard gunshots,' said Amir, as Blackbeard heaved himself over the bulwark, using the rope that had been thrown down. Michael was already on board the *Gallant*, shivering as he nodded in thanks to the Barbary pirates, who had crowded round him with looks of concern on their faces. 'When I woke up, your ship was gone, and so was the *Brave*. So I gave the order to weigh anchor and follow. What happened?'

Blackbeard looked from Amir to the crew and back again. He wondered if he should have a private word, but thought better of it. He wanted the Barbary crew to sail right into unimaginable danger – it was only fair that they knew exactly what that danger was.

'We've been double-crossed,' said Blackbeard. 'That Spaniard, Luis, drugged my crew. Yours, too –

he said he was going to share his meal with the boys on the *Brave*. They're all in deep sleeps. I don't know if they'll *ever* wake up – that's if they don't get...'

Amir's head leaned forward, his face tight and anxious. 'What?'

'I know what killed your man Nasir and his crew. I know what frightened the very life out of my quartermaster. Monsters...wrapped in shrouds, stiff with death – walking corpses.'

Amir turned away, as his crewmates within earshot gasped and muttered among themselves. 'Mummies?' he hissed. 'I thought them merely legends.'

'They're real,' said Blackbeard. 'And they're going to eat the insides out of my crew unless we catch up with them.'

Amir nodded, turning back and hollering orders in his native tongue. His crew hesitated, but when he mentioned Nasir's name, they obediently got to work. Blackbeard had to give it to the North African mob – they were as brave and loyal as any captain could ever hope for.

Soon the *Gallant* had picked up speed, sailing south as the Nile Delta seemed to draw it in like a gaping mouth.

Chapter Thirty-two

The *Gallant* was lighter and faster than the *Queen Anne*, and so should have caught up with Blackbeard's vessel within a few miles at the very most. But it took them several hours to catch sight of it. By this time, the sun was at its peak and gushing an almost unbearable heat.

The *Queen Anne's Revenge* was stranded in the Mediterranean, seeming to emit a sense of foreboding and desolation, which made a mockery of the sprawling, tumbling banks of papyrus plants that swished and danced like the waves themselves.

It should have been a beautiful sight. Instead, the only feeling in Blackbeard's gut was a knot of tension and fear.

'Why has it stopped?' asked Omar, coming to stand by Blackbeard at the bow. 'And where is the Brave?'

'Why are you asking me?' snapped Blackbeard. 'How am I supposed to know what goes on inside a mummy's brain?'

'Mummies don't have brains,' said Omar. 'It's pulled out through the nose during the process.'

Blackbeard shook his head and stomped away

towards the waist-deck, reminding himself that he should not chuck Amir's First Mate overboard, however much he wanted to.

He walked along the starboard side, finding Amir leaning over to survey the motionless ship they were approaching. 'Are your men ready?' he asked.

'As ready as they can be,' said Amir, 'to face mummies.'

'I saw only three,' said Blackbeard. 'There should be no more than five. That's how many coffins we had onboard. They're relentless, but they're also slow – if we all stay light on our feet, and keep our wits about us, we should survive.'

'Survive to do what?'

Blackbeard hesitated, recognising that, while many emotions were charging through him – anger, a desire to reclaim his ship, to save as many of his crew as he could – the one thing he lacked was an actual plan. After all, he had put bullets into these monsters, and it didn't even knock them over. Michael had stabbed a blade through one of their bodies, and it didn't slow down.

Just how did he hope to fend them off now?

'You don't have to join me,' he said to Amir. 'But I won't abandon my crew to the fate that awaits them.

Draw up alongside, and me and the boy will board.'

Amir shook his head. 'These things killed a captain in my fleet,' he said. 'For that, they will get a second death. And I will make it more painful than the first.'

Blackbeard smiled, despite the tension tingling in his chest. 'I like the way you think.'

As the *Gallant* slowly slid by the *Queen Anne's* port side, the Barbary pirates slung their grapnels over the bulwarks, lashing the two ships together. As Amir's crew clambered onto their gunwale, ready to walk across the rope, Omar turned and regarded Blackbeard and Michael with a smug look.

'Do you two need help across?' he asked.

Blackbeard glared back at him, resisting the almost overwhelming urge to see how well his skull stood up to a pistol blast. Beside him, Michael leapt up onto the gunwale from a standing position.

'It's easy, Captain,' he said, taking his first step onto the rope. 'It's just balance.'

The Barbary crew murmured in respect as Michael walked calmly across the rope onto the waist-deck of the *Queen Anne*. Blackbeard looked at the rope, which bounced as it straightened itself out. He was six-foot-six, and bulky with it – he did not expect that a thin, measly rope would hold his weight.

But the thought of giving that skinny little twerp Omar even the smallest of victories filled his chest with a hot, prickly bile that he wanted to spit into his face.

He felt a large hand grip him firmly at the elbow. Amir appeared on his other side, a wry smile on his face. 'This is hardly becoming of men of our rank,' he said, pulling Blackbeard along the deck. 'Come.'

Blackbeard turned and saw two of Amir's crew pushing out a wide, wooden board, which was grabbed by two more Barbary pirates onboard the *Queen Anne*.

Amir gestured to Blackbeard that he should go first. As he heaved himself up onto the gunwale, Blackbeard mumbled over his shoulder: 'Someone's going to give him worse than a clump one day, you know that?'

'It just takes about six years to get used to him,' said Amir.

'I ain't got six years,' said Blackbeard, as he walked across the board to the deck of his ship.

The weather-decks of the *Queen Anne's Revenge* were deserted – no sign of the mummy he had seen at the helm, nor the two he had shot without success.

The sun beat down on the oak, revealing no blood or torn flesh, or any other sign of a struggle between the pirates and the mummies.

Blackbeard drew one of his pistols as he made his way towards the ladder at the quarterdeck, which led down to the sparred gallery. Behind him, he heard the thumping of feet on the deck, the scrape of steel leaving scabbard, and the dull rub of pistols being wrenched from holsters. The sea bandits were marching as one, right into God only knew what hideous hell.

If a fight hadn't taken up on deck, then that meant that the mummies had left after stealing his ship – or they had gone back down below and...

Blackbeard shook his head clear of the dreadful thought. This could not happen. It just *could not* happen.

Not on board *his* ship.

He climbed down the ladder into the sparred gallery, walking side-on towards the gun-deck, where he had last seen his crew. The narrow passage was filled with a stale, stuffy air that teased sweat from his face. His heart was pounding. He had to grit his teeth to keep his breathing under control. He allowed himself to feel a flicker of hope to realise that he could not detect the stench of decomposing corpses.

The crew would still be there, in the deep sleep they had been left in by Luis's tainted supper.

The sunlight from outside dragged itself through the darkness, rippling with the shadows of the pirates following Blackbeard as it revealed more of the gallery until he came to the end of it.

The darkness of the gun-deck was absolute. The gunports were closed. As he stood at the entrance, Blackbeard listened for the sound of breathing, but he could hear nothing. But there was nothing unusual in that, he told himself. The lap of the waves, the roar of the wind, the chaotic, clumpy footsteps of the pirates behind him, forcing their way into the narrow passage, would veil anything.

He stepped into the gun-deck, slowly and carefully. 'Mateys,' he called, hoping to rouse someone.

But there was no response.

He took another step, and felt his right boot slide involuntarily forward, heard the slick sound of his sole scraping the deck.

It was wet – and Blackbeard had the sickening feeling that it was not seawater.

'To the walls,' he mumbled. 'Open the gunports.'

Michael and the Barbary pirates blindly fumbled and fanned out in the darkness. Blackbeard closed his eyes as he listened to the squelching steps before, one-by-one, the twenty-four gunports were thrown open, the whine of their hinges sounding almost like a cackle as they let the sunshine leak in.

He knew it was going to be awful, from the gasping and groaning he heard all around him. He blinked his eyes open, expecting to see thirty dead bodies.

Instead, he saw the pieces of them.

The walls of the gun-deck were awash with blood, the crimson mess shining gruesomely as it seemed to swallow and then spit back the sunlight. On the deck itself, it collected around scalps that had been torn from their heads and tossed aside. The rest of the men's heads lay where Blackbeard had last seen them, when he tried to wake them up, their eyes closed and their expressions peaceful – which meant that the men had never emerged from their slumber. As he walked numbly along the blood-wet aisle between the cannons, Blackbeard could see through men's chests and guts, the planks of the deck clearly visible beneath torsos that had been torn up and now resembled open trap doors, while their broken skulls were as bare as an empty bowl.

His stomach churning, his soul shuddering, Blackbeard stepped around a discarded eyeball – he could not tell whose – to stand in the middle of the deck, turning on his heels and taking it all in.

'Is this everyone?' asked Amir, his voice raspy with shock and dread.

Blackbeard shrugged helplessly. 'Do you want to do a head count?'

Amir stepped forward more forcefully, his boots slapping the bloody oak. 'Mr Teach! Is this every man on board?'

Blackbeard started to nod. 'It looks like it...' Then he stopped, his mind drowning in the most horrible thought of all. 'Mary!'

He barrelled through a hastily made gap in the group of pirates, out of the gun-deck and back down the sparred gallery. Without breaking stride, he kicked open the door to the small cabin next to his.

It was empty. But it was clean.

'No!' he cried, punching the wall and feeling the wood cave beneath his fist, almost as if the ship herself had lost the will to be strong. And who could blame her? Their new, ungodly enemies had stolen away his half-sister, after killing his entire crew.

'Captain?'

Blackbeard started at the voice. It was coming from his cabin, to his left. He turned and reached for the handle, throwing it open.

Chris Claw, Handsome Harry and Chaplain Charlie were crouched behind his desk, their eyes and the barrels of their pistols peering over the edge. When they saw him standing in the doorway, the three of them stood up with a relieved sigh. They looked paler and more haunted than they had on the day they had deceived Percy. Their wide eyes didn't blink, and their voices shook with an almost spiritual terror.

'Thank God it's you!' said Chris, holstering his pistol.

Blackbeard stepped into his cabin, hearing the familiar, heavy footsteps of Amir joining him.

'What happened?' he asked.

Chris, Harry and Charlie shared an awkward glance. 'We woke up,' said Charlie, 'and saw...' His head dropped, his chubby face folding in on itself as he bit back an anguished sob that wanted to burst from him.

Handsome took up the story. 'Walking dead, sir... In some sort of funeral bandages... They were...'

But even the hardened old pirate, whose skin bore more scars than pores, could not finish the terrible tale. It was left to Chris Claw to say:

'They were eating the crew, Captain. And, for our

shame, we were fortunate enough to come to, just in time to see it. We tried shooting them, but it did not stop them – it did not even slow them down.'

Harry was staring at the desk, disgrace showing in his single eye. 'So… we hid away, and hoped they would leave.'

'Please believe us, sir,' said Charlie. 'There was nothing we could—'

'I know,' he said. 'I don't blame you.' He forced the next two words out of his mouth like he was running out a cannon: 'And Mary?'

It was Harry who answered, his voice a slick rasp, wet with grief. 'They took her.'

'Who did?'

'That Spanish dog!' Harry snarled, anger crushing his sadness. 'I heard him from the other side of the door. He said, "She must not be harmed".'

'We think he was directing the bewitched crew of the Brave,' said Chaplain Charlie. 'We heard lots of talk in the Barbary tongue, sir.'

Blackbeard said nothing. His heart was full of futile hope – Mary was still alive. But for how much longer?

Behind him, he heard Omar muttering something in his own language, which drew a sigh from Amir, who tapped Blackbeard on the shoulder.

'Your hold is empty,' said Amir. 'The treasure is gone.'

Blackbeard nodded as he walked over to his hammock, where his hat still lay – right where he had left it when he had gone to investigate the strange bumps in the night. He put it on his head, instantly feeling just a little bit stronger. 'And we know where its gone,' he said. 'Nothing's changed, Mr Barbarossa. You can continue leading us to the pyramid of Sakhmet, as we planned.'

'Captain!' Harry came round from the back of the desk, his fear replaced with incredulity. 'Surely, this proves that we should leave here immediately? We're meddling with dark forces that ought not to be—'

'One more word out of you,' said Blackbeard, leaning forward so that he was nose-to-nose with the older pirate, 'and I'll have your other eye. I don't care what they are, or how powerful – they have my father's daughter. My sister. That's not the sort of thing I'm going to just let go.'

He turned to Amir. 'Lead the way, Mr Barbarossa. We'll sail on the *Gallant* the rest of the way. The *Queen Anne's Revenge* is no more.'

Blackbeard stood at the starboard bulwark on board

the *Gallant* as it sailed away from the *Queen Anne's Revenge*. His magnificent ship, whose muscular hull and dextrous sails had stolen for him many a victory over his innumerable enemies in the New World.

But it would not survive the Old.

Amir Barbarossa appeared by his side. 'Are you sure you want to do this, Mr Teach?'

Blackbeard did not take his eyes off his beloved ship. Its three masts with the sails rolled up, the skeleton of the rigging exposed beneath the harsh sun in the clear sky over the coast of Egypt. The motley-shade of the hull that had survived broadsides fired by rival pirates and the British Navy.

But not the next one.

He nodded to Amir, who bellowed a single word in command. Blackbeard didn't need to know Amir's language to know what he had shouted.

'Fire!'

The ten cannons on the *Gallant*'s starboard side unleashed their fury, shunting the whole ship to port as they battered the *Queen Anne's Revenge*. The shooting flames of the ten cannons collided with each other, as the broadside converge on the same area of the lost ship – just beneath the port bow.

The powder magazine.

The storm of lead tore through the oak, bringing forth a shower of flame spraying upwards like a fountain as the stored gunpowder caught alight. The vessel seemed to bounce on the surface of the sea. The decks seemed to fold in half, mizzenmast and foremast slamming into the main on both sides.

Then the sea claimed her – and everyone on board.

Part Four

Chapter Thirty-three

The *Gallant* fought its way through the Mediterranean, into the Nile Delta itself. Over the course of the three days that it took to clear it, Blackbeard's eyes took in sights that should have lifted his heart, and got his nomadic blood flowing faster through his veins. But the swell of the sandy hills placed improbably next to the silty plains of the Delta may as well have been the bilge of his ship. The view of the roofs of limestone high-rises in a bustling town held no promise of fun or adventure. The curious birds, with feathers of more varied colours than something Mister Peters might once have cooked on board the *Queen Anne*, whose names Blackbeard knew he would probably never even discover, were neither cute, nor fascinating. They were just incidental to this strange region of the world, which had brought Blackbeard nothing but tragedy – unless they started up with their singing, then they were an utter nuisance.

I picked the wrong time to come to Egypt, he thought – more than once.

'There is one thing that troubles me,' said Omar, on the fourth day. 'How do we know your sister wasn't the one who betrayed you – and the crew of the *Brave*?'

Blackbeard had stopped contemplating how hard it would be to smooth things over with Amir if he threw Omar overboard. Much more from the mouthy little runt, and he'd be fish food.

They had dropped anchor, even though there was little need with the Nile air being so calm. Blackbeard stood at his usual place, at the bow of the *Gallant*, staring beyond the carved cobra figurehead, and taking in the sights of the riverbanks, sights he still struggled to get excited by. Amir had told him, they were at a place called Giza. Over the riverbank towards the west, Blackbeard could see closely-built limestone buildings arranged into a township that seemed to have knelt down to a raised, rocky plateau, atop which sat...

Pyramids.

The ancient tombs of legend. The impossible architecture – square-based, yet triangular, their perfect points jabbing towards the clouds.

Even Blackbeard could not deny, they were impressive.

Blackbeard pulled his eyes away from the scenery, turning from the bow to fix Omar with his fiercest glare. 'I know my sister,' he said. 'There is no way that she is a part of this. And Luis... I knew there was something funny about the way he looked at her, that day he translated Nasir's logs. I should have known...'

'So she could be in the thrall of Luis,' said Amir, who leaned back against the helm, his muscular arms crossed. 'If... If she's still alive.'

Blackbeard nodded. 'She has to be alive,' he said. 'Luis said she was not to be harmed. She's probably held prisoner now, in Sakhmet's pyramid.' Blackbeard pondered his own words for a moment, then regarded Amir. 'Can I speak to you in private?' he said, gesturing that they should walk to the very stern of the *Gallant*.

Amir unfolded his arms, nodding as he walked beside Blackbeard. At the stern, they stopped and Blackbeard let out a sigh as Amir resumed his crossed-arm pose. The man couldn't help showing off his physical strength. 'This is...'

Omar had drawn up alongside them, skinny arms folded in a rather comical imitation of his leader's. Blackbeard kept his eyes on Amir. 'I said, in private.'

Amir gave Omar a flick of the head, gesturing that he should leave. Blackbeard heard him give a petulant huff before he stomped across the quarterdeck.

'This has become very personal to me now,' he said, as the wind blowing south whipped his long hair and beard away from his face. Opposite him, Amir's plaited ponytail writhed like the long neck of the cobra drawn on his torso. 'It's not just about lifting the curse off my head. In fact, I doubt it can do much worse to me at this point. But if there's a chance of saving my sister, I will do anything it takes. I will understand if you take me as far as the entrance to the pyramid, and then turn your crew back.'

Amir looked away from Blackbeard, at the outline of the Nile river that curved away to the north, feeding the vast sea that had seen so much death and destruction over recent days. His right hand drifted almost unconsciously to the ivory handle of the dagger that had been tucked into his waist ever since Blackbeard met him. When he looked back at Blackbeard, he was shaking his head.

'If you think you can con me out of the treasure,' he said. 'Think again. We make this journey side by side.'

As Amir made to move away, Blackbeard shot out

a hand and took him by the arm, almost startled to feel the rock-like strength in the muscles. He hoped it didn't show on his face.

'Why?' he asked.

Amir frowned. 'Why what?'

Blackbeard took a step closer, glaring at him under the brim of his hat. 'Why, when you've seen what these things are capable of, would you so willingly risk your life to steal from them again?'

'Because the treasure belongs to *me*,' said Amir.

Blackbeard smirked and shook his head. 'Liar. You seem to have forgotten that I know for a fact you were delivering the treasure to the Sultan. Now, with him so far away, all the way over in Constantinople, why is a renowned and feared pirate going to such lengths to honour an agreement with him?'

Amir grit his teeth, clearly angry at being caught out and challenged. But beneath the anger, there was something else – his eyes flashed with something that Blackbeard had last seen in the eyes of his three Spanish prisoners.

Desperation.

'It's personal for you, too,' he said. 'Isn't it?'

Amir sucked air in through his gritted teeth, closing his eyes and scratching his shaved head. 'The Sultan holds my son,' he said. 'My ten year-old son. He will release him only in exchange for the treasure.'

'Why does he want it?'

Amir laughed bitterly, turning back to the stern bulwark. He leaned on it and stared out at the river again, his arms taut with frustration and fury. 'Why does any powerful man want anything?' he said. 'More power.'

Blackbeard joined him, casting his eye over the riverbank, staring into the clusters of palm trees that bobbed and rustled in the wind. They were beautiful, but Blackbeard could have done without them for the time being – they veiled the surrounding area, making Blackbeard feel like the Nile had walls.

Pirates, as a breed, tended not to like walls.

'So here we are, then?' he said. 'Two great pirates, willingly undertaking a suicide mission because we have no other choice.' He clapped Amir on the shoulder, which was so muscular the gesture was almost painful. 'You know, if we pull this off, they won't stop singing songs about this for a hundred years after we're dead.'

Amir snorted. 'Maybe in your part of the world,' he said. 'In mine, we're not that fond of singing.'

Blackbeard held out a hand, which Amir took in

his own. 'You fight alongside me here, I'll accompany you to Constantinople. The least I can do.'

Amir nodded. 'Yes, it is.'

Blackbeard held the man's eyes for a moment. He was still an impressive presence, even standing among the exotic scenery beneath an unforgiving sun. But his face sagged a little, his eyelids drooping and his cheeks and jaw hanging just a little lower. It was like the exhaustion and weariness of his efforts to rescue his hostage son were finally being released.

With nothing more to say, Blackbeard gave a nod and began to walk over to the waist-deck, where he would fill the remainder of his crew in on what their plans were. Amir's voice stopped him at the ladder, at the foot of which stood Omar, scowling up at him.

'Mr Teach.'

Blackbeard turned. Amir had his back to him, still facing out over the stern.

'When you sailed into my territory, you destroyed one of my fleet, killing most of the crew and stopping them from completing the mission I so desperately needed them to complete. You stole the treasure and then brought it back to me. A traitor in your midst bewitched another of my fleet, and they will probably die – if they haven't already. And now, you leave me no choice but to venture into the pyramid again to try to steal that treasure back from a vengeful Goddess who has now awoken from a sleep of three thousand years.'

Blackbeard let the silence wash over him for a moment. Then he shrugged. 'What's your point?'

Amir half-turned, aiming at Blackbeard a look of sheer rage. 'Has it not crossed your mind that – for me – *you* are the curse?'

Chapter Thirty-four

'This heat is just not necessary,' said Handsome Harry, as he adjusted the white bandana around his head. The Barbary pirates had handed one each to Harry, Chris, Charlie and Michael, saying they would need them in the desert.

They weren't joking. It seemed like every ten yards Blackbeard was removing his hat to wipe the sweat from his brow, before it ran into his eyes. At this rate, Amir would not have to worry about keeping his promise to kill Blackbeard if they made it out of Sakhmet's pyramid alive.

The desert would beat him to it.

It felt like since they had docked the *Gallant* at Cairo they had done nothing but walk, and try to avoid the scorching grasp of the pitiless sun. They had trudged as a ragged group, Amir leading them first along the green and sedimentary plains of the riverbank, through papyrus plants that literally tickled the pirates' bellies; then along a dirt road that fed them to the city itself. Amir had marched them around the high walls of the city because, he said, the price on his head in Cairo made him suspicious of everyone – even his mother, who lived there.

So they had skirted Cairo, the sounds of the hustle and bustle, the haggling of the markets, the general city chaos, splashing over the walls like sea spray over a bulwark.

Once they had cleared the city, the Egyptian landscape spilled away to...nothing.

That was the only word that came to mind for Blackbeard when he caught his first glimpse of the desert. An endless sea of sand and dust, baked by the sun, which seemed so hot, Blackbeard would not have been surprised if he had looked up to see it falling to earth.

On and on they walked now, the European pirates following the Barbary mob. Up steep inclines that levelled out to rocky plateaus for miles, before tumbling down into sandy depressions. Whether the ground was rocky or sandy, it remained scalding hot, to the point where Blackbeard would not have been surprised to look down and see the soles of his boots melting. Once or twice, Blackbeard raised his spyglass to check their progress, but all the magnifier did was increase the blurriness of the heat haze, which veiled the horizon. Blackbeard shoved the spyglass into his waist belt and trudged on.

Chris Claw nudged his arm. Blackbeard could see that he had a slight tear in his bandana at the left temple, where he had been scratching it. 'Are you sure we can trust them?' he asked. 'How do we know they're not just luring us into the desert to kill us?'

Blackbeard sighed, giving it a moment to see if Chris's brain would catch up. But it didn't. He would have narrowed his eyes at him witheringly, except that he was already squinting constantly against the sun. It was hot, and getting hotter.

'Would you walk all this way into the desert just to kill someone and then have to walk all the way back?' he asked. 'And, besides, if that was their plan, they'd have done it on board their ship.'

'Yeah, I suppose,' said Chris.

Blackbeard trudged on in the wake of the Barbary pirates, trying his best to walk in their shadow, snatching any shade that he could.

His hand went to his pistols when he caught a flicker of movement out of the corner of his right eye. Michael had broke from the group, running at an angle.

'Oi!' Blackbeard called. 'Where are you going?'

Up ahead, Omar had stopped and turned, the Barbary pirates walking around him. In the crook of one arm, he held the canvas sack in which Amir had placed the fourth canopic jar, the map for which they would need once they were underground.

If they ever got there.

'Desert madness,' he said. 'He's probably seeing a lake that isn't really there.'

Blackbeard ignored the smug tone of his voice, and the smile on his face. He stopped and called out to Michael.

Twenty yards away, Michael fell to his knees. Fearing that the heat was killing him, Blackbeard took off, hearing Chris, Harry and Charlie following, their ragged, chaotic and exhausted steps almost obscuring the curious consternation of the Barbary mob's shouts.

'Michael!' Blackbeard cried, as he came upon the boy. He was on all fours now, peering at the ground as though he had just discovered the most wondrous, precious treasure.

'Look, Captain,' he said, pointing. 'Look!'

Blackbeard stooped to follow his point, and saw what he had picked out. A small creature about the size of a ship's rat, with a body of green, overlapping scales that shone in the desert heat. It was about fifteen feet away, its long, tapering tail flicking and writing as it slithered over the cracks in the rocky ground, walking on four short legs that moved rather like wheels as it made a steady course to God only knew where.

'It's a lizard!' said Michael. 'I've never seen one before.'

Blackbeard shook his head, turning to the Barbary pirates, none of whom had stopped. 'These things dangerous?' he called.

It was Omar who turned around. 'No,' he answered.

Blackbeard turned back to Michael, reaching to grab him under the arms. 'They're dangerous, lad,' he said. 'Come on.'

'It's amazing!' said Michael, standing up and following the others as they hurried to join up with the Barbary mob.

As they rejoined the pack, Blackbeard saw that Amir had slowed his own pace to let them draw level with him.

'I get the feeling,' he said, 'you Europeans don't exactly belong here.'

Blackbeard snorted. 'You could say that. The sooner we find this pyramid, the better.'

Amir smiled grimly, cocking a thumb over his broad shoulder. 'Well, you're in luck. Take a look.'

Blackbeard reached for his spyglass and held it up again. The heat haze filled his vision for a moment, but as he focused, he saw it. A few more miles of sand dunes, their curves gently rounded, rising and falling like suspended waves.

And beyond it, curious dunes with sharper edges, ending in points that seemed to stab for the sky. There were three of them, just like Amir had suggested. Three Egyptian pyramids.

Which meant, the fourth one – the sunken pyramid of the Goddess Sakhmet – was now close.

Chapter Thirty-five

'Must have had some big old ruckus here once upon a time, eh?' said Blackbeard, as the group came to a stop outside the ruined walls of a city that had probably been melted away by this wretched sun hundreds, or thousands, of years ago.

The walls were made of brick the same shade as the sand, looking not man-made, but natural – as though sprouting from the desert itself; it seemed that, every ten yards, there was a break, a breach, the whole structure looking like a giant set of broken, rotting teeth.

It did not take much for Blackbeard to believe that this place could eat people alive. In its own way, it probably had.

Amir gave a grunted command in his own language, and led the group through one of the gaps in the walls, into the empty city. Stumps of stone foundations marked where dwellings had once stood, and thin depressions in the dusty earth suggested an old road. But it was ruined, abandoned – deserted.

They were walking towards the trio of pyramids, which, Blackbeard had to concede, were rather spectacular. They were square at the base, with four perfect triangular sides rising to a capstone that looked so sharp, Blackbeard felt they would impale the sky if ever it were to fall. The whole structure was made of a limestone that gave it a white glow, even in the brightness of the open desert.

'Bet you have nothing like this in England,' said Omar, switching the canvas sack from one arm to another.

'I wouldn't know,' said Blackbeard. 'It's been years since I was there.' Of course, he knew that there was nothing of the sort back home. The construction of the pyramids was an instant mystery to him – how could this have been pulled off?

But he wasn't going to tell Omar that.

They were almost at the base of the pyramids. By now, the heat was so oppressive, Michael was standing behind Blackbeard at all times, using his huge shadow as a shield. Blackbeard could sense tension among the Barbary mob, could hear concerned mutterings. He didn't need to know their language to have a general idea of what they were discussing – they had been here once before, and knew what was coming.

Amir came to a stop, right where a thirty-foot

chasm opened up between the bases of two of the pyramids. He turned to the group and drew his pistol. Blackbeard heard the Barbary boys do the same. He drew one of his own guns, as Amir said:

'From this point on, we must be alert. Whatever you see, try to stay calm.'

Blackbeard nodded. 'Don't worry about my boys,' he said. 'We've seen things you—'

His voice was drowned out by a startled cry. Omar stumbled forward, seeming to be struggling with the canopic jar in the canvas sack, as though it was trying to escape him somehow. As he wrestled with the artefact, he gave Amir a look of confusion and helplessness. All around them, the Barbary pirates were backing away.

The sack began to writhe and swell in Omar's arms, a sharp point poking out of the sides. Blackbeard felt Michael clutching at his arm as the sack opened up a tear in itself from the inside, and the sharp, gleaming bronze-tipped head of a spear thrust out, slicing a gash in Omar's leather waistcoat as he hopped backwards, letting the canopic jar fall to the desert ground.

It hit the dust and flattened, not with the sound of cracking or smashing marble, but with a low thud. The sack and the jar inside seemed to crumble, the spearhead rising up in another stabbing motion, as the whole group scattered like broken glass.

The canvas was torn to shreds from within, as a seven-foot tall Egyptian warrior stood up out of it.

Chapter Thirty-six

Blackbeard backed away with the rest of the group, but was unable to take his gaze off the soldier. His face was exactly like the one that had been carved into the marble jar that Omar had been carrying all the way through the desert and, from the way his form seemed to suck in and contain the desert sunlight, throwing it back out in sword-sharp rays that caused some of the Barbary pirates to shield their eyes, Blackbeard instinctively knew that this was not a flesh-and-blood foe.

This soldier's 'flesh' was made of marble.

He was bare-chested, bare-headed and barefoot – the only clothing on his body was the pristine white kilt wrapped around his waist. In his right hand, he beat the shaft of his bronze-tipped spear on the desert, rhythmically and threateningly, while his left hand held a shield in the familiar kite shape, made of wood and ox-hide. On its face was a painted image of Sakhmet.

The soldier regarded the intruders gathered around him, his painted eyes showing no expression at all. He jabbed his shield out at the pirates nearest him, who all hopped back to avoid the blow.

Then he turned and ran.

His stride was slow and deliberate, but his long legs carried him forward quickly.

Amir gestured to the group to chase the soldier.

'You want to *follow* that thing?' shouted Chris Claw, as the Barbary pirates hesitantly filed past him. Then he looked to Blackbeard questioningly.

Blackbeard shrugged. 'He surely can't do much worse to us than mummies, eh?'

They ran across the desert city, the group charging in the gap between the two pyramids. As soon as he rounded the corner, Blackbeard looked up ahead for the marble warrior – but he was nowhere to be found.

'He's gone below ground,' said Amir, at the head of the group. 'He's gone to her.'

But Blackbeard was barely listening. His attention was focused on the sight at the end of the wide alley between the pyramids. 'What is that?' he said.

A stone structure seemed to grow from the ground, a statue without a plinth. Its strong legs ended in claws, and its body was carved to look powerful, muscular. It was the body of a lion. But its head was something very different – its mouth was long, and held open in a silent roar, its innumerable teeth as sharp as swords.

Amir sighed as he put his pistol back into his waist-belt. 'Ammit,' he said. 'Devourer of the Dead. She consumes the souls of the wicked.'

'And you brought us here?' exclaimed Handsome Harry. 'What were you thinking?'

Beside Amir, Omar was checking himself, making sure he had not incurred a mortal wound when surprised by the marble warrior. 'You'll be all right,' he said, 'as long as you don't die.'

Blackbeard shook his head. Even amid their desperate situation, Omar couldn't stop being an annoying little twerp, it seemed. He turned to Amir. 'What now?' he asked.

Amir rubbed a hand over his shaved head, which glistened with sweat that ran down his face and dripped off his chin. 'We keep going,' he said. 'The last canopic jar came to life, to return to Sakhmet – which means that Sakhmet's power grows ever more powerful. We must be careful.'

He set off again, towards the statue of Ammit.

One by one, they descended the stairs, into the dark tunnel that plunged steeply away from the door that Amir had opened in the right hind leg of the terrifying statue of the Devourer.

At the foot of the stairs, the tunnel ran in both directions, lit by torches that had been stabbed into holes that dribbled dust. 'They're new,' said Chris, scraping at one with a long, black fingernail.

Amir nodded. 'We're walking in the footsteps of Sakhmet and her minions,' he said. 'Even without the map on the canopic jar, we should find the tomb easily.'

'It's what happens once we get there that we have to worry about,' said Blackbeard.

The tunnel was so narrow that the crew could only walk two abreast. On either side, the torches stretched out like flaming archways, making it seem all the smaller. The only sounds were their echoed footsteps, their procession sounding like rumbling thunder.

At the head of the group were Omar and Amir; Blackbeard was in the second pair with Chris Claw, young Michael walking alone just behind them. Handsome Harry and Chaplain Charlie were the last pair of European pirates before the rest of the group was taken up with young Barbaries who, even though they had been here before, walked with no more confidence than the foreigners.

Turning after turning, Amir guided them from memory. It seemed simple. It seemed like everything was going to work out.

Amir took the sixth turning without looking back. Blackbeard followed, keeping an eye out for danger, although he didn't know how danger might strike effectively in such a cramped space.

'*Oof!*'

Blackbeard felt Omar's bony shoulder slamming into his sternum. He backed up into Michael, planting his feet for balance and glaring at Amir's First Mate. 'What you turning round for?'

'Something's different,' said Amir, as he turned in a slow circle, lips curled in thought, fingertips rubbing his forehead as though he might tease the memory out of his mind.

Blackbeard stepped up to him. 'What's going on?'

'Something's missing,' said Amir. 'Omar…' He looked to his First Mate, who nodded, his spindly arms wrapped around himself in fear, his chest heaving with panic.

'The skeletons,' said Omar.

Blackbeard looked at both of them. 'What skeletons?'

'The skeletons of the labourers,' said Amir. 'The ones who died building this very tomb. When we were last here, we had to step over them very carefully, so as not to disturb their bones.'

'We're probably just coming up on them,' said Chris Claw.

But Amir was shaking his head. 'No,' he said. 'We should have seen them by now.'

Blackbeard looked around for any signs of disturbed bones. He saw nothing on the ground except dust and pirates' boots. 'There's nothing,' he said, looking up at Amir. 'Maybe Chris was right...'

But Amir did not return Blackbeard's gaze. He was looking over his shoulder, over the heads of the group – back the way they had come.

And for the first time since he had met him, Blackbeard saw fear in Amir's eyes.

'We have big trouble!'

Chapter Thirty-seven

Skeletons.

Dozens of moving skeletons, armed with the hammers and chisels they had clutched since their deaths, however many thousands of years ago that had been. Their bony faces were locked in hideous grins as their blackened teeth clattered together in a rattling laughter that made Blackbeard's throat tighten in terror.

And they were rushing right towards the pirates in the tunnel, their arms jabbing and scything with their deadly tools.

'Run!' Blackbeard called out, turning around and charging as fast as he could down the tunnel, following Omar and Amir, hearing Chris Claw just behind him. The panicked cries of the pirates filled the tunnel with a deafening, disorientating noise, the thundering of their feet sending tremors through the ground and walls.

A shrill cry emanated from the back, freezing the blood in Blackbeard's veins. Blackbeard chanced a look over his shoulder, seeing the flash of pale bone as it hacked at a helpless victim.

Blackbeard felt Chris Claw's fingernails poking through his doublet as he shoved him forward. 'Captain! Don't slow down!'

'What *are* they?' cried Michael.

'Guardians,' Omar shouted, still running. 'They served Sakhmet in life, and now they serve her in death. She commands them. Just like I told you.'

'What do we do?'

Blackbeard half-turned, reaching behind him and taking Michael by the shoulder, dragging him forward. 'We keep moving!'

'We should fight them,' Amir shouted.

'And kill them how?' said Blackbeard. 'They've already died once and now they're just walking bones. We need to get clear, not risk more lives trying to kill things that probably can't be killed again. Everyone keep moving!'

Michael, the youngest and nimblest of the group, was streaking ahead, racing through the stripes of light and dark cast by the torches in the walls. His head was down as he dug deep for all the speed he could muster.

He did not see the frayed rope nailed into the walls, stretching across the tunnel at ankle-height.

Blackbeard desperately stretched to grab a handful

of Omar's leather waistcoat, trying to drag himself forward – trying to reach Michael. 'Michael, stop!'

But the boy didn't stop. He kept running, looking up only to glance over his shoulder at Blackbeard.

The rope snapped free with a dull *twang*, its nails spinning away down the tunnel. Now, Michael froze, looking down at his feet just as it dawned on him what had happened.

A trap.

He looked up at Blackbeard again, his face a picture of horror. 'Capt—'

With a low rumble, the ground beneath Michael seemed to cave in on itself at five points. Spikes sprouted from beneath the earth, cruel and vicious.

Two of them stabbed right through the soles of Michael's feet, bursting through his boots in a shower of blood and leather.

Michael screamed.

Chapter Thirty-eight

Michael screamed and gasped, hyperventilating; for a moment, he looked like he might try stepping free of the trap.

'Don't!' said Blackbeard, lumbering to a stop just in front of him. He had barged past Amir and Omar, who scampered after him. He barely heard them, or the other group of pirates, as they came to a stop, colliding with each other on all directions. From the rear, the sound of the Barbary boys fighting valiantly against the skeletons, the echo of their battle-cries, cannoned off the tunnel walls.

But Blackbeard barely heard any of it. The only thing he knew was that Michael was done for. There was no point in trying to free him, as there was no way he would be able to keep up with the rest of the crew as they ran, and any man who carried him would be too vulnerable to whatever else awaited them in these tunnels. And, even if Michael tried to run by himself, he would not get very far. The spikes had torn a hole in both of his feet. Blood was draining from severed veins. The boy's eyes were already growing distant from the blood-loss.

He had minutes, at best.

Michael gritted his teeth so hard that Blackbeard thought they might crumble. 'Get Miss Bonny back,' he said.

Blackbeard reached out a hand to tousle Michael's hair, but changed his mind and just held the boy's head against his chest for a moment. 'I'm sorry,' he whispered. 'I made you a promise, that I'd see you right, and I haven't. Forgive me.'

Michael pulled away from him, smiling through his pain. 'There's nothing to forgive, Captain. I'm proud to die a real pirate. I *am* a pirate, aren't I?'

Blackbeard squeezed Michael's shoulder. 'Aye, son. One of the best.'

Michael stretched his arms out either side of him, sliding the nearest two torches free of the walls. 'Keep going. I'll hold off these bony lubbers.'

Blackbeard tousled Michael's hair for the very last time, as he led the crew onward down the tunnel. As he walked, her heard the other pirates – European and Barbary – offering their gratitude and good wishes to Michael.

As Amir lead them down a left turning, Blackbeard head Michael's voice echoing along the tunnel. 'Good luck, mateys!'

The crew jogged in silence, following Amir's direction, until the sound of Michael's defiant battle cries, and the swishing of his flaming torches as he set his skeleton enemies ablaze, could no longer be heard.

As soon as the silence fell, Blackbeard pushed past Chris Claw to the head of the group. He tapped Amir on the shoulder.

And when Amir turned around, Blackbeard slammed his fist into his nose.

Chapter Thirty-nine

'Why didn't you mention that there were skeletons!?' Blackbeard roared, swatting away an attempted attack from Omar, and shoving him into the waiting arms of Chris Claw, who wrapped him up in a restraining chokehold, his fingernails resting threateningly on the skin around his jugular.

Amir had been sent sprawling along the tunnel by Blackbeard's punch. He sat up, wiping his bloody nose with his knuckles. 'I didn't expect them to come to life,' he said. 'Sakhmet was not so powerful that she could raise the dead last time – but now she is.'

'Well, you could have warned us that might happen,' said Blackbeard, flexing his sore fist, ready to swing again if Amir pounced. 'Thanks to you, I've lost another member of my crew.'

'And thanks to *you*,' said Amir, getting to his feet and dusting off his breeches, 'I've lost about fifty of mine. I'm sorry the boy died, but we're all risking death by walking these tunnels. Now, is your man going to let mine go so we can continue, or am I going to have to command the rest of my crew to fill your chest full of bullets?'

Blackbeard glanced over his shoulder, seeing that the Barbary pirates had drawn their guns. Handsome Harry and Chaplain Charlie had backed off, with their hands held up. He reminded himself he did not have the numbers.

He looked back at Amir. 'Lead the way, Mr Barbarossa,' he said, gesturing to Chris Claw that he should release Omar.

Blackbeard drew up alongside Amir, as the group got going again. 'Is it broken?' he asked.

Amir lightly touched his nose, which still trickled with blood. 'Don't worry about it. You remember my promise?'

'To kill me if we made it alive? Oh yes, I remember.'

'You've just earned yourself a slower death.'

The crew moved quickly, but carefully, eyes on the ground looking out for more trip ropes. But as the tunnels sloped downwards, the only thing that troubled them was the occasional rat and scorpion, scurrying harmlessly by.

Soon, they came to another right turning. As the next tunnel stretched away into the darkness, he and Amir came to a dead stop beside each other. Blackbeard felt Chris and Harry bump into his back.

He heard a gentle wave of murmuring wash over him from the rear of the group.

'Is it another trap, Captain?' asked Harry.

'No,' said Blackbeard. 'It's about thirty of them.'

Trip rope after trip rope stretched out in front of them, more than he could count. But unlike the one that had ended the life of Michael, these weren't ankle-high, but thigh-high. Well, thigh-high to Blackbeard – waist-high to almost everyone else. All of the pirates stepping over them could take hours.

'We have to crawl,' said Amir. 'Everyone must stay very low.'

'What will happen if we break one of the ropes?' Blackbeard asked him.

'No clue,' said Amir. 'If I would have done that the last time, my own corpse would be lying there right now, wouldn't it?'

'I suppose you're right.'

They moved in single file, Amir going first, with Blackbeard second. Omar was just behind him, with Blackbeard's three remaining mates next in line. Amir's knees dragged through the dusty ground, making shallow tracks in which the others followed.

Blackbeard had to give it to him. He was a strong man, that was for sure. They hadn't made it fifteen yards when his own knees began to feel like they might collapse, but Amir didn't seem to be tiring at all.

Blackbeard looked up ahead, seeing that there was still a long way to go, and many ropes to pass under. The tension, the anxiety about rising too high and tripping one of the ropes made him feel as though a heavy, invisible hand was pushing down on his back.

'Keep going, lads,' he called out. 'And stay low. I don't want to know what these ropes will trigger if they're broken.'

He continued to crawl, getting into a rhythm. With every tenth pace, he looked up and quickly surveyed the path ahead, if only so he could see, in good time, if any more rats, or scorpions – or, worse, lizards – were heading their way. Having them run past his feet was fine enough, but he did not fancy being face-to-face with the nasty, spiteful little creatures.

But each time he glanced up, all he saw were the ringed stripes of light and shadow cast by the endless rows of flaming torches.

'I think we're close,' Blackbeard said. But as he heard his words be passed in two languages from pirate to pirate, all the way to the back of the group, he froze.

Had he seen something up ahead?

Amir had not stopped, and Omar seemed to take this as his cue to slither past Blackbeard into the second link in the chain of crawling pirates. As Chris Claw drew up almost alongside him, hissing over his shoulder at everyone to halt, Blackbeard leaned to his left, placing his face against the wall, the better to peer as far along the tunnel as he could.

'Captain?' said Chris, joining him in peering up along the tunnel, into the pulsing pools of fiery light. Behind them, Harry and Charlie had stopped, also, forcing the rest of the Barbary mob to halt, much to their muttered chagrin. 'Why have we stopped?'

'We need to be careful,' said Blackbeard. 'There's something up ahead...something...'

They saw it at the same time. A six-wide row of bodies, carved out of wood, walking slowly towards them. As they passed under the torches, the fiery light made their painted armour glint and gleam, as well as the spears and swords held tightly in their fixed, immovable wooden fists. They moved with purpose, paying no heed to the trip-ropes, because they were short enough to walk safely below them. As they got closer and closer, Blackbeard could see the expressions on their faces – fixed into twisted snarls of hateful, violent intent.

'The *Shabti*!' Amir gasped, as he and Omar crawled backwards, their heads coming dangerously close to the bottom of the ropes.

'Get down!' Blackbeard hollered at them. The Barbary pair dropped, laying almost flat as they kept on crawling. Blackbeard and Chris reached forward in the tunnel to grab them by the legs, hauling them back.

'The *Shabti*,' Amir said again. 'The servants created to guard Sakhmet in the next world – they've come to life to protect her corpse from intruders.'

'Stone me,' said Blackbeard. 'You know something? If you Egyptians didn't play around with all this sort of nonsense, we'd just have a simple walk-in-and-steal-something mission. Bread-and-butter stuff. But no!'

The six moving statues of the *Shabti* passed through the rings of light and dark in a deliberate march, each step accompanied by the creaking sound of splintering wood. Behind them, more and more soldiers marched – it was a whole platoon of the things! Their faces remained unnervingly fixed in their carved expressions of fearsome scowls.

'What are we going to do?' Blackbeard heard Chaplain Charlie cry.

Normally – if there was such a thing – Blackbeard would have had no fear of tackling six, sixty or six hundred two-foot-tall wooden statues. He'd just stomp, stamp and kick them all over the place.

But that was hard to do when forced to fight on all fours.

Blackbeard wriggled to draw his cutlass. Up ahead, Amir and Omar drew curved swords. 'Fight as best you can,' he called to the men. 'Keep moving forward!'

As the *Shabti* started running, Blackbeard swung his cutlass from left to right, striking at the statues that had avoided Amir and Omar's swipes. It was the only move he could make, given the position he was in and the space he had. His blade slashed through the wooden soldiers, sending heads and limbs ricocheting off the walls.

But by the time he had made his strike, the next line of *Shabti* were scurrying past him, jabbing the points of their spears and swords at his arms and ribs. His doublet was thick and their weapons were small, so the blows were not fatal, but Blackbeard had to throw up his free hand to prevent a tiny sword scratching his eye out as the wooden army overwhelmed the vulnerable pirates, falling upon them like a swarm of bees. The cacophony of fearful cries shook Blackbeard's soul.

He heard the crunch of fist and blade on tough timber, followed by triumphant yells – that swiftly grew into shrieks as more of their innumerable enemies piled in.

Two of them had charged at Blackbeard, clambering onto his back. He released his cutlass and threw his hands up over his head, his most vulnerable part, as he felt the pricking of their spears up and down his spine. With a roar, he rolled over, sending them tumbling into a wall. He placed both hands on the top of the nearest soldier's head and ripped it off.

But the second one flew at him again, spear thrusting right for his throat. Blackbeard caught it in his mighty palm and, with a twist, snapped it in half. He turned the spearhead in his hand and drove it right between the eyes of the second statue, feeling a rush of elation when its face exploded into a shower of splinters.

Blackbeard moved forward, away from the mess of fighting, crawling in the wake of Amir and Omar, sweeping aside wooden heads and limbs as he went. Mercifully, no more *Shabti* were charging from up ahead, but when he looked over his shoulder, Blackbeard's eyes fell upon the most bewildering horror he had ever seen.

The pirates were wrestling, writhing on the ground, with the squad of animated wooden statues. Each time they batted one away, another would leap from the shadows, thrusting and scratching at them with their spear.

Cries of effort and exertion became wails of pain. Blackbeard saw eyeballs tumble from sockets, saw blood spray from slashed throats.

Saw Chaplain Charlie rising too high as he tried to scramble away from his three sword-wielding attackers.

'No!' Blackbeard yelled. 'No, Charlie, don't—'

But it was too late. As he blindly got to his feet, Chaplain Charlie's bleeding back tripped three ropes, all at the same time.

Chapter Forty

The walls either side of them opened up with countless holes, making them look diseased. A storm of spears came shooting out in any and every direction.

There was no escape. They slammed into pirate and *Shabti* soldier indiscriminately, breaking all bodies in their path – be that body made of wood, or flesh and blood.

Blackbeard scrambled away from the spears, feeling no triumph when he saw that he had cleared the last of the higher trip ropes, nor any relief when he was finally able to stand up straight. Beside him, Amir was restraining Omar, who was trying to run back to the massacre.

The only thing Blackbeard felt was an impotent rage, as pirate after pirate was impaled on spears. Chaplain Charlie had been pinned to the floor, while a pair of Barbary pirates had been stabbed into the wall. *Shabti* soldiers exploded, their frames not even slowing the spears down as they continued on, slamming into another prone pirate.

'Captain!'

Blackbeard snapped out of it when he saw Chris

Claw and Handsome Harry frantically crawling forward, the spears missing them by sheer luck – luck Blackbeard thought had long run out.

He lunged forward, crouching by the last of the trip ropes and extended both arms underneath it. Chris and Harry clutched at his wrists with both hands, their desperation so pure they almost yanked him forward into the last rope. But Blackbeard dug his heels in to the stony ground and threw his weight back, roaring in determination as he dragged his two friends clear.

An unbearably heavy silence fell over the group after the last of the spears clattered off the stone walls. Nobody beneath the trip ropes was moving. If the *Shabti* hadn't killed them, the spears had finished the job. Their ragtag crew had been reduced to five – and one of them didn't even have all his fingers to begin with.

'I'll kill you!'

Omar broke free from Amir's grip and lunged at Blackbeard, driving him into the wall. Blackbeard was so stunned, so numbed by what he had seen that he offered no resistance, nor did he feel any pain from the hooked punch that slammed into his jaw.

'You got them all killed!' Omar yelled, as Chris Claw pulled him off and slammed him into the wall, one forearm holding him still, the other arm raised with his clawed hand poised to rip out Omar's throat.

Blackbeard snapped out his own hand to clutch at Chris's wrist, just as Amir Barbarossa placed the point of his blade against his throat.

'No, Chris,' said Blackbeard. 'He's right.'

Chris released Omar, who turned around to attack him, stopping only at the restraining palm of Amir, who was placing his blade back into his waist-belt.

Blackbeard's sore, aching knees collapsed beneath him. He put his head in his hands and growled through gritted teeth. 'What have I done?' he said, over and over again, barely feeling Handsome Harry's efforts to pick him up off the ground. 'I've got them all killed – and for what? To rescue my sister, who's probably already dead? Oh, she was right – I should have retired when we left the Atlantic.'

'Oh, be quiet!'

Blackbeard looked up into the eye of Handsome Harry, who stood over him, shaking his head. 'A pirate is prepared to go to Hell, if that's where his voyage takes him. We all knew that when we set sail. Now, we came here to settle a score, did we not? We came here to lift a curse off ourselves. Are we going to follow that through, or are we going to sit here sobbing like a bunch of landlubbers?'

Blackbeard said nothing. He had no idea how to respond to Harry's chastising. The will to fight had deserted him.

'On your feet, Captain,' said Harry.

Blackbeard did not move.

'Fine,' said Harry. 'You sit there. You sit there and feel sorry for yourself, and die underneath the Egyptian desert. Die knowing that you were a fraud – that, when it came time for you to live up to your legend, you lost your nerve.'

The energy and will to fight began trickling through Blackbeard's body, like blood returning to a numbed limb.

Harry crouched in front of him. 'What was it you used to call yourself? What name struck fear into the hearts of merchant, pirate and naval commander alike?'

'Man From Hell,' Blackbeard whispered.

'I didn't hear you.'

'*Man From Hell.*'

Harry gave him a smile – a smile that was all gum. 'Right you are, Captain. You were the Man From Hell. Look around you... You're home.'

Blackbeard pushed himself to his feet, gritting his

teeth again – but this time, it was a different kind of rage he was feeling. It was a focused rage – a determined rage.

A rage that he was going to unleash on Sakhmet, her mummified minions, and anyone else who tried to stand in his way. He reached into his pocket and found the long, stiff lengths of fuse that he had not used since he'd turned his back on the Atlantic.

'Aye,' he said, beginning to place the fuses beneath the brim of his hat. He placed the last one against the flame of a torch in the cave wall, then used it to light them. He felt the familiar gentle heat pulsing on his cheeks and beneath his eyes; he saw the smoke drifting away from him to blend with the shadows.

Somehow, he was feeling like his old self again.

'Let's go,' he said. 'Now, we finish this. No one who died here will have died in vain. I swear it.'

Chapter Forty-one

They followed Amir as he led them through the last of the tunnels. Blackbeard knew they were close when the rows of torches stopped. Now, the only light in the tunnel was from the floating orbs of Blackbeard's slow-burning fuses, the heat kissing his face and matching the internal fire of rage he felt in every inch of his body.

Amir dropped into a crouch, looking at the group. 'Be ready,' he whispered. 'We are too few to steal the treasure and run for it. Now, we must fight – fight to the death.'

'How do we kill folk who are already dead?' asked Chris Claw.

Amir smiled grimly. 'We finish their death,' he said. 'Look in the tomb for a papyrus scroll. In our culture, it is called The Book of the Dead – a guide to outwitting the Gods of the Afterlife. While she has this, Sakhmet is immune to the wrath of the Devourer. If we can destroy it, the Goddess will be at the mercy of the Gods – she will face the justice that she should have done three thousand years ago.'

Blackbeard nodded. 'And with her, all...devoured,

like the curse will be lifted, and you can take the treasure anywhere you want?'

'I hope,' said Amir, turning back to the wall of darkness that would lead to Sakhmet's tomb. Even in the veil of shadows, Blackbeard could see that his uneasy ally did not look entirely convinced.

Amir led them in a crouching walk through the last of the tunnels as, up ahead, a faint pool of light seemed to shimmer. An archway in the tunnel, leading to some kind of clearing. Blackbeard felt a flutter of relief in his chest at the prospect of getting out of these cramped passages. He drew two of his guns from his waist-belt. He knew the odds of survival were slim, and so was content to charge in and blast away. Even if bullets would not harm the mummies, or whatever other sorts of demonic forces Sakhmet commanded, he could die content that he had raised some Hell... one last time.

'Do hurry up.'

The surviving pirates froze at the sound of the voice swimming down the tunnel. It was a single voice that somehow sounded like two. Like a string instrument playing two notes at the same time, the sounds at once blended and distinct. Luis's voice, combined with the soft, snake-like tones that he had adopted the day he offered to translate the mess of notes for Blackbeard. Just before he betrayed them all.

'We've been waiting for you.'

The group stood up, weapons still held ready, as they walked faster down the tunnel, through the archway and into a brightly lit chamber.

Into the tomb of Sakhmet.

Her golden sarcophagus had been placed dead-centre of the tomb, only now it stood upright. It no longer wore the cracks of time, the splotches of worn paint, the dullness of old gold. It gleamed and shone in the light of the torches that lined each of the four walls, row after row of them disappearing into the blanket of black that veiled the ceiling. At her feet stood all four of the canopic jars, bearing the heads of a jackal, falcon, baboon and warrior. The four coffin-pillars on plinths were arranged around the sarcophagus like guards keeping a vigil. Which, Blackbeard supposed, they were.

Egyptian soldiers lined the wall to Blackbeard's left. Thankfully, they were not all seven-foot tall like the marble maniac that had burst out of the canvas sack; they were average height, with the same outfit of a linen kilt covering their lower body; they had swords or bronze-tipped spears in one hand, ox-hide shields in the other. Blackbeard would have reckoned on the shields, with their three-thousand-year-old covering, giving off the foulest stench in the room. But whatever pungent stench wafted off the face of the shield was buried beneath the rancid reek of the soldiers themselves.

Each of them was an impossibly gaunt and shrivelled figure, their skeletons covered in the thinnest layer of decomposed, rock-hard skin and flesh in a maddeningly mottled shade of black and grey. They scanned their tomb with milky, dead eyes, their heads turning in synchronised, lazy arcs that made their dead bones creak and their rotting flesh crack, faint specks of skin breaking through and tumbling down their bodies in a pathetic avalanche.

Standing by the opposite wall, were more shrivelled, half-decomposed figures, wearing similar linen kilts, but their shorter statures and bulbous pot-bellies indicated that they were not soldiers. They didn't carry weapons, but curious square wooden buckets.

Only two figures inside the tomb seemed to have any real flesh on their bones.

The first was the smirking figure of Luis, stood between the sarcophagus and a table, which lay adjacent to it. The second was the figure on top of the table. She was tied with thick rope, though the bonds seemed unnecessary – she was unconscious, her face having the same serene, peaceful look as Blackbeard's pirates after they had eaten Luis's tainted meal.

Mary.

Chapter Forty-two

Blackbeard reached out to the wall and snatched up a torch. His companions did the same. They did not really need them in the well-lit tomb, but a weapon was a weapon. Blackbeard knew bullets and blades had little effect against the minions of Sakhmet – maybe fire would succeed where they had failed.

The pirates stepped slowly towards the centre of the tomb, every one of their strides watched by the line of soldiers, the creaking and cracking of their dried out bones filling Blackbeard's ears.

He shuddered when he looked closer at their faces. The skin around their cheeks and mouths had half decomposed, exposing their yellowed teeth and blackened gums. As one, they raised their swords and spears, looking ready to charge if commanded.

Blackbeard turned to Luis, who leaned over Mary, his hands flat on the table, forming an arch over her head. 'I'm here to barter,' he said, trying not to let his own gaze fall too sharply on what he could now see in the crook of his sister's right arm.

A papyrus scroll.

Luis smiled, that two-tone voice echoing throughout

the tomb: 'Sakhmet does not barter.'

'Not even when she is threatened with being served up to the Devourer?' said Amir.

Luis's smile faltered, but only for a moment, his head half turning to his right. He looked like he was thinking it over – or getting instructions from the lady inside the sarcophagus.

Maybe both.

Luis looked back to Blackbeard. 'No.'

Blackbeard was stunned. He heard Chris and Harry shifting uncomfortably, either side of him. What could he do?

He looked to Amir, and saw the same thought in his eyes – if they were going to go out, they may as well go out like pirates.

In style.

'It's quite simple, Luis,' said Blackbeard, rolling his shoulders to release the tension he felt. He could not fight these corpses when he was as stiff as they were. 'You let my sister go, and we'll all walk out of here, and leave you to whatever it is you're planning to do with this rather lovely group of lads you've got here. Refuse, and we'll burn this place to the ground and not care if we go up in flames with it. Your choice.'

Luis said nothing. He just looked to the sarcophagus.

Then he looked to the soldiers. 'Kill them all!'

The shrivelled soldiers lurched away from the wall, coming towards the pirates in a chaotic charge, swords and spears raised high. In place of battle cries, they gave agonised groans, as though they were dying every second.

But that didn't mean Blackbeard could take them lightly. Their weapons moved so fast, the torchlight barely caught the flash of steel. Blackbeard used his own pistol to flick one strike away, feeling another scratching at his ribs. An inch to the left, and it would have broken his flesh.

He charged forward, spinning in a wide arc and hearing his doublet snag and tear on a spearhead. He shoved the pistol back into his gun-belt and drew his cutlass, just in time to slash at the body of a lunging soldier, seeing a spray of blackened, dusty rotten skin fly off its chest.

His blow had little effect.

Chris Claw was swiping his vicious hands with all his might. He ripped off chunks of skin and revealed the grey bones beneath.

But it did not slow the soldiers down.

Handsome Harry had dropped the torch that he had been holding in the crook of his arm, and was swinging the remains of his limbs like clubs, knocking soldiers this way and that.

But each one he put down got straight back up again.

To Blackbeard's left, Amir and Omar fought back to back, swinging their curved blades at the dead soldiers, lopping off hands at the wrist, puncturing guts and chest, the withdrawing of their blades accompanied by slick, sucking sounds.

But each soldier that fell simply got back up again, no matter what wound they suffered.

Three more came at Blackbeard, teeth chattering in the same horrific, groaning death rattle as the skeletons in the tunnel. He stepped forward, his roar burning through his throat as he slashed his sword from left to right, using all the strength that he had. He heard the blade rip along all three necks. He felt a thrill of triumph when he saw their skin break apart, the wound stretching all the way around, exposing their vertebrae. He almost cheered when he saw their heads lean back, back, back, as though they were going to fall off.

He growled in frustration when the three heads fell forward again, lolling, barely attached – but attached enough that they came forward in another charge.

Blackbeard backed up, swinging his sword in wide slashing arcs that did nothing to warn them off.

They just kept coming forward. But as long as he kept them in his line of sight, he reckoned he should have stayed alive long enough to—

A flash of steel on the edge of his vision – by his right eye. Blackbeard recoiled, spinning away to his left – and straight into the path of another soldier, looking to skewer him.

He dived for the floor, his flaming torch and cutlass flying out of his hands. Instinct had taken him over, his body moving before he even began to think about forming a plan.

He had rolled over onto his back, drawing and firing two of his pistols before his brain could tell him they probably would do no good.

'Ha!' he cried, jubilant, as he saw the bullets smash through the exposed vertebrae of two of the soldiers, their heads bouncing on their shoulders once, before tumbling to the ground and breaking like eggs. The rest of the soldiers' bodies crumpled to the ground.

Dead at last.

'The heads, lads!' Blackbeard cried out. 'Try to take off their heads!'

He scrambled for his cutlass again, swinging it

two-handed at everything that came towards him. Soldiers' heads went flying in every direction, until – one by one – they all fell down.

His chest heaving with exertion, his shoulders aching from all the slashes and hacks with his sword, Blackbeard turned back to Luis. 'You had your chance,' he said. 'Now, it's your turn to—'

Blackbeard's words died in his throat when he saw the four wooden standing-coffins begin to shudder – just before their lids opened with a hideous creak.

Luis smiled at him, speaking in that two-tone voice. 'You will die here,' he said, his eyes dropping down to Mary. 'You will *all* die here.'

The coffin lids swung open, revealing Sakhmet's four mummified minions, standing stock still for just a moment, before the twin pools of black where their eyes should be seemed to flicker. As one, they took lumbering steps out of their coffins, arms raising with the creaks and cracks of bones that were defying an eternal state of rigor mortis.

Like the soldiers, their mouths emitted their agonised groans – that endless, continuous death rattle. The last breath of life that would never end.

'This is no problem, boys,' said Blackbeard. He and the other pirates drew together, weapons facing outward – a protective circle. 'They should fall the same way that them soldiers did. All he we have to do—'

The mummies' death rattle rose to a snarling roar. The loose strips of shroud shot forward like fishing lines thrown into a river, the linen unrolling itself from the limbs of the corpses, the edges getting closer and closer to the pirates.

Before Blackbeard could move, one of them had wrapped around his neck. From the strangled gasps to his left, he could tell that Chris and Harry were in the same predicament. He looked to his right, and saw that Amir and Omar had fared no better. He followed the length of shrouds that wrapped round their necks, following them all the way back to a single mummy, the one wearing the jade pendant.

Blackbeard's eyes watered as nausea filled his neck. He couldn't breathe. His temples pounded, and his vision swam in front of him. He limply tried to swing his cutlass, to cut the shroud, but he just felt another length wrap around his right wrist, squeezing it so hard his fist burst open. His blade dropped to the ground with a clang that Blackbeard didn't even hear. His ears were roaring, his whole skull feeling like it was going to burst.

Blackbeard blinked his eyes clear, just as the linen shrouds retracted, reeling the pirates in towards the rotting carcass.

He batted at the shroud around his neck with his free left hand, expecting it to rip and tear at his strike. It was thousands of years old – it should have fallen apart.

But it held.

He tried to dig his heels in to the dusty, desert earth, and throw his bodyweight backwards.

But he did not even slow down his progress.

He was within three feet of the mummy now, its hands open like the jaws of a shark about to tear through its prey.

'Down!' Luis's voice was faint and distant – as though Blackbeard was underwater and the bewitched Spaniard was screaming at him from the shore.

The mummy obeyed the command. Blackbeard felt a sudden jolt of pressure at his neck, the shroud yanking him down to the ground.

He looked up, his vision swimming again. The mummy was slowly leaning down over him.

Was this it? Was this going to be the end for the greatest pirate of them all?

Not today!

Blackbeard still had his left hand free. And he still

had four more pistols in his gun-belt. He fumbled for the highest one, in the third holster. He drew it and took aim.

He fired.

The mummy's head exploded like a melon struck with a hammer. Chunks of flesh and shards of skull flew in every direction. But no brain.

Because there was no brain left.

Blackbeard felt the dusty, dry air rush into his lungs as the shroud slackened around his neck. He felt the blood rushing back into his right hand.

'No!' Luis roared.

Blackbeard tossed his spent third pistol aside and drew his fourth, taking aim at Luis. The Spaniard ducked and scrambled behind the golden sarcophagus before Blackbeard could get off his shot.

'Ca... Ca... Capt...'

Blackbeard wheeled around, seeing that Harry and Chris were almost within reach of their two mummy attackers. He drew his fifth pistol, coming to stand in between the two shroud-wrapped corpses. He held his arms out to the sides, his body forming a perfect T-shape.

The twin shot sent a shiver through the tomb. The two mummies collapsed, as did Harry and Chris.

Blackbeard dropped his guns and crouched over Harry to help him untangle the shroud from around his neck, while Chris practically ripped his own off.

Opposite them, Amir and Omar had used their blades to slice through the shroud, before scrambling away, coughing and spluttering.

'I'm almost out of bullets,' Blackbeard told the others. 'But I don't need them to kill— Whoa!'

His left foot flew out from underneath him, and he landed flat on his face. Dazed for a moment, he felt Harry reaching for his doublet.

But the old pirate had not the hands to get any purchase and was powerless to stop him being dragged towards the fourth mummy, the one with the jade amulet. 'Captain!'

Blackbeard was being dragged along the floor of the tomb, his body crashing through the remains of the shrivelled dead soldiers as the fourth mummy reeled him in. He tried grabbing for one of the carcasses, but succeeded only in pulling it with him.

He tried turning over and crawling in the other direction, but the mummy was too strong.

The dust from the ground was kicking up, filling his eyes and nose, making him cough and gag.

There was nothing he could do now. He knew it. He

had had one lucky escape, two was asking fate too much.

He stopped trying to crawl free. He stopped trying to make his body dead weight against the irresistible pull of the mummy's shroud.

He let his body go limp, and waited for the death he couldn't avoid, at the hands of Sakhmet's last mummified servant.

BANG!

Blackbeard came to a dead stop. He struggled into a sitting position, wiping the dust from his eyes and saw Chris Claw standing beside him, smoking pistol in hand.

Then he saw the headless mummy falling forward.

He rolled aside, just as the lifeless corpse slammed into the ground with a dull thud. Blackbeard heard bones break on impact. He freed his foot from the loosened shroud and stood up.

'Thanks,' he said to Chris, as a breathless Harry appeared beside them. Then he turned around and let his eyes rove over the chamber for Luis.

But he didn't find Luis. Instead, his gaze settled on a sight that turned his guts to what felt like a writhing mess of sludge.

In his desperate struggle to stay alive, Blackbeard had not heard the lid of Sakhmet's sarcophagus slide off.

Chapter Forty-three

Countless lengths of linen shroud rose up out of the sarcophagus like looming snakes, stretching over the edges and coiling around the prone body of Mary.

'No!' Blackbeard cried, stepping towards them, only to feel himself repelled by an invisible hand that plucked him from the ground and tossed him across the tomb. He crashed into Harry and Chris, the three of them rolling back.

'What...?' Blackbeard spluttered as he struggled to his feet. Amir and Omar drew up beside him, their faces frozen in fear. Blackbeard looked back to the sarcophagus. The lengths of shroud had almost completely mummified Mary. Out of the golden coffin, Sakhmet walked with a ghostly grace.

Her body was as shrivelled as the other mummies, but it had a poise and a purpose that the others did not. Her head and neck was more mobile, turning in the direction of her helpless victim, Mary, as though she was observing and appraising.

She stood up in the coffin, as the shroud unwrapped itself around her, revealing the true extent of her long-dead corpse.

It was hideous. Tall and thin, with withered, leathery skin, that flaked and peeled as the last of her rotten swaddling came off. Above a nose that was just a ragged hole in her face, were the two crystal blue eyes that gleamed with intelligence and purpose. Sakhmet's meaty tongue rolled and squirmed behind a yellow-toothed grin. She raised her arms and emitted a slick, gurgling hiss towards the ceiling of the tomb.

Luis reappeared from behind the sarcophagus, gazing at the hideous Goddess in awe. 'Sakhmet will live again,' he said. 'She will reclaim the physical world!'

Blackbeard felt his stomach slowly turn when he saw Sakhmet's flesh begin to pulse and heave, her blackened skin begin to lighten; bristles of dark hair sprouted from her skull.

'Oh no,' gasped Chris. 'Captain, she's...'

Chris couldn't finish his sentence. Blackbeard didn't need him to. He could see very clearly what was happening.

Sakhmet's rotted form was transforming into Mary's. It made sense to Blackbeard now. That look Luis gave Mary after he had translated Nasir's logs and maps – the appraising look.

He *had* been. He was appraising her as a vessel

315

for his Goddess's transformation. That was why Mary had been taken, and all of the other pirates left onboard. Sakhmet did not want to rule anything – this world or the next – in her shrivelled form that had been dead for thousands of years. She wanted to cross over young, vital and beautiful.

Luis and Sakhmet laughed in a hideous, triumphant chorus. Blackbeard saw that Mary's form had almost completely overtaken Sakhmet's, as though Mary's skin and features were a cloak.

The face that turned to look at him was his half-sister's – but the voice was the Goddess's.

'I am reborn!'

Sakhmet gave a shriek so loud, Blackbeard's legs wobbled beneath him as he covered his ears. Either side of him, Harry and Chris had slumped to the ground, hands and arms wrapped around their heads. Amir and Omar had reeled away from the noise.

Blackbeard looked back towards the sarcophagus. Sakhmet's crystal blue eyes, set into his sister's face, were fixed on him, her teeth bared in a frenzied grimace. 'Brave pirate,' she roared. 'I hope your death today satisfies your foolish pride.' She gave a hideous, sickening sound of wet, hissing laughter as she turned away from him.

She waved her hand over the canopic jars lined in front of her sarcophagus. A flare of blue light, the same shade as her eyes, drifted over the carved heads of the jars, dying as they landed upon them. The marble containers stretched and swirled upwards like clay being moulded by an invisible hand, forming fully-grown and moveable marble statues.

They stood before their Goddess, poised to maim and kill at her command.

'It begins!' Sakhmet shouted, casting her eyes to the ceiling and spreading her arms.

The entire tomb rumbled like giant hands were shaking it from the outside. Blackbeard collapsed like a rotten tree, barely able to get his arms up in time to protect himself. The other pirates staggered around, falling on top of each other.

'What is it?' cried Harry.

'An earthquake!' said Omar.

'Sakhmet rises!' Amir cried. 'It is over.'

From the hidden ceiling of the buried tomb, a thick blade of brilliant blue light stabbed down into the dusty earth, tearing a chasm and burrowing down and down and down until Blackbeard wondered if it might burst out on the other side of the world.

He felt an irresistible force tugging at his body, the

strongest current he had ever known. His body was flipped and flung onto the writhing, spiralling waves of earth that descended into...where? Hell?

Amid the rumbling from above, he could hear the screams of his friends Harry and Chris, the wailing of Luis the Spaniard, begging for his Goddess to save him.

And the laughter of that Goddess as she, too, was dragged into the Abyss, along with everything in her tomb.

Blackbeard closed his eyes, aware of nothing but the sensation of plummeting, and the sounds of Sakhmet's laughter rising over the anguished cries of the other pirates, and the rattling death-groans of her corpse minions.

'Fight them!' he heard Amir yell. 'Kill as many as you can! Go out in glory!'

Blackbeard heard the faint clanging of steel against steel, heard a wild gunshot fired in the maelstrom, the sound no more threatening than when someone would knock on his cabin door. He didn't even open his eyes. He just let his body fall, expecting to never land.

So it was with a shock that he felt the air driven from his body as his ribs slammed into hard earth.

Blackbeard lay there for several minutes, catching his breath as his senses came back into focus.

He was almost annoyed to still be alive.

He no longer felt the heat of the fuses at his cheek. He had finally lost his hat.

Blackbeard opened his eyes for what felt like the first time in days, blinking away the stinging sand and dust that made them water. He found himself back in the empty city, by another stretch of broken, ruined rampart. He struggled up to his feet, turning around to see that Sakhmet's maelstrom was not over.

Where Blackbeard had previously seen the statue of Ammit, there now rose a tornado of sand and stone, spinning and twisting in the air, stretching all the way up to the sky. It lashed like a snake in the breeze, scattering clouds of sand and chunks of rock.

'What now?' said Chris Claw, who was crawling across the desert towards him. Blood streamed from a wound at his temple, which Blackbeard guessed he had acquired during his landing.

'Should we run, sir?' Handsome Harry was at Blackbeard's side, appearing no more mangled than he usually did. In any other situation, Blackbeard might have laughed – that old codger had to be invincible.

'We can't run,' he told them, bending to help Chris

to his feet. 'The desert will kill us.'

'But then wha—'

Handsome Harry's words died at the sound of an anguished wail, elsewhere in the desert. Blackbeard followed the sound. Omar knelt at the foot of a pyramid, oblivious to the rocky debris that was raining down over him, cradling the head of Amir.

The Barbary King's chest was gushing blood.

Blackbeard found strength he did not know he had and ran over to Omar and Amir. As he stood over them, he could see that there was no hope for Amir. His chest had been torn open, a shred of a bronze spearhead glinting amid the pool of blood that leaked from him.

He had indeed fought to the end.

Blackbeard reached down and took two handfuls of Omar's bony shoulders, as the young man's body heaved with sobs. He tried to pull him to his feet. 'Come on, lad,' he said. 'There's nothing you can do.'

'A pirate does not leave his Captain,' said Omar, his face slick with tears, mucus and drool, his grief unleashing all of it in a stream that almost matched the bloody one coating Amir's torso.

'Your loyalty is admirable, son,' said Blackbeard. 'But this is not the time for it. We have to go.'

'Why?' said Omar.

Blackbeard cast his eyes down the wide aisle between the pyramids, towards where he had seen the stone statue of Ammit the Devourer. It still stood there, the odd mix of lion and crocodile, cruel mouth open, ready to consume anything in its path. It was impressive, monstrous...

But not as monstrous as what had formed behind it. The dust of the tornado was dissipating, to reveal a second statue – twice as tall as Ammit and, to Blackbeard, far more frightening.

The familiar, malevolent beauty of Sakhmet had risen from the site of her sunken tomb. It stretched up and up, higher than the pyramids, the teal-and-white robes Blackbeard remembered from the sarcophagus painted onto the limestone in brilliant, perfect colours.

And at her feet, her army of dead marched. All of them – the skeleton labourers from the tunnel, the cursed *Shabti* dolls, the shrivelled soldiers, the animated marble forms of the canopic jars.

And the four mummified minions, trailing lengths of shroud along the desert as they shuffled forward at the rear of the dead army.

Everything that the pirates had killed below the ground had been restored. And they were marching down the alley between the pyramids, with a deliberate purpose.

Blackbeard knew that that purpose was to finish off the final four pirates.

He clutched Omar tighter, forcing him to his feet. '*That's* why we have to go,' he said.

Chapter Forty-four

'There's nothing for it,' said Omar, standing over the body of his leader, whose eyes stared vacantly into the sun. 'We cannot beat them.'

'And we can't run,' said Harry. 'As you said, the desert will kill us.'

Blackbeard nodded, stepping away from Amir's body and coming to stand at the edge of the alley between the pyramids, enjoying the blessed cool cast by the long shadows. Sakhmet's army still marched towards them, as though the statue was spitting them out.

'Hand me my cutlass,' he said. Chris Claw stooped to pick it up from where it had fallen when Blackbeard was ejected from the sunken tomb. He handed it to him. Blackbeard tested the weight of it in his palm, let his eyes sail over the dust-covered blade, which was scuffed and chipped from the earlier escapades. But it would still work if he swung it.

Keeping his eyes on the marching dead, who were led by the line of skeletons, close enough now that their rattling teeth could just about be heard in the vast expanse of searing hot nothing that was the desert, Blackbeard felt around his gun-belt. There was just the one pistol left, the one hanging lowest, right at his gut. He drew it with his left hand, although he had no plan to put the bullet into any of these things that were moving relentlessly forward.

Just like he had no plan to lift the curse from himself. He knew his mission was over. There was no way to save Mary, which meant he cared not if he ever lifted this curse from his head. Sakhmet could curse the entire world, and everyone in it for all he cared now.

The bullet in the barrel of the gun in his hand was meant for Blackbeard's own head. That would be his little victory – to decide for *himself* when this would be over.

And before that, he would finish the deaths of as many of these cursed souls as he could.

'Omar,' he said. 'Look at it this way – any one of this lot could have been the one that struck Amir the killing blow. It seems only right that you deliver vengeance to all of them, doesn't it?'

Omar's face seemed to clear, as he at last looked away from Amir and glanced at Blackbeard. He used his forearm to wipe his face clean and it was like he had swept his grief-stricken expression entirely off his face, replacing it with a look of determination.

'Yes, Mr Teach,' he said. 'I agree with you.'

Blackbeard looked at Handsome and Chris. 'How about you boys?' he said. 'Ready to avenge our crew in the only way we know how?'

Blackbeard's three remaining companions stepped towards him. 'Aye, Captain,' said Chris.

'I don't fear death,' said Harry.

'Of course you don't,' said Blackbeard. 'Look at you – you must have experienced it eight times over.'

Harry laughed as, behind him, Omar bent to snatch up his fallen leader's weapon. He was armed with two swords, and an expression that said he planned to slay at least ten times that number with them.

Then the four pirates stood in a line, and waited for death to fall upon them.

Chapter Forty-five

When the marching dead were within thirty feet, Blackbeard gave the command to charge. As one, the pirates ran, with the lighter, more nimble Omar in the lead, swinging his twin blades at the first line of skeletons, aiming for their heads and scattering their bones over the heaving, fighting pack.

Blackbeard was next, slashing his cutlass to keep his enemies at a distance, and using his pistol as a club at the head of any who did manage to get in close. He saw skulls shatter and skeletons collapse. He heard the tearing of long-rotted flesh as Sakhmet's soldier guards tried to swarm him, thrusting their swords and bashing him with their shields, driving him back into the waiting arms of a skeleton, whose tight grip made him drop both of his weapons. The *clack clack clack* of the skeleton's rattling laughter swamped his senses as, at his feet, a pair of *Shabti* stabbed their tiny blades into his thighs.

Blackbeard stamped his feet onto the heads of the *Shabti*, crushing them to splinters, before slamming an elbow into the bare, exposed ribs of his skeleton attacker, feeling them cave in and then snap. He turned around and thrust out his hand, his thumb and index finger slipping into the empty eye-sockets of the skull. Yanking his arm back, Blackbeard used the skeleton like a staff, slamming the reanimated bones into anything that he could reach, watching toes and feet, legs and pelvis, arms and ribs break apart and rain upon the corpse-soldiers and mummies, who lingered at the rear of the pack, groaning with a vicious, violent intent.

A hunger for the flesh of the four last living men in this desert.

His skeleton weapon destroyed, Blackbeard weighted the skull in his hand and slammed it onto the head of the nearest corpse-soldier. The skull shattered in Blackbeard's hand, leaving behind a deep crater in the soldier's head, revealing a brain strewn with dead maggots. He then ducked to pick up his gun and cutlass, resuming his relentless resistance.

He didn't know how much longer he could keep it up. But he would swing and stab, cut and slash, until he physically could not do so anymore.

To his left, Chris Claw cut a path through the first and second lines of attackers, ripping out chunks of torso and gouging out eyes. Beyond him, Handsome Harry – without the hands to hold any type of weapon

– clobbered everything in his path.

Omar punctuated his twin strikes with ferocious snarls, and bellowed insults in his own language. Blackbeard forced his way towards him, hacking with his cutlass and sending bone, skin and wood crashing to the desert earth.

He helped Omar cut and swipe his way clear of the corpse soldiers, fighting their way through to the rear of the pack, feeling the limp flesh of his enemies batting and clawing at his doublet.

But what slammed into his chest was not limp.

In charging a way through the mess of enemies, Blackbeard and Omar had stepped into the path of Sakhmet's marble protectors. The head of the baboon had butted Blackbeard just below the sternum, sending him flying, while the rigid fist of the marble warrior had knocked Omar into the air and over the heads of everybody.

Blackbeard landed in a chaotic heap on the desert earth, Omar landing on top of him and bouncing clear. As he sat up, catching his breath, Blackbeard saw the sky darken for a moment, as the falcon and winged-jackal soared, carrying the flailing bodies of Handsome and Chris, who they had plucked from the battle and now dropped beside Blackbeard and Omar.

'Guess they've never heard of "fighting fair",' said Blackbeard, drawing dark, grim laughter from his companions. 'What say you, lads? I've still got a lot of fight left in— Whoa!'

Blackbeard cried out in surprise as he felt a harsh tug at his feet, and felt the skin of his legs and back burn as he was dragged along the scorched desert ground. Behind him, the other three pirates gave similar cries of shock and despair.

None of them had noticed the shrouds of the mummies slip around their ankles.

Blackbeard sat up as he slid along the earth, casting his cutlass aside as he tried to reach for his ankle. But he couldn't. Each time his fingers touched the shroud, it would tighten, and he would feel a fierce yank on it from the mummy that was reeling him in. Behind him, the rest of the dead army had stopped their relentless pursuit, standing to attention to watch the grisly end of their victims.

Suddenly, the pistol in Blackbeard's hand felt heavier than he had ever known. The pistol he had retained in order to preserve his choice – his minimal control over his own destiny. Was this the moment?

'Don't do it…"brother".'

Blackbeard looked back towards the mummies,

back towards the death to which he was being inexorably pulled. Two more figures were walking arrogantly around the line of four mummies, who were dragging the pirates towards them with their arms held out, gnarled hands extended – ready to tear flesh and consume organs.

The first was Luis, clutching the papyrus scroll – the Book of the Dead with which Sakhmet could outwit the Gods of the Afterlife. The second was Sakhmet herself, wrapped in the human cloak that was Blackbeard's half-sister. She spoke in a two-tone voice, Mary's mingled with the snake-like hiss that Blackbeard knew to be Sakhmet's.

'Such a tragic end is hardly becoming for a pirate,' she called.

'It is all over, Blackbeard,' said Luis, pointing with the papyrus scroll. 'Yours will be just the first of thousands of souls that my Goddess consumes as her power grows. She will rule *everything*.'

'Not if I have anything to do with it,' said Blackbeard, finding new strength to throw his body backwards, resisting the pull of the mummies. He succeeded only in slowing down his progress. The shroud gripped his ankle tighter as it fought against him. Blackbeard could not feel his right foot anymore.

Luis kept the papyrus scroll pointed at Blackbeard. 'But you won't!' he yelled. 'You are weak, worthless in comparison with Sakhmet.'

Blackbeard sat forward and held out his pistol, squinting as he looked along the barrel. He took a deep breath and pulled the trigger, seeing Luis's fingers fly free from his hand, the bottom of the papyrus scroll exploding in a shower of dust. The treacherous Spaniard fell to the ground, staring at the space where his fingers used to be, his scream of pain hollow and pointless in the vast, almost totally barren desert.

Sakhmet gave an unearthly gasp – there was no trace of Mary's voice anymore.

'*No!*'

The Goddess turned, as the four mummies relaxed their grips on the pirates, who struggled to free themselves. Blackbeard pulled himself to his feet, as he and the others stood close together, watching as another cloud of dust and stone was teased from the desert ground, dancing and spiralling around the statue of Ammit, the Devourer.

And behind the pirates, the dead army were groaning and grunting in utter confusion and fear.

'What have you done, Captain?' asked Chris.

Blackbeard's body was overcome with an uncontrollable laughter. 'Woken up someone who's been wanting to get their hands – or, should I say, *teeth* – onto Sakhmet for a long, long time...'

The long, deadly stone jaws of Ammit snapped shut, with a crack that echoed along the alley between the pyramids like a cannon being fired. With a rumble of stone, the Devourer's head turned from side to side, as her body began to swell and grow to a size even more immense than the statue of Sakhmet. Colour began to seep through Ammit's form, her lion's body becoming a golden yellow, and her crocodile head a blend of brilliant green and red scales.

With a ferocious roar, Ammit the Devourer leapt into the air, her body eclipsing the sun and casting everything in thick shadow, as she opened her jaws, gaping wide, revealing the inside of her mouth to be as red as blood.

Sakhmet cast her face up to the sky, Mary's features twisted with hate and petulance. She spread her arms out to the sides as she emitted a terrified shriek.

The Devourer dive-bombed, seeming to swallow Sakhmet, Luis and the four mummies whole as she smashed through the desert ground, sending up rippling waves of tremors that tickled Blackbeard's feet through his boots.

Blackbeard and the pirates backed away as the tremors intensified, and the fissure in the earth widened.

'Now should we run?' asked Chris.

But before Blackbeard could answer, the desert ground where Sakhmet had burrowed unleashed a stream of stone and earth that cannoned towards the sky, writhing in a torrent of blood that was spreading out across the air.

Blackbeard knew there was no outrunning that. He consoled himself with the knowledge that he had destroyed the evil Goddess, and avenged both his sister and his crew, as his vision, his senses, his whole being, was drowned in red.

Chapter Forty-six

This had to be Hell.

Only Hell could have been this hot. His cheeks felt like they were on fire, his skin breaking out in blisters that had already burst, oozing pus that trickled over his beard and into his lips. Blackbeard coughed and spat, rolling over and placing his palms on earth that was scorching – and *soft*.

He opened his eyes and shielded them with his hand against the glare of the Egyptian sun.

He wasn't in Hell.

He was on a sand dune. He could just about see the peaks of the three pyramids in the distance, beyond the ruined walls of the empty city. He could not see the statue of Ammit, but he somehow sensed it was there, back to its normal size – not the mammoth form it had taken just before it had devoured Sakhmet, whose statue was now nowhere to be seen.

He pushed himself up onto his knees, slapping himself about the face and chest. The flushes of pain told him that this was not a dream – it was real. 'Ammit must have decided to let us off,' he said to himself. 'Well, I was due some luck eventually.'

He began walking down the sand dune, stopping dead when he saw four familiar figures sat cross-legged at the bottom, scooping up handfuls of water from a lush oasis nestled in the depression. He smiled.

'Oi, you lot! What is this – sunbathing?'

Mary, Handsome Harry, Chris Claw and Omar turned towards him, their faces showing relieved smiles. Mary scrabbled to her feet and ran up the sand dune, with a speed and energy she should not have had – considering that, the last time Blackbeard had seen her move anywhere, it was deep into the Egyptian desert, in the mouth of a vengeful god.

'Edward!' she cried, throwing her arms around him. 'You're alive!'

'What do you mean?' asked Blackbeard, catching the relief in her tone. 'Was I not before?'

'It was hard to tell,' said Harry, as he and Chris joined them. Omar had stayed where he was, head down and arms crossed. 'You weren't moving or breathing. But then, neither was Chris at one point, and he woke up.'

Chris grinned. 'So we decided to wait it out.'

Blackbeard cast a look back towards the pyramids. 'You know,' he said, 'I've been thinking. I don't think the Old World is for us.'

His friends laughed as they set off down the sand dune, back towards the Nile.

They passed Omar, who did not look at them. Blackbeard stepped up to the young man. 'What will you do now?' he asked.

Omar shrugged. 'I don't know.'

Blackbeard smiled. 'I think I do,' he said. 'Why don't you come with us?'

Omar's head bounced up, his eyes narrowed in incredulity. 'Me?' he said, a sly smile on his face now. 'Sail with *you*?'

'Why not? Neither of us has a full crew anymore. And I know you're handy to have around...even if you annoy me.'

Omar laughed, looking off into the distance. Blackbeard could see him thinking it over. Finally, he shook his head – but not in refusal, but it in disbelief at his own decision. 'Very well, Mr Teach,' he said. 'I will sail with you.'

Blackbeard clapped him on the shoulder. 'Glad to hear it,' he said, setting off again, Omar following. 'After all, we'll need to take the *Gallant*.'

Beside him, Mary clutched his wrist tightly. 'What do you mean, we're taking the *Gallant*? What happened to the *Queen Anne's Revenge*?'

'Long story,' said Blackbeard.

'But... But... You promised me...'

'I know, I know,' said Blackbeard, trying not to laugh. 'But I really did have no choice.'

Mary sighed. 'Fine,' she said. 'I'll just be Captain of the *Gallant* then, after you retire.'

Blackbeard paused at the bottom of the dune. Mary took two steps and wheeled around.

'Don't tell me—'

Blackbeard gave a sheepish shrug. 'There's just one more thing I have to do first.'

Epilogue

Constantinople

Beni Barbarossa looked through the window of his bedchamber in the Sultan's palace. It wasn't a cell in the dungeon – that was deep beneath the complex – but it might as well have been. Three guards were outside his door at all times, and the window he looked through offered a view of the courtyard – four floors below.

The only chance of escape was if his father, Amir, completed whatever task the Sultan had set for him. But it had been a year now, and Beni was still locked up.

How much longer would the Sultan wait?

'*Ooof!*'

Beni turned away from the window when he heard some kind of scuffle on the other side of the door. Were his guards fighting each other? Or was the palace under attack?

The sounds of the scuffle died as quickly as they had started.

The door to his bedchamber flew off its hinges,

revealing a giant of a man in a red doublet, standing in a doorway that was too small for him. Six pistols ran diagonally across his chest, the uppermost pistol half hidden behind the longest beard Beni had ever seen.

Beni backed away from the door. 'Who are you?' he asked, his voice quivering in fear.

The giant in red just smiled. 'They call me Blackbeard,' he said. 'Your father sent me.'

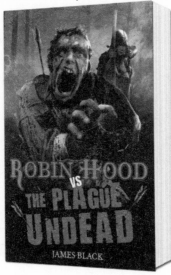

Little John stopped several paces from his house. 'I saw my Ruth die,' he mumbled. 'How is this possible?'

The figure in the shattered doorway certainly looked like Ruth, but all the traces of the kindly woman Robin had known were gone. Its gown and hair dripped with black sludge and the bones of its right hand were completely exposed, the flesh torn off halfway up its forearm. Its pallid, boil-covered face was set in a snarl, its cheeks almost caving inwards. Its nose flared in hungry snorts and grunts as it turned to face the Outlaws. It moved slowly, but as deliberately as a predator.

Robin felt bile rise in his throat, and heard Marian gasp: 'Oh, my Lord!' The fiend's left eye wept thin tears of blood that split into two when they struck the boils, the red trails like rambling tree roots down one cheek. Its right eye seemed clouded with a dull, greyish film. Blood and drool dribbled over its slack bottom lip, and the only sound it made was a wet snarl.

The breeze carried the stench of the fiend – a stench that turned Robin's stomach over.

'The dead walk!' cried Friar Tuck. 'They rise as Undead! My Lord God, is this the end of all things? Is this the Day of—' Friar Tuck's words rose to a shriek as the Undead Ruth sprang forwards, hands clawing at the air.

'Run!' Robin shouted.

The Outlaws turned and fled the scrabbling creature. Robin didn't need to look back to know that it was close – he could almost taste death in his mouth, and wished he'd not left their weapons behind.

'To the gate!' Robin called, grabbing John's sleeve in an effort to speed him up. Marian and Much streaked ahead, and behind him Friar Tuck was scampering as fast as his fat legs would carry him.

'*Argh!*'

Robin turned without stopping, almost losing his balance and scraping his hands on the beaten-earth road. 'Oh no...'

Will Scarlet's age had caught up with him.

The old Outlaw was lying face down in the road, with the fiend-Ruth clinging to his back. Will desperately tried to crawl free, his eyes wide with fear as his fingers dug for purchase. He threw back his elbow, slamming it into the Undead lady's face.

But it did not let go.

With a desperate cry, Will kicked his legs, trying to push himself clear.

But it did not let go.

Robin swung his boot at the fiend's head, sending it tumbling over to one side.

But it did not let go.

The fiend dragged Will with it, man and moving corpse rolling across the road. Will drove his elbow into its ribs once, twice, three times.

But it did not let go.

Robin picked up a piece of timber from the broken door and plunged it down into the fiend's face. He felt its skull cave in; he yanked the wood free to reveal a sunken crater between its eyes and mouth.

But it did not let go.

As Robin raised the wood for another strike, he saw the fiend's mouth open and its teeth clamp down on Will's neck, biting through his shaggy grey hair and sending out a spray of blood that splashed Robin's knees. Will's eyes widened with pain, his mouth opening to cry out but the sound was stolen away by the pure shock of what had happened.

Robin swung the jagged piece of wood like an axe at

the fiend's skull, over and over again; each strike made a bigger dent until clumps of what was once Ruth's brain burst and sprayed free. The fiend was finally still, its grip on Will loosening. Robin used the lump of wood – dripping blood, flesh and brain, and studded with shards of bone – to work Will free of the fiend's clutches.

As Robin reached down to help Will to his feet, the old Outlaw shoved him back. Robin fell into the sturdy frame of Little John, who braced him.

'Will!' Robin gasped. 'Let us help you—'

'No use,' said Will, with a bitter laugh. 'There's no use, Robin. Fate has a sense of cruel humour this day. "One last ride" indeed.'

Will crawled back from the fiend and came to a stop a few feet away, on his knees as if in prayer. His head hung forward, and Robin could see blood streaming from the hole in his neck.

'Will, we must go,' said Robin. 'We must get out of this cursed town.'

'Yes, you must,' said Will, 'and you must leave me here.'

Robin stepped towards Will, but the old Outlaw flashed him a look so fierce Robin became still even before he spoke.

'Do as I say, for once!' Will shouted. 'Get out of Nottingham. Raise the alarm, and take as many people with you as you can. And don't come back – not ever.'

'But Will, I don't understand,' said Robin.

Will Scarlet gently raised a hand to the wound in his neck. 'It burns, Robin,' he said. 'It burns on the inside.'

'No...' Robin breathed, shaking his head. 'No...'

'*Yes*,' said Will, raising his head to look at Robin, his eyes showing bitter amusement at his bad luck. 'I think poor Ruth passed her Plague to me, through her bite. I am infected... You must get away from me, and quickly. This infection is going to kill me... I might become like Ruth... I might attack you...'

Robin ran his hands through his hair, holding on to his head as if to stop it bursting. He felt anguish like a rusty blade lodged in his chest.

'Good God, no!' cried Little John. He was looking back up the road, towards his house.

Peter was crawling out through the doorway. Except he wasn't Peter anymore.

And he wasn't the only one.

Door after door all the way up the street was forced open. They clattered to the ground, flipping and tumbling, breaking apart as they collided with each other.

Fiend after fiend stumbled out of the dwellings and into the road on legs that barely seemed to work. As one, they turned in the direction of the stunned Outlaws, their faces set in shared snarls of ravenous, cannibalistic intent.

'What is happening?' Robin breathed. 'How is this possible?'

Will looked over his shoulder, then back at his Outlaw brothers for the last time. He struggled to his feet and reached for the lump of wood Robin held. 'I'll hold them off for as long as I can. Raise the alarm – get the people out. Otherwise everyone in the town will be end up like these creatures. Do it!'

Will turned and ran towards the fiends. The old Outlaw swung the wood, hitting skulls and jaws, jabbing it into chests, not caring for how many times he was scratched by flailing Undead hands.

As Will disappeared among the writhing mass of corpses, Robin tore his eyes away, seeing Friar Tuck gazing to the sky, as if Heaven would answer his questions.

Robin led his group at a trot back down the street, keeping his eyes peeled for any more fiends. 'Everyone gather themselves,' he said. 'Much, Marian, you're the fastest on foot. Go to the inn, find the Butcher and have him bring the cart back to the main gate. We'll meet you there. Tell everyone that you pass that they must leave Nottingham, right now. Tell them, to stay means death – *worse* than death!'

'But the gate is closed,' said Much, wiping his nose with the back of his hand, his eyes as red as a fiend's. 'How will we get past the sergeants?'

'We'll get past them,' Robin said. 'Whatever it takes. Go!'

Marian set a brisk pace through the streets and Much followed.

Robin addressed Little John and Friar Tuck. 'We make for the gate, and we make as much noise as we can. And we get that gate open...one way or another.'

The three Outlaws made a chaotic course through the town. They lobbed stones at front doors, and bellowed the word 'Plague!' over and over again.

'Everyone make for the gate!' Robin hollered as he barrelled down the last residential road before turning on to Silk Street.

He skidded to a stop in the middle of the road. No one was moving – the merchants packing up for the day simply looked at the three men with confused expressions.

'You must listen to me,' said Robin. 'A plague has fallen on the town. Everyone must leave if they wish to live.' A few of the sellers looked uneasily at each other, but still no one moved. 'To stay is to die,' Robin shouted. 'And die in the most awful of ways. Please, listen to me.'

A murmuring moved through the merchants.

'He's mad!' said one.

'Probably drunk!' said another.

Robin shot an anxious glance at Friar Tuck – how were they going to convince people to flee?

'Get away, you drunkard,' said one of the merchants. 'Stop causing trouble.'

'I swear to you, I'm not making—'

'*Argh!*'

Everyone looked towards the blood-curdling scream. A woman had fallen on to the dirty cobbles. An Undead man was ripping at her face. Robin almost wretched when he saw the fiend swipe off a handful of the woman's cheek, then force it into its mouth.

They eat flesh, he thought, feeling sick.

MASH UPs
Competition

Win one of twenty copies of the first blood-curdling Mash Up, *Robin Hood vs the Plague Undead!*

To enter the draw, simply send the answer to the following question, along with your name, address and telephone number to:

Mash Ups Competition
Orchard Books
338 Euston Road
London
NW1 3BH

or email ad@hachettechildrens.co.uk

Competition will close 31st October 2011.
Only available to UK and Eire residents.
For full terms and conditions go to
www.orchardbooks.co.uk/TermsAndConditions.aspx

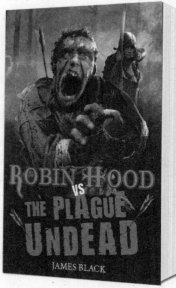

978 1 408 31388 6 £5.99 Pbk   978 140831 549 1 £5.99 eBook

ORCHARD
www.orchardbooks.co.uk

ANTHONY
HOROWITZ
HORROR

Collection of horror stories by No 1 bestselling
author Anthony Horowitz.

It's a world where everything seems pretty normal.
But the weird, the sinister and the truly terrifying are
lurking just out of sight. Like an ordinary-looking
camera with evil powers, a bus ride home that turns
into your worst nightmare and a mysterious
computer game that nobody would play...
if they knew the rules!

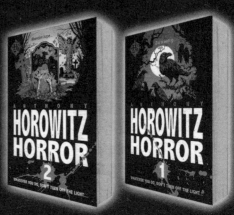

ORCHARD BOOKS
www.orchardbooks.co.uk

ANTHONY HOROWITZ
GRAPHIC HORROR

An instant hit of horror from best-selling author, Anthony Horowitz. Scare yourself silly with these four haunting graphic novels:

978 0 7496 9510 1

978 0 7496 9511 8

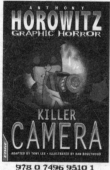

978 0 7496 9512 5

978 0 7496 9509 5

OUT NOW!

www.franklinwatts.co.uk.

iHorror

Fight your fear. Choose your fate.
Battle the undead in these
power-packed interactive adventures!

Available as eBooks

978 1 40830 988 9
978 1 40831 479 1 (eBook)

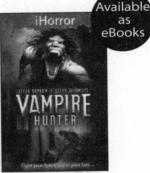

978 1 40830 985 8
978 1 40831 476 0 (eBook)

978 1 40830 986 5
978 1 40831 477 7 (eBook)

978 1 40830 987 2
978 1 40831 478 4 (eBook)

STEVE BARLOW ✝ STEVE SKIDMORE
OUT 2011

www.orchardbooks.co.uk

ORCHARD BOOKS